HOLLY JAMES

THE BIG FIX

KENSINGTON
PUBLISHING CORP.
kensingtonbooks.com

KENSINGTON BOOKS are published by

Kensington Publishing Corp.
900 Third Avenue
New York, NY 10022

Copyright © 2025 by Holly Rus

All Kensington titles, imprints, and distributed lines are available at special quantity discounts for bulk purchases for sales promotion, premiums, fund-raising, educational, or institutional use. Special book excerpts or customized printings can also be created to fit specific needs. For details, write or phone the office of the Kensington Special Sales Manager: Attn. Special Sales Department, Kensington Publishing Corp., 900 Third Avenue, New York, NY 10018. Phone: 1-800-221-2647.

Library of Congress Control Number: 2024949547

KENSINGTON and the K with book logo Reg. US Pat. & TM. Off.

ISBN: 978-1-4967-5174-4
ISBN: 978-1-4967-5829-3 (trade)

First Kensington Hardcover Edition: April 2025

ISBN: 978-1-4967-5175-1 (ebook)

10 9 8 7 6 5 4 3 2 1

Printed in the United States of America

This one is for me.

CHAPTER 1

An estate sale at a dead guy's suburban mansion was not how I'd planned to spend my first Saturday of summer break.

"I can't believe you talked me into this," I said to my sister as I followed her up the house's front path. A sign stuck up from the lush front lawn like a proud, little goalpost advertising that the vacant house's contents were up for grabs to anyone interested in browsing. "We both know I can't fit anything else into my apartment, and you need exactly zero things from an estate sale, Libby. Your spartan husband isn't going to let you keep anything you find anyway. He's allergic to clutter."

As we approached the house, the lively but overgrown yard rolled and curved in vibrant shades of green and pink on either side of us. The old Victorian sat waiting with doors open like a tired parent exhaling a dramatic breath amid the youth of its own garden. As if we'd caught its sagging porch and faded shutters midsigh while the bounty of early summer freely blossomed around it.

Libby shot me a glare over her shoulder while managing to keep an eye on her son toddling near the untamed rose border and the stroller that she was pushing with one hand aimed straight. "John is gone for the summer, so he can't stop me anyway. Max, don't touch that." She hardly broke stride to scold her son before continuing. "And besides, you could use a little adventure in your life. You're always so busy studying and working and being responsible. I know the most excitement you get is trivia night with your socially stunted professor friends. Max! I said no!"

I scoffed in offense. "First, we dominate trivia night, and second, how is an estate sale an adventure? It's just a yard sale where they were too lazy to drag everything outside."

"One person's junk is another's treasure. I've always wanted to see inside this house; I think he's a creepy old hoarder," she said without bothering to lower her voice.

"Can't you be a normal neighbor and spy, instead of waiting until he's dead and hauling the whole family over?" I whispered, but not quietly enough based on the scandalized look the woman carrying a gaudy gold lamp down the front steps gave me. "Sorry," I muttered as she passed.

The comment earned me another glare from Libby as she nosed the stroller's front tire to the bottom step. The three-wheeled rover built for a moon landing surely could have scaled the old wooden steps on its own, but Libby pushed it into a position I knew well. "Spying on your neighbors only leads to trouble. Grab that." She pointed to the handle at the front of my infant niece's stroller and rocked it back on its hind wheels.

I dutifully circled to the front end and hooked my hand into the strap, lifting Ada like royalty in a cushioned throne to help carry her up the stairs. For fun, I puffed out my cheeks and crossed my eyes at my niece, and the sound of her giggle pierced the air like a sunray.

While Max looked like his father—long and wiry even for a three-year-old—Ada looked, oddly, like me. Libby's chemically lightened blond hair bobbed on the side of her head like a golden sticky bun, while mine was the color of chocolate and matched the sprig pinched into a little pink bow on Ada's downy head. We both had blue eyes, Libby's were green, and a propensity for blushing deep shades of scarlet when called upon to do so by social interactions.

"Max, come on. Inside," Libby called toward the fourth member of our brood.

Max abandoned the rose border and bounded up the steps behind us, green sycamore leaf from one of the yard's enormous twin trees in hand. He victoriously and silently presented it to me once I set down the stroller.

"Thanks, pal," I said, and poked its stem into my jeans pocket, accustomed to accepting his small, random gifts.

He dashed through the front door, on a mission, and skirted a man exiting with a pricey-looking ceramic vase, which surely would have shattered, had it fallen from his grip.

"Slow down!" Libby called, but Max had already disappeared.

"Lib, maybe we should leave the stroller outside?" I offered as she rocked it back again to lift the front wheel over the front door's lip.

"Only if you want to carry Ada," she said, and charged forward with the resolve of her son.

I followed her into the foyer and had the sudden sensation of being swallowed by the enormous house. Most California homes were airy, light-filled celebrations of sky and sea, with panels of glass built to suck the heavily taxed sunshine right inside and hold it in place. This house was a celebration of wood. Polished, shiny, dark wood. And wallpaper in shades of burgundy and emerald, with tiny gold pinstripes. A staircase curved from above, unfurling itself with a red tongue runner and landing several feet from a round table, which a man in a tweed jacket was currently inspecting. Rooms branched off to either side of the foyer: a dining room to the right and formal living room to the left. A hallway stretched like a throat into the dim reaches of the house's belly, perhaps to a parlor or an office.

It was simply stunning.

"Guess he wasn't a creepy old hoarder after all," Libby mumbled under her breath.

"I'd say not." I craned my neck to take in the chandelier dangling from the ceiling like an elegantly beaded tonsil.

Libby had told me her neighbor had died the week before. She'd slipped it into a conversation between news of Max starting swim lessons and the sponge cake recipe she was thinking of trying for their neighborhood potluck, as if it fit like any other fact from her busy life.

"Which neighbor?" I'd asked, knowing it was no one from her inner circle, given her casual delivery.

"The grumpy one on the north. Mr. Griotti."

"Huh" was all I'd said because I had never met Mr. Griotti and didn't know him beyond being the grumpy neighbor who lived in the big, old Victorian to the north of my sister, and I occasionally saw him coming and going when I visited.

She'd made no more mention of it until last night when she called to invite me to the estate sale this morning. I'd balked because estate sales were not part of our regularly scheduled activities, and because I'd already had plans to spend the day lounging by her pool, sipping lemonade and listening to an audiobook, as I was prone to do on weekends in summer. Alas, her insistence had gotten me out of the city, where I lived, and down the San Francisco Peninsula to her suburban kingdom several hours sooner than I normally would have shown up on a sunny Saturday. I had to assume it was due to her insatiable need to snoop inside her dead neighbor's mansion, and not wanting to do it alone.

Standing inside the yawning foyer, I could not deny that I'd always wanted to see the inside of the house too.

"So, how does this work?" I asked as we drifted toward the living room. "We grab stuff and stick money in a box or something?"

"Not exactly. There should be someone running the sale."

She turned her head and spoke toward the room like she expected to see the ringleader there waiting for us. "He should be around here somewhere . . ." She mumbled the last part and pushed off with her stroller like she saw someone she knew.

Despite my reluctance to come, the idea of an estate sale fascinated me. The going-out-of-business, everything-must-go mentality applied to the contents of someone's life felt at once enormously sad and wildly ripe for opportunity. Everything from their furniture to their dishes, the decorative baubles and utilitarian tokens, available to be picked over by scavengers. Walking the halls where someone had lived, with most everything exactly how he'd left it, felt like one step above looting. Breaking and entering with permission.

I had imagined we'd find a fair amount of junk inside the old house, but there was no junk in sight. The inside was elegant and prim, as if only the casing around it had gone to seed.

I lost sight of Libby and made my way into the living room toward a bookshelf crowded with spines and trinkets. It stood neck-high and held an assortment of artwork on its top.

"I've seen these on an antique show before," a nearby woman quietly hissed to her husband. She held a pair of gold candlesticks and leaned in conspiratorially. "These are worth *at least* five hundred for the pair."

"There are no price stickers on anything," her husband said.

They were midsixties, retired-looking. She wore a matching blue tracksuit set, and he, khakis and a polo shirt. I didn't recognize them from the neighborhood. From the looks of them, they were bargain hunters and had sniffed out the sale from miles off.

"Yes, that probably means he doesn't know how much anything is worth," she continued in a whisper.

I bent my ear their direction and pretended to take interest in a small, framed oil painting perched atop the bookcase.

"Or he hasn't gotten to pricing anything because his uncle just died," the husband said.

"Well, his lack of preparation is to our advantage, then, isn't it," she said in a callous tone, which sent an uncomfortable chill up my spine.

A shuffle of noise drew our attention to the doorway leading back into the foyer. A man had appeared, holding a box and looking harried. He wore black jeans and a black T-shirt and black boots, with the tiniest heel, like he'd stepped offstage at a rock concert. Whatever was in the box must have been heavy, given the flex of his arms and the slight sheen of sweat on his forehead. A small bead had greedily latched on to one of the dark waves framing his face and adhered to his temple in a curled J.

He was, quite possibly, the most beautiful thing in the room, maybe the whole house.

"Perfect—that's him," the woman with the candlesticks said. She bustled over toward him, brushing past me at the bookcase, with her husband in tow. "Excuse me, young man? I'll give you fifty dollars for these." She waved the candlesticks at him, one in each hand like a pair of gilded batons.

Fifty dollars? More like a rip-off than a bargain.

The man with the box glanced at her and the candlesticks, catching sight of me in the background. I stole a closer look at his face and noticed matching purple half-moons beneath his eyes. He looked like he hadn't slept in days. A dart of sympathy hit me in the heart that this poor, exhausted man, who'd just lost his uncle, was about to get ripped off by a pair of local hucksters.

He opened his mouth to respond to her offer, and I stepped in before he could speak.

"I'll give you five hundred," I blurted. An embarrassed flame curled into my cheeks. I did not have five hundred dollars to drop on a pair of candlesticks I'd never use, and now the beautiful, tired man with the box was staring at me.

The woman swiveled around and glared at me hard enough to make me flinch. "These are mine. I found them first."

The man with the box eyed her, and then me, and then back to her. He nodded his head once and said, "A hundred for the pair, and they're yours."

The woman beamed and bounced up on her toes. She snapped her fingers at her husband, who pulled out his wallet and stuck a wad of cash into the man's hand that was still clutching the box. The thieves skipped off, grinning, and left me gaping.

The man walked toward me with his box and set it on top of the bookcase. Books. No wonder it was so heavy.

"You're either really bad at math or really bad at haggling," I said to him.

He cast me another glance, and without the box in his arms, I realized how broad and tall he was. A specimen, surely. And definitely no one I had ever seen in my sister's neighborhood.

"Sorry, but I knew you weren't going to buy those. You don't look like someone ready to drop five hundred bucks on a pair of candlesticks."

I flinched, shocked. "Okay, that was *rude.*"

"Just being honest." He pivoted on his heel and stalked back toward the foyer.

I followed, suddenly feeling the need to explain myself. "Well, I was only trying to help. I'll have you know, I overheard your customer conspiring to rip you off because she knew the true value of those candlesticks, and I thought, as a dutiful neighbor, I would intervene and drive up the price to closer to where it should be."

He paused, and I almost ran into his back. He turned to eye me. "You live around here?"

A flush returned to my face. His disarming gaze was heavy

and prickly and made me feel like I was being x-rayed. "No, but my sister does. I'm visiting for the weekend. Do *you* live around here?"

"Well, now I do, but it's only temporary while I deal with all this." He waved his hands at the room and then combed one hand through his mop of hair. It promptly fell right back into disarray. The stubborn, sweaty J still stuck to his temple.

I was about to ask him if he was from a place where neighbors were rude to one another when Libby reappeared with the stroller, still aimed out in front of her like the bow of a boat. "Pen, have you seen Max? I can't find—Oh, I see you've met." A smile spread across her face, lifting her eyes into a telling, scheming sparkle, which I knew well. "Penny, this is Anthony. Anthony, this is my sister, Penny."

The man—*Anthony*—suspiciously eyed Libby and the stroller, and though he'd done nothing to make me expect a welcoming smile and handshake, I was still surprised when I didn't get either. Instead he arched a thick, dark brow at Libby. "And who are you?"

His reaction did not faze her in the least. She politely laughed a charming sound. "I'm Libby. We met last night in your driveway. I'm your neighbor."

As soon as she said it, everything clicked.

It was a setup. Libby's latest form of meddling and attempt at playing matchmaker. This brooding—yes, attractive—but *rude* man fell from the sky and landed next door, and she lured me on false pretenses to come meet him. We were not at this estate sale to browse the home goods selection. We were here to browse the tall, dark, handsome man selection, of which there was one option. This was the adventure she'd been referring to.

A look of chagrin passed over Anthony's face with the speed of a blink. "Sorry, it's been a haze these past few days. I do recall the, um, *pie* you brought over."

I fought not to roll my eyes.

Libby placed a loving hand on his arm. "Yes, well, hopefully things calm down soon. I'm sure you're dealing with so much. My sister, Penny—"

"Can I talk to you for a minute?" I cut her off, and grabbed her extended arm to drag her away before she could further force me upon this man, who clearly had no interest.

She tsked at me, once we were a few paces away. Anthony stayed close, distracted by another looter asking how much for a decorative glass bird.

"A *pie,* Elizabeth?" I scolded her. "May I ask what exactly you think you're doing?"

She rolled her eyes in that dismissive *I know what's best for you* big-sister way she'd honed over a lifetime of bossing me around. "Yes, *Penelope.* I baked him a pie. The poor guy flew in from New York yesterday, and he's dealing with the loss of a family member. I was simply being a kind neighbor."

"Yes, and the fact that you've dragged me along, and essentially served me up on a platter, is coincidence?"

She didn't even try to deny it. "Well, in case you haven't noticed, he's rather attractive. And you're rather single." She looked over at him negotiating with the bird lover like she was peeling a banana with her eyes.

Both facts were undeniably and unfortunately true. I'd dated in grad school, and even then, had limited time for a social life. But as soon as I'd landed a faculty job with a ticking tenure clock, I'd forgotten to look up, and somehow five years had passed with nothing more than a few coffee dates, despite Libby's best meddling efforts. She'd made attempts to set me up with her husband's coworker, their pediatrician, and the guy who sold organic chard at their farmers market. None of those failed missions had been as sly as this one though. Her premeditation was growing more sophisticated.

"Yes, and he's also very rude," I said. "Did you hear what he said to me about the candlesticks?"

"No, I didn't. Max! There you are. Please don't touch that . . ." She scooted away, cutting our conversation short, and with the stroller leading the charge. I'd lost her to the duties of parenting once again, but what was she expecting, bringing a grabby three-year-old into a museum of a house?

I turned back around to see Anthony pocketing another handful of cash and apparently done with the bird man. I crossed my arms and glared at him. "Why didn't you take my offer on the candlesticks?"

He looked up, as if he'd forgotten I was standing there, and at once seemed exasperated that we were apparently still having this conversation. "Look, I meant no offense to you." He stepped closer, and the smell of him hit me in a heady rush of dark, spicy notes and a hint of something feral. Like throwing a handful of cinnamon and amber on a campfire. He lowered his voice. "The truth is, I don't care what anyone pays me for any of this stuff. I just want to get rid of it. The sooner I do, the sooner I can sell the house and leave."

If I'd taken him for a sentimental man, I was mistaken. As was I mistaken about his size. Standing so close, I became intimately aware of his height and the expanse of his chest. I wondered what he did back in New York. Perhaps modeled underwear or trained professional athletes.

"Oh" was all I could summon.

Anthony's dark eyes suddenly shot over my shoulder. He stared down the hall with a look of stricken panic. "Stay away from there!"

I flinched at the loud boom of his voice, so suddenly changed from the raspy whisper he'd spoken in moments before. I turned to see Libby hoisting a crying Ada out of her stroller, already bouncing and shushing, while simultaneously trying to stop Max from opening the door beneath the stairs.

Anthony charged down the hall like an angry bull, and I rushed to catch up, having no idea what kind of experience he had with children and not wanting him to lift my nephew off the floor by the collar with one of his enormous hands.

"I'll get it," I said, and shoved past him. The brief contact of our bodies, a mere bump, hit me like lightning. I thought he might have felt it too, with the way he bounced off me, but that might have been due to the limited space. The hall, much narrower than I realized, now that it contained Libby, the stroller, a crying baby, a rebellious toddler, and the two of us, seemed to shrink with every step.

"Max, buddy, leave that alone. This isn't our house. We can't go touching things and opening doors without permission!" I called to my nephew.

He stood with both chubby hands wrapped around the glass emerald-green knob protruding from the door like a big, shiny jewel. Even a house as old as this one was unlikely to have a basement in California; the door must have led to a closet beneath the stairs.

"Please don't do that!" Anthony called again. The sharp fear lacing his voice like barbs made me wonder exactly what was in the closet.

"Max, don't!" Libby halfheartedly scolded, her true attention tuned to Ada and her scrunched, howling face blooming a furious shade of pink.

"Max, leave it alone!" I echoed.

The devilish glint in Max's eye said clearly that he was not going to obey. If all the adults wanted him to stop, that could only mean whatever he was about to get into must have been good.

"*No!*" Anthony bellowed, his voice a thunderclap in the cramped, wooden space right as Max yanked on the knob with both hands.

The door swung open with more force than a small child

could have exerted, as if something had been leaning on it from the other side ready to fall.

Indeed, something fell out, crashing to the floor like a collapsing drawbridge, and landed with a dead, heavy thud between us. Anthony and I stood on one side, Max, Libby, the stroller, and the still-screaming Ada on the other.

We collectively stared at the object: an oblong shape haphazardly covered in a sheet. It took me a surprising amount of time to realize that the limp, gray thing sticking out from one side of it was a hand, and the pale, gaunt moon at the top, a lifeless face, and that I was, indeed, staring at a dead body.

And then we were all screaming with Ada.

CHAPTER 2

I'd never been in an interrogation room before, but I suddenly found myself sitting in one across from a detective.

The police had arrived promptly on the scene, surely having a lack of other calls to tend to on a quiet Saturday in paradise. I wasn't even sure who summoned them, seeing I was too busy losing my mind in the hall. Before I knew it, Libby was dragging me in one hand, Max in the other, and somehow still pushing the stroller out the back door of the house. The estate sale ended, crime scene tape was unspooled into a yellow barrier like a scar on the pristine neighborhood, and we were asked to come down to the police station to give a statement.

Now I sat across from Detective Daryl Warner, a man I'd seen at a handful of holiday barbeques and once very drunk in an ugly sweater at a Christmas party. In a community where everyone knew everyone, it was only suitable that the detective was my sister's best friend's husband. He was Libby's age, late thirties, with dark skin and a face like he could be your best friend or break you in half with his bare hands, depending on his mood. The mood and the face were, thankfully, friendly at the moment.

We'd left Libby in the lobby with the kids, partly because Ada was asleep, but mostly because Warner said he wanted to talk to me first. Alone.

He pulled out a pen and clicked it before resting his hand atop the yellow notepad, ready and waiting with a fresh page. He started off casual. "How are you, Penny?"

I snorted, unsure if he was sincerely asking or trying to break the tension. "Well, I mean, I just saw a dead body fall out of a closet, so you know."

He kindly smiled at me. He had young kids of his own and lived a few streets over from Libby. His wife, Nicole, founder of an extremely lucrative online skincare company, spent a fair amount of time poolside with us in Libby's backyard. She made a mean strawberry margarita and always had the best book recommendations. "You're only here for the day?"

"That was the plan. I come down most weekends in the summer to swim with the kids, but Libby invited me to the estate sale today."

"You're still up in the city?"

"Yes."

Although there were several to choose from in the Bay Area, *the city* most commonly referred to San Francisco. The seven square miles where people piled on top of each other and paid eye-watering prices to climb the wind-whipped hills and live in the fog. My apartment in the Outer Richmond was a solid seventy-five-minute drive to Libby's house in a peninsula suburb.

"You're still teaching at the school?" Detective Warner continued with his line of questioning, which felt more like a catch-up at a backyard barbeque than anything to do with discovering a dead body.

"Yes. Finalizing my tenure case this summer."

"Hey, congrats. Still computer sciences?"

"Uh-huh. Are we going to talk about the body, or what?"

He gently laughed. "Getting there, don't worry. I wanted to know what you're up to these days. I haven't been around to any gatherings this summer to find out."

"Well, we're only a few days in. There's hardly been a chance yet."

Classes had recently ended, and I'd submitted final grades before diving headfirst into my tenure case, which had to be completed by the end of August. I had three papers to finish, a grant to write, and a book chapter to revise—all in a three-month window. Weekend escapes to my sister's pool were about the only thing I had to look forward to this summer. I had no time for adventures, especially the amorous kind Libby wanted me to have.

Detective Warner smiled again. "Well, let's hope today's incident doesn't derail any normal summer activity."

I blinked at him, unable to imagine how that could be possible. As if dead bodies fell out of closets in this neighborhood all the time.

He clicked his pen again and pulled the pad closer, ready to get started. Something notably shifted in his voice. "How well do you know Anthony Pierce?"

"His last name's not Griotti?" I asked in surprise.

He flipped a page of his notes, scanned something, and looked back at me. "No. Lou Griotti was his mother's brother, so different last name."

"Huh." The name Anthony Griotti had been spiraling around my head like a marble in a jar since we'd left the house. As had the theory that he'd murdered his own uncle to inherit his house and stuffed him in the closet, though I knew that couldn't be true. The man in the closet was about twenty years too young to be Mr. Griotti, and he certainly had not been dead for a week, like Mr. Griotti had been.

"Tell me what you know about him," Warner said.

I shrugged. "Honestly, hardly anything. I met him this morning at the estate sale."

"Really?" His brows lifted in dubious arches.

"Yes. Why do you ask?"

"A few witnesses mentioned they noticed what they referred to as *chemistry* between the two of you."

"*What?*" I cried, glad my sister was not present to pounce on his statement. "*Multiple* people mentioned that?"

He referenced his notes. "Yes. In fact, one referred to you as his girlfriend. They said they 'saw him arguing with his girl-friend over the price of candlesticks,'" he quoted from his notepad and looked up at me for an explanation.

My mind went blank and spun at the same time. "How could I be his girlfriend? I met him this morning for five min-utes."

"I'm only reporting what people were saying."

"Well, they're wrong."

"Hmm," Warner hummed, and scribbled on his pad. I got the acute sense he didn't believe me, and that fact made for an uncomfortable realization.

"Wait, am I being accused of something?" I replayed his earlier questions about my job and what I was up to this sum-mer, and the fact that he'd wanted to question me alone, with-out Libby, who'd witnessed everything I had—and was the mother of the child who instigated the whole situation. "Do you think I'm somehow part of this? An accomplice or some-thing?"

Warner didn't answer, but instead moved on. "Describe your argument over the candlesticks."

My skin prickled in annoyance at the memory of the interac-tion, but also in concern that Warner was already using the other witnesses' description of it being an argument. The latter did not bode well for extracting myself from whatever this tan-gle was. "Well, I offered to buy some candlesticks because I overheard this couple discussing how they were going to swin-dle him by offering way below their value, and he sold to them despite me offering much more. I thought I was being helpful and that it was a nice thing to do for someone new to the neighborhood—a person, mind you, *I've never met before.*" I emphasized the end of my statement.

He made another note on his pad. "Anything else?"

My annoyance bubbled again. "Truthfully, he was pretty rude through the whole thing. I confronted him about why he didn't take my offer, and he said he didn't care what anyone paid for anything. He only wanted to sell it all so he could sell the house and get out of town."

"He said those words? 'Get out of town'?"

"Um . . ." I paused, hesitating and unable to recall exactly what he'd said. "I'm not sure, but that's what he implied."

He continued scribbling on his pad in loops and curls, which I couldn't make out, upside down, from across the table. "Okay. Did you notice anything that seemed off about him during your interaction?"

I snorted with another comment about his manners spring-loaded on my tongue, when I remembered there was something that had been off. A few pieces clicked together in my head. "Yeah, actually. He was sweaty."

He paused writing and looked up. *"Sweaty?"*

I thought back to that little, curled J pressed against his damp temple. He had been wearing black, so the sweat wasn't readily evident elsewhere, but I had definitely seen signs of it. "Yes. Around his face, as if he'd been exerting himself. He was carrying a box of books when I first saw him, but not one big enough to really make anyone sweat with the effort."

Detective Warner held my gaze. From the look in his eye, I got the sense we were thinking the same thing.

Not sweaty enough for carrying books, but sweaty enough to have shoved a body into a closet.

"Describe finding the body. How did that play out?"

The dull thud of it hitting the floor echoed in my mind. The term *deadweight* would never be the same again.

"There wasn't much to it. Max pulled open the closet door, despite all of us telling him not to, and the body fell out. It was wrapped in a sheet, but not very well, as I'm sure you saw."

"You were telling him not to open the door?"

"Yes. Anthony was the first to tell him to stop; he was really concerned about it. I thought he didn't want a little kid opening random doors in his house, but then he charged down the hall to stop him. He obviously knew the body was in there, because why would he have cared so much otherwise?"

The detective subtly nodded, as if he didn't want to commit fully to agreeing with a statement that would have been called speculation in court. "Did he say anything to you after the body was exposed?"

I swept my memory for an answer, but shock had mostly blanked out that section of the story. "I don't think so."

"Okay. Anything else you can think of that might be important?"

There was something that jumped out, but I was still struggling to make sense of it.

The thing was, I swore I recognized the man in the closet.

Since we'd left the estate sale, I'd been racking my brain, scaling the chutes and ladders of my memory, only to come up empty. I taught hundreds of university students each year and worked with dozens of faculty members and had spent plenty of time in Libby's neighborhood, but the man in the closet wasn't a match for anyone I could think of.

I hadn't even told my sister yet, and with Warner's suspicion that I might have somehow been an accomplice, sharing with him didn't seem like the greatest idea.

"No. I can't think of anything else important." I paused before asking, "Do you know who the body is?"

Warner let out a tight breath and tapped his pen on his pad, studying me. "We haven't made a positive ID yet. Are you *sure* you didn't know Anthony Pierce before today?"

"A thousand percent positive. Why? Did he say we've met before?"

I could feel the cogs of his brain working in the silence, which spanned what felt like an eternity. "We haven't had much chance to talk to him yet. We took a brief statement at the house, but he requested a lawyer before saying anything more. We're waiting on them to come down to the station now."

"Oh."

The fact that Anthony had lawyered up so soon did not bode well for his innocence—though I would have called in help if someone had found a dead body in my closet too, even if I hadn't put it there.

I couldn't fathom why I was mentally trying to defend him. All evidence pointed to a situation to run far away from.

"Can I go now?" I asked, ready to leave the small room, which had me feeling jumpy.

Warner reached into his suit jacket pocket and pulled out a crisp white business card. "For now. Your sister has my number, but here's my card anyway. Call me if you think of anything else."

His tone left me unsure which side of the suspect-witness line I fell on. I took the card and uneasily poked its sharp edge into my fingertip. "Thank you."

Warner led me down the hall and back into the main room where phones rang, and conversations bubbled. Back out in the lobby, we found Libby in a chair, with Max limply draped over her chest like a vest, sound asleep. Ada was still napping in her stroller. Libby looked up at Detective Warner with the threat of death in her eyes if he dared suggest she wake her sleeping children so that he could question her.

He got the message and stepped back, mouthing, *We'll do this later.*

Libby nodded and rose from the chair without disturbing Max. I wrangled the stroller as we prepared to leave. Other neighbors from the area still lingered, waiting to be questioned, and I saw them in a new light, wondering which of them might accuse me of being Anthony's girlfriend.

Speak of the devil, we ran into Anthony waiting near the entrance when we exited the building. He hadn't changed out of his black uniform, but he now wore a flush in his tanned, olive-toned cheeks and a pair of sunglasses, which showed me my own reflection.

"Hey," I said, and marched right up to him. Libby took the stroller and headed for the minivan parked in the front row. A few other people milled about the front of the building. News of what had happened was already grapevining its way through town.

Anthony flinched at my directness and the finger I pointed in his face.

"The cops think I'm your girlfriend and that I'm somehow involved in this, so you need to go in there and clear all that up right now."

My statement clearly unsettled him. "What? How in the world would they get that idea?"

"I don't know. I guess the other witnesses said they noticed *chemistry* between us when we were discussing the candlesticks."

He stepped back like I'd hurled an insult at him. I stepped forward and, not seeing the edge of the curb, tripped.

For two belly-dropping seconds, I was weightless. The pavement quickly rose to greet me in a dirty gray rush, and I thought all was lost until Anthony threw out his arms to stop my fall.

"Easy," he said as I landed in his grip, already wanting to die before I even came to a full stop.

I regained my footing, but not my dignity. I was not the most graceful creature. Tripping off a curb was not new to me, and I honestly would have preferred to land hands and knees on the bird-poop-stained police station parking lot than in Anthony Pierce's arms, because not only did I now owe him thanks, but my nose was also an inch from his chest, which smelled positively divine.

"Thank you," I said on a flustered breath when I stood up.

"No problem." He sounded genuine and not as annoyed as I would have expected. The warmth of his large hands still lingered on my rib cage when I gathered myself enough to look up at him. Of course I saw my own reflection because of the sunglasses. I was flushed, with my lips parted and hair in my face. My cheeks burned deeper in embarrassment.

A deep voice interrupted from our left, putting an end to our awkward confrontation. "Anthony, good man. Always helping out a lady, just like your uncle."

Anthony dropped his grip and pivoted to the newcomer. The man wore a slick suit and had even slicker hair. His outfit screamed *lawyer* and *expensive* with the enthusiasm of a bullhorn. I could see his gold watch winking from his wrist. I wondered if he'd somehow teleported in from New York, or if Anthony had local connections to get him here so quickly.

"Mr. Mitchell," Anthony said. He stuck out his hand to shake the man's. "Thank you for coming."

"Of course. And who's this?" He turned to me with a charming smile, which felt only a tad greasy.

"Oh, um. This is my uncle's neighbor's sister," Anthony said. I noticed he put as many degrees of separation between us as possible when he could have simply said my name.

"Dr. Collins," I said, and stuck out my hand, not because I particularly wanted to make this man's acquaintance, but because I felt the need to label myself something other than the several-degrees-removed *lady* in distress who Anthony had helped.

I felt Anthony's eyes bounce to me at my use of *doctor.*

"Pleasure to meet you, Dr. Collins," Mr. Mitchell said. He

turned back to Anthony, all business. "I assume they are expecting us inside?"

"Yes," Anthony said right as Libby called to me.

"Pen! Let's go!" She stood on the runner outside the driver's door and leaned on top of the minivan, keys dangling from one hand. I'd missed the circus of loading two small children into a vehicle: the collapsing of the stroller and then strapping, belting, and securing into car seats.

I nodded at her and turned back to Anthony and his lawyer. "Please make sure you clear up any confusion in there."

Grinning, Mr. Mitchell clapped Anthony on the shoulder. "That's what I'm here for."

I watched them enter the building and was certain we were not talking about the same thing.

The crime scene tape still flapped in the breeze when we pulled the minivan back into Libby's driveway. The kids miraculously stayed asleep through our station exit and journey back home. I helped Libby nestle them into their crib and bed, and then joined her in the kitchen for a drink.

"Well, that wasn't how I expected this day to pan out," she said, pouring a luscious stream of lemonade into matching acrylic glasses. She poked neon-pink straws into each and shoved one my way.

I sat on the opposite side of the titanic granite island in the middle of her kitchen. The house was an airy aviary compared to the wooden tomb next door. We sat in a white-on-white room with tiled floors, slick countertops, and shiny appliances, which openly spilled into the dining room on one end and the toy-littered family room on the other. A bouquet of fresh lilies stood in a slender vase at the island's end, and I could see the backyard and pool through the dining-room windows, a slap of vibrant color against all the white. The space felt profoundly alive, perhaps because we'd spent the morning in a place marked by death.

"Indeed, it was not," I said, and took a swig of lemonade. The way it pinched my throat was pure summertime bliss. We'd hardly spoken on the car ride home, since the kids were asleep. I hadn't yet told Libby that the police thought I was involved with Anthony or that I thought I might have recognized the body. Admittedly, I was biding my time to figure out how to do both.

"You're not saying something. What is it?" Libby asked, reading me like a book.

I huffed like she might have been wrong when we both knew she wasn't. She was my big sister and had been fluent in my mannerisms since the day I was born.

I sipped my lemonade again and carefully set it on the island. "I have to tell you something, but I don't want you to freak out."

"Why would I freak out?" Her brow curved in an arch, which was at once curious and cautious.

I gave her a knowing stare back; I was fluent in all the subtle languages of sisterhood too. "Just don't, okay?"

She shrugged with a bulge of her eyes in silent agreement.

I opted for what I thought was the more important of the two facts. "So I recognized the guy next door. The body in the closet."

"*What?!*" she screeched, right on cue. "Why do you recognize the dead guy in the closet?"

"I don't know!"

She glanced over her shoulder toward the house next door; it was plainly visible through her kitchen window. Her voice dropped a few decibels to a conspiratorial level. "Penny, this is serious. I thought it was some freak accident that we happened to be there, but you think you *know* who it was in there?"

Her question sent a hot rush barreling up my neck into my face like I'd done something wrong. At the same time, I mentally shook my brain for the memory like a piggy bank, trying to get the lone coin to fall out of the slot. "I don't know, Lib. But I swear, I've seen him before. It's like it's on the tip of my tongue. Detective Warner said they don't have a positive ID yet, so he couldn't show me any photos to confirm."

She leaned back on the island, crossing her arms. "Well, I've never seen him before, so he's not from around here. Maybe you know him from your school?"

"Maybe, but that narrows it down to a few thousand options."

Libby's lips twisted and she went quiet in the way she did when she was thinking.

I sipped my lemonade for courage before continuing. "There's more."

"Oh?" she asked, wide-eyed.

"Yes. The police somehow have the impression that I'm Anthony's girlfriend. Warner was questioning me like I might be involved."

"*What?!*" she screeched again. Her face paled in shock and then flushed red in anger. "You told him you're not, right?"

"Of course I did!"

"Good!"

Both of our voices had risen to howler monkey levels. Libby took a breath and fished her phone out of her legging pocket. "This is absurd. I'm going to text Nicole and tell her to tell her husband that he's way off base."

"I already told him."

"Well, he needs to hear it from multiple sources." She angrily tapped her phone like it had thrown a punch at her.

"Lib, relax. I told Anthony to clear it up when he talked to them. That's what we were talking about in the parking lot at the station."

She scoffed. "And you trust him?"

It was my turn to scoff. "Need I remind you that you were trying to *set me up* with him mere hours ago?"

"Yes, but that was before I knew he was a serial killer!"

"He's not a serial killer!" I said, surprised to hear myself defending him. "I don't think . . ."

Libby glared at me. "Penelope, we found a *body* in his closet! Who has bodies in their closets? *Serial killers.*"

"You watch too many true crime documentaries. And he's a really bad serial killer if he stashed a body in his closet and then had an estate sale the same day. Most serial killers are smarter than that. *And* serial means many, not one."

She narrowed her eyes in another glare. "How do you know serial killers are smart if you don't watch true crime docs too?"

I let out an exasperated huff and rounded the island into the dining room to look out the wall of French doors. I could see the backyard next door. The crime scene tape circled the house's whole perimeter like a big, loose rubber band. The back door Libby had dragged me and her children through, as if the house was on fire, still stood open. Police officials came in and out, snapping photos and placing little yellow markers on the ground. I wondered if the body had been removed yet. A detached garage sat back from the back porch. It shared the same jade green siding and faded white trim as the main house. The car, a boat of an old green Cadillac, always sat in the driveway, so I had to assume the garage was not used for parking.

Thoughts of what might be in there made me shudder.

Libby came up behind me and stood on her toes to rest her chin on my shoulder. She was older, but I'd been taller since a growth spurt in high school. "Will you stay here with me and the kids? Please? I don't want to be alone with him next door."

I had the feeling she was going to ask. I couldn't blame her, what with her husband currently five thousand miles away. "Tonight?"

I felt her shrug against my back. "At least."

She was being vague on purpose, and I knew one night could turn into all summer if she unleashed her expert persuasion skills on me.

"Anthony said he's only staying until he sells the house," I said.

She snorted. "Yeah, and who's going to buy that house, now that everyone knows they found a body in it?"

It was a solid point. "Why don't you ask Mom to come stay with you and the kids?"

Libby dramatically groaned. "Oh, *God.* Sign me up for an axe murderer neighbor before Mom."

That was a fair comment. Libby was a bit of a black sheep in our family. Our mother was an English professor, and I could easily coexist in the same house with her, given we were both prone to long bouts of solitude and silence while engaged in reading or studying. Our father, a renowned mathematician, wasn't much different. A man of very few words and a mind full of equations, he found opportunities to teach and to learn at every turn. A social creature, Libby thrived on conversation and constant company and stimulation. She and our parents exhausted each other in opposite ways.

"What else do you have going on anyway? It's summer."

I cast her a glower over my shoulder. "I'm trying to make tenure, remember?"

"Ah, right. Truly, our parents' child. Well, you can do that remotely, can't you?" The plea in her voice was almost a whine. I hated saying no to her, and she made it near impossible. She circled in front of me and gripped my shoulders. "Listen, it's either you stay here, or I pack up the kids and haul all three of us up there to your apartment, and we all know the latter would be a disaster."

She was right. I had one bathroom, a kitchen the size of a

postage stamp compared to hers, and my spare room was a glorified nook I'd converted into an office by way of adding a fern and a desk to it.

The look on my face must have given me away. She saw me swaying and pounced.

"Yes! You're going to say yes. I can see it in your eyes!"

I rolled my eyes and moved out of her grip to walk back to the kitchen. "I'll stay *tonight,* but, Lib, he's probably not even going to come back home. I mean, the house is a literal crime scene, and even if that lawyer looked fancy, I doubt they're going to let him go so quick—"

My sentence stopped midbreath. At the proper angle, we could also see the neighbor's driveway through the kitchen window. And at that moment, a shiny black sedan pulled up and parked. Anthony Pierce climbed out of the passenger side while the lawyer from the police station climbed out the driver's side. They shook hands at the hood of the car, and then the lawyer turned around and waved at the police officers still on the scene. His gold watch glinted in the sun.

Two officers came over to talk to him, and after a brief discussion, they nodded and promptly removed the crime scene tape.

Anthony stood on the porch and watched it all happen like the director on a film set. Even from a distance, I could see a small smile playing at his lips. The sight of it, along with the police scurrying about like ants to erase evidence that something nefarious had taken place, put an unsettling weight in my gut—a stone dropped from afar and left to slowly sink.

"How is that possible?" Libby said what I was thinking, in the same stunned tone that I was thinking it.

"Must be a good lawyer," I said, shocked that they hadn't arrested him.

Something about the whole scene felt off. Like when putting

a shoe on the wrong foot or missing the bottom step on a staircase. It didn't fit, and watching it unfold made me feel like that stone in my belly had lifted only to fall even harder.

The unsettling feeling only grew when Anthony turned, looked right at us through the window, as if he knew we were watching, and waved like a friendly neighbor.

CHAPTER 3

True to my word about staying, I spent the afternoon exhausting the kids in the pool before I helped with dinner and bath time. I read Max a bedtime story while Libby rocked Ada to sleep in the next room over.

I'd just finished our book and was going to turn off Max's bedroom light when I caught glimpse of something small and shiny on his floor. He had plenty of toys, but the object lying near a herd of stuffed animals seemed out of place.

I crossed the room to pick it up and saw that it was a key. A small gold one that looked suited for a mailbox or maybe a bike lock. I turned it over and saw no distinct marking, no engraved initials or indication of what it might open. It was entirely nondescript. He must have found it somewhere and had kept it as treasure, as he was prone to do.

I pocketed the shiny, little choking hazard and turned off his light.

I left his room and crept back downstairs. The cavernous house stood silent and softly glowing like a caramel-orange sky in the moments after the sun sinks below the horizon. My brother-in-law had it rigged with lighting that optimized circadian performance, which basically meant it was hazy golden orange at night and crisp white blue in the morning and daytime. John funded their life with a career in robotics engineering that even I struggled to understand half the time, and that often took him away on business. Like right now, when he was spending three months in Tokyo to work with a team that was going to build something to save the planet in one way or another.

The living-room lights turned on with a slowly rising glow rather than a harsh flick when I entered, another one of John's tricks. My eyes easily adjusted as I sank down onto the couch.

It didn't take long for Libby to join me and fall asleep watching old sitcom reruns with her feet pressed into my hip, despite having the length of her enormous sectional to stretch out on. She hugged a pillow and quietly snored through a canned laugh track and set of familiar jokes playing on a TV screen big enough to be seen from outer space. I wore a pair of her borrowed pajamas—cotton shorts and an oversized T-shirt. The lights were low, all the doors locked. I was nestled and comfortable and pulled out my phone to do something I'd been wanting to do all day, but hadn't gotten the chance.

Stalk Anthony Pierce on social media.

I went through the major platforms, one by one. There were dozens of Anthony Pierces, ranging from teenagers to business professionals, gym rats to retired old men. I clicked through a few and didn't see his smoldering eyes staring back at me from any of the profile photos.

After several fruitless minutes, I frowned and set my phone down. Plenty of people didn't do social media; it didn't have to mean anything suspicious. But the lack of a digital footprint coupled with everything else that had happened had me reaching for my laptop I'd left on the coffee table to dig a little deeper.

The episode playing on TV ended and Libby stirred. I'd just typed *Anthony Pierce, New York* into a browser when she suddenly sat up and spoke.

"Oh no, she's still missing?" she said in a sleepy drawl.

"Who's missing?" I asked without looking up from my screen. My eyes widened. My search returned more results than I expected.

Libby pushed herself up to sit and reached for the remote balanced on the coffee table. "Portia Slate. Don't you watch the news?"

The name rang a bell, but not because I'd heard it any time recently. "Sorry, end of the semester has been a little busy."

The volume on the TV rose, and a news anchor's voice cut into the room's quiet hum. I looked up from my screen.

". . . missing since last Saturday. The tech billionaire's wife was last reported seen at the couple's home in Woodside, the affluent community west of Palo Alto. Her husband, Connor Slate, CEO of EnViSage, reported her missing after she did not return from a jog. Local authorities have been searching the wooded area around the Slates' property. A missing person report has also been issued and shared with regional and state-level authorities. Mrs. Slate was reported to be wearing black leggings, a dark blue fleece sweater, and blue running shoes when she was last seen. The news of Mrs. Slate's disappearance came just days after her husband made headlines for EnViSage's failed acquisition of StarCloud. We will continue updating on the story as we learn more."

"Rough week for that guy," Libby muttered. "He loses a multibillion-dollar deal *and* his wife goes missing? I bet he killed her."

As the news anchor spoke, a brief carousel of images cycled through: Portia in a smart pantsuit with her blond hair pulled back into a low ponytail, waving at a crowd from a stage at a convention. Portia in a sparkling gown, with her famous husband in a tux, on a red carpet. Portia in a bikini on a boat, surrounded by a shock of teal water, squinting for a vacation selfie in the bright sun. Portia on a sidewalk in jeans and a baseball cap, looking like she was trying to blend in on a coffee run. She was young, beautiful, and married to one of the richest men on the planet.

"Oh, my God," I said in shock. The dawn of realization hit me like a sledgehammer. Pieces snapped and clicked into place so quickly, I lost control of my breath.

"What's the matter?" Libby asked as I sat up.

I reached for the remote in her hand and tried to stop the images on the screen. "I know her," I said in a daze as I frantically jabbed at buttons. It wasn't only Portia. There was someone else in the periphery of each photo that I needed a closer look at, and the images were going by too fast. "How do I pause it?"

Libby snatched the remote away, giving me a flashback to our youth when we used to squabble over control of the TV. "What's going on, Pen? You *know* Portia Slate?"

The pieces continued crashing together as the news story transitioned into another topic. "I don't *know* her, know her. But I've met her, and I think . . ." I trailed off and opened a new tab on my laptop, lost in the chaos of my own thoughts. I jammed in *Portia Slate public* and hit an image search.

Libby gave me her full attention. She sat at the couch's edge and leaned over to see what I was doing. "You think what? And when did you meet her?"

I was half listening, half remembering the day of our brief interaction. "She came to campus once. The Slate Foundation donated a new computer lab to the school last year, and they sent her for the occasion. She met with the university president and the department deans, and then they made me take her for coffee. I guess because they think only young women can socialize with other young women. Or maybe they were all too intimidated, I don't know. But it wasn't only her, it was also . . ." I trailed off again, scanning the grid of images that had populated my screen. Many of the photos were the same ones we'd seen on TV, but now I could zoom in, look closer, and take my time to connect the frayed threads unspooling in my head.

"You had coffee with a billionaire's wife and never told me?" Libby said, glomming on to a truly trivial element, given the situation.

"It was a work thing; I didn't think you'd care," I muttered, and kept scanning.

She sputtered in disagreement right as my eyes landed on what I was looking for. My heart surged up into my throat and beat there with a force that strangled my voice.

"No way. It *is* him."

"Him who?" Libby demanded, elbowing her way closer to my screen.

She didn't need to, because I refined my search to *Portia Slate bodyguard* and turned my computer to face her.

"*Him.*" I pointed at an image of a broad man with buzzed hair wearing sunglasses and a black T-shirt. He was a shadow, a background prop, a houseplant. Invisible in every photo unless you went looking for him. The search results ranged from casual sidewalk candids to black-tie events, his wardrobe adapting from streetwear to a tux. But one constant remained: He was always an arm's length away from Portia Slate.

"That's why I recognize him, Lib. He's Portia Slate's bodyguard! He was with her that day on campus. And he was . . ." I swallowed hard, only daring to imagine the full implications of my realization. "He was the body that fell out of the closet."

Libby stared at me with eyes wider than the moon. Her mouth popped open and slowly closed a few times before she could summon words. "Are you sure?"

"Yes. You saw him too. Don't you agree?"

She squinted at my screen with a look of unease. "I mean, that guy was dead, and this guy is very much *not* dead. He's *huge.*" Her eyes popped again, and I could see her remembering the size of the body that had fallen at our feet. She shook her head in shock. "If it's him, what does it mean?"

I looked back at the photos as my certainty that it was the same man, and my uncertainty over what it meant, both grew to unsettling proportions. I could think of several scenarios that would explain why Portia Slate's dead bodyguard was in Anthony Pierce's closet, and all of them were too chilling to voice aloud.

In our stunned silence, the next news story spilled out into the room. The female anchor narrated.

"A local estate sale was cut short today when a body was found inside a closet in the house. Authorities were called to the scene just before noon. The homeowner, the late Lou Griotti, passed away last week. His nephew, who recently inherited the house, Anthony Pierce, was hosting the sale and has been questioned by police. Authorities have not yet released the identity of the body or named any suspects in the incident, though Mr. Pierce is a person of interest. He can be seen in this photo captured outside the police station today, along with his lawyer and the woman believed to be his girlfriend."

My jaw dropped through the floor. It was me. In Anthony's arms. Looking like a distressed damsel right in the moment after he'd caught me, and before his lawyer had interrupted us.

"What. The. Hell." Libby voiced what I was thinking. "Who took that picture? And how did it get on the news?!"

My heart was pumping too much blood to my ears to hear straight. My vision began to blur. All I knew was that the two news stories on TV were connected, and the man next door had turned me into the glue.

Despite my sister's protests, I shoved on flip-flops and marched over to Anthony's house. The bulk of the Victorian sat dark, sucked into the backdrop of inky night, except for a few lights on the first floor, which had the house eerily glowing like a jack-o'-lantern. I knew he was still up. Libby tried to force me to take a can of pepper spray, but I didn't have any pockets. All I had was my phone and a raging fury propelling me into the warm night. I swore to her that I wouldn't go inside, and I knew she would supervise our entire interaction from her kitchen window.

My borrowed rubber sandals smacked the same path I'd walked up that morning when I existed in a world without dead bodies and mysterious neighbors. Everything had changed, and I hoped a conversation with the person responsible would be enough to change it back. I could *not* afford a police investigation this summer. The only thing that could tank a tenure case faster might have been plagiarism.

The arthritic front steps creaked under my feet, announcing my arrival before I even reached the doorbell. When I pressed the button, it chimed like a church organ into the gulch of the house.

Nothing happened.

I shifted my weight and glanced over at Libby, where I could see her hovering inside her kitchen window, backlit by the recessed lights and chewing her lip. Crickets chirped; trees rustled. A car engine purred in the distance.

A pang of guilt hit me that I might truly be disturbing Anthony so late at night. I let it go with an annoyed huff, thinking of all the ways he'd already disturbed my life, and knocked.

After a solid minute that almost made me give up and turn home, the door cracked open an inch. Anthony's dark eye filled the narrow gap. He blinked a few times and then opened the door farther.

"Oh. It's just you," he said.

"Were you expecting someone else?" My hand landed on my hip of its own accord. I felt his eyes take in my pajamas and flip-flops, my hair in a messy bun, and phone gripped in one hand.

He pulled the door all the way open and scanned the street behind me. His sharp gaze almost made me turn around to see if there was anything there worth looking at. "At eleven p.m.? I can't say I was expecting anyone to ring my doorbell."

"Well, I won't take much of your time. I came over to say you *obviously* didn't clear things up with the police, because I saw *on the news* that I'm supposedly your girlfriend!" My voice cut the night like a blade. He leaned back from it and from my phone that I shoved in his face. "'Anthony Pierce, person of interest, *and his girlfriend* outside the police station,'" I quoted from the news article I'd pulled up. The same photo from TV filled the screen.

He blinked at the bright screen in the dim porch light. He reached out for my wrist to hold my hand steady so he could read the small print. "Oh. I'm very sorry about that."

I wasn't expecting an apology. I bit back the next bullet loaded on my tongue ready to continue my rampage. I swallowed and composed myself. "You should be. What are you going to do about it?"

He looked at me like he was really considering a solution. It gave me time to notice he was still in all black, but this time, a pair of joggers slung low around his hips and a T-shirt. He wore only socks on his feet, and something about seeing him shoeless set the air on an intimate edge, which made me shift my weight again. He hadn't let go of my wrist. His long fingers circled it in a gentle loop like he might have been checking my pulse. I hoped he wasn't, because it was beating at a rather embarrassing pace.

He opened his mouth to speak, but snapped it shut just as quickly. His hand clamped down on my wrist with a suddenness that stole my breath. Before I could even throw a desperate glance at Libby, he yanked me inside his house.

I stumbled over the threshold with a yelp, my flip-flops smacking the hardwood floor and my free arm cartwheeling. I almost landed on my face. "What are you doing?!" I demanded as he let go of me and threw the door shut. I spun around, ready to defend myself, but he wasn't looking at me. He was pressed up against the door, peering out the peephole.

My heart absolutely jackhammered my ribs. It was fit to beat out of my chest, and the manic wailing on my bones only compounded when I saw what was tucked into the back waistband of his joggers.

A gun.

I froze as if I'd been dropped into a pen with a tiger. If I stopped moving, stopped breathing, maybe he wouldn't notice I was there.

As the seconds ticked by, a primitive chamber of my brain screamed at me to run. But to where? He was blocking the door, and there was no way I could shove a man of his size out of the way to get by—especially if he had a gun.

Why did he have a gun?!

I realized then I didn't really want to stick around to find out. Libby had probably already called the police. For the second time today, the house would be crawling with authorities any minute.

In its spiral of panic, my brain managed to remember it *was* the second time today that I'd needed to escape this house. The first time, I'd gone out the back door, and I could do it again.

With Anthony's attention still out the front door, I took a step back, deeper into the foyer. When my flip-flop smacked on the floor, I winced. As quickly and as quietly as I could, I removed each shoe and prepared to silently run for the back door. The hardwood floor was smooth and cold beneath my bare feet, like a river rock in the shade. I crept backward a few more steps, cautiously pressing the balls of my feet into the floor and praying it didn't creak. When he didn't turn around after three steps, I pivoted and sprinted for the hall.

Shadows lurched out of every corner in the dim house. I passed the living room and then the closet, with its shiny green knob protruding like a gemstone. The hallway was put back together, as if nothing had happened. I flew down it toward the door at its end. The only other light spilled out from the last room on the left. The door stood open, and a golden swath painted the hall from a glowing lamp.

I stomped to a stop when something inside caught my eye. The room, a neatly appointed office, had dark green wallpaper, the same wooden floor I stood on, a hulking desk, and a leather chair, which was nothing short of a throne. None of that was out of place. What caught my eye was a crowbar on the desk and the painting swung out into the room, a secret hatch to reveal a safe nestled into the wall. A safe with a keyhole. A golden keyhole that looked suited for the small key I'd found on Max's bedroom floor.

"Penny! Wait!" Anthony called from the other end of the house, far enough away to sound like he was shouting down a tunnel.

My heart had never stopped pounding, but it picked up pace again at sight of him coming my way.

I bolted for the back door and tore it open. The back porch creaked the same as the front porch, and soon I was padding over the concrete of his driveway, still holding my shoes. I turned left and ran straight toward Libby's backyard gate. A strip of cool grass momentarily soothed my feet when I reached the side yard separating the two lots. The gate only opened from Libby's side, and there was no way I could reach over to lift the latch. I was ready to scale the fence barefoot when the gate flung open. Libby stood on the other side, her face awash with panic and anger.

I plowed into her, never having stopped running.

She took the hit like a tackle and fell back onto her lawn,

with me on top of her. "Penny! What are you doing?" she demanded, and tried to sit up.

"What are *you* doing?" I gasped, out of breath and shocked, but thankful to see her.

"I was coming to get you! I saw him pull you inside, and when you didn't come back out the front door, I figured I'd go in through the back door."

I pushed up off her and noticed then she was holding a tennis racket. "And do what, hit him with your backhand?"

"It was this or John's nine iron. You know we don't have any weapons in the house," she said as she sat up.

By *weapons,* she meant *guns.* Any number of things in her house could serve as a weapon in a pinch: sports equipment, kitchen knives, pruning shears, a handful of Max's Legos strategically strewn about. The thought of the gun in Anthony's waistband made me shudder.

I flinched when the light from his back porch flicked on. Libby took the cue from me and reached for my hand. Like we were fleeing a searchlight, she hunched over and led me back to her house. My speeding heart only began to slow once we were inside behind her locked doors.

"I told you that was a bad idea," she said, and set the tennis racket on the dining table.

I released a long breath in agreement. "What was in the street when he pulled me inside? All he did was shut the door and look out the peephole."

"He didn't hurt you? You didn't have to escape?" she said with unmistakable relief.

"Well, I mean I kind of escaped. But he wasn't trying to stop me. He didn't tie me up or anything." I felt my wrist where he'd held it, the warmth of his hand a fading memory.

"Good. Now I don't have to kill him."

A weak laugh popped from my mouth, though I didn't think

she was kidding. "What was he looking at?" I repeated my question.

"A car drove by. That's all I saw."

"Did you recognize it?"

"It's pretty dark, but it looked like a normal car."

"Normal?"

She lifted her shoulders in a shrug. "I don't know, Pen! A black car, with dark windows. I didn't pay too much attention, because I was too worried about my idiotic little sister getting snatched!"

"I didn't get snatched." *But he has a gun.*

I didn't say the last part out loud because, surely, she would begin screeching again and perhaps attack me with the tennis racket.

"Well, not for lack of trying. You're not allowed to go over there again," she scolded, and pointed a finger at me like I was a rebellious teenager sneaking out to see my boyfriend.

I couldn't promise her I wouldn't. We still had to sort out the girlfriend issue, and my curiosity about the key Max had found belonging to the safe in that back office was gnawing, to put it mildly. Not to mention, moments before I'd discovered the world believed me to be Anthony Pierce's girlfriend, I'd identified the body in his closet as Portia Slate's bodyguard.

The pieces were enough to make me shudder. Part of me wanted to run far away from it all and another part wanted answers. But the biggest part—that was connected straight to my heartstrings—had me wanting to stay with my sister and quell the look of terror in her eyes.

"I'll be careful, Lib," I said. "And I'll go up to the city tomorrow and get my stuff to stay here for a while, okay?"

Her shoulders sagged with relief. "Thank you."

We said good night, but I knew I would be chasing sleep for hours.

Back upstairs, I resumed the internet search that got cut off when the news had come on. *Anthony Pierce, New York.* The tab I'd opened was still there waiting for me. As it turned out, the hefty haul of results I'd seen was due to the news breaking about the body, not anything to do with Anthony in general. In fact, his absence on social media bled over into any kind of digital footprint. Other than stories about the estate sale, he didn't seem to exist. I even used a VPN to hide my sister's IP address before combing a few dark corners of the Web, locations I'd learned from an old grad school roommate who was poached out of our program to go work for the NSA. Even in those unseemly places, nothing.

I frowned all over again. Existing in today's world without any kind of digital footprint was near impossible, and a feat only accomplished by conspiracy theorists or people who had legitimate reasons to stay offline. While mysterious and cagey, the man next door did not strike me as the type to hole up in a basement with canned goods and a doomsday clock. Anthony Pierce was invisible on purpose.

A list of the types of people to be invisible on purpose ran through my mind, and I quickly cross-referenced it with who might also have a body in their closet and a gun in their pj's: a spy, a black-ops agent, or, the most likely option, a criminal.

I swallowed a thick lump.

As invisible as Anthony was online, I, on the other hand, was very visible. A simple search of my name would bring up my faculty profile, lists of publications, conference presentations, ratemyprofessor.com ratings. There was no way I could scrub myself from the internet, and all it would take was someone recognizing me from the photo for the already-moving snowball to gather speed into an avalanche. I was already battling stereotypes as one of the only women in my department. I couldn't give them any reason to doubt me, and showing up on the nightly news in suspicious fashion would not work in my favor.

I weighed the options of getting out in front of it by notifying my tenure committee versus keeping quiet and hoping they didn't notice. The latter seemed unlikely, given it was already all over the internet *and* on TV. Dr. Benson, my committee chair, watched the nightly news like religion. He'd probably already seen it and was drafting my termination letter.

The thought hadn't even fully formed in my mind before my email *pinged* with a message that sent a shock wave of terror through me.

Dr. Benson had watched the evening news and felt compelled to reach out about it. He was notorious for emailing at all hours, and the expected response time was nothing short of instant. His preferred style of communication was short bursts of speech or text that the recipient was responsible for interpreting: Concerning story on the news tonight.

He didn't have to say more because we both knew what he meant.

I blinked at my screen until my eyes were dry, silently panicking over how to respond. The idea of late-night messaging with my committee chair about dead bodies and fake boyfriends was nearly as terrifying as the dead body itself. I had a vision of him giving me one of his stern stares that made undergrads cry and felt my career circling dangerously close to a drain.

I took a bracing breath and typed out a response.

Hi, Dr. Benson,
It's all a misunderstanding. My sister lives next door to the house where the estate sale was, and we happened to be there at the time of the incident. I had no part in it, other than being a witness. I don't even know Anthony Pierce and we certainly aren't dating.
Penny

I hit send and considered diving under a pillow.

His response came almost instantly: **Good. I'd hate for there to be any distractions that could complicate your tenure case, and the school doesn't need any bad press.**

Even if he didn't mean it as a threat, I took it as one: **Of course, Dr. Benson, there won't be. I'll take care of it.**

I hit send on my reply and shut my laptop with a snap. I wished I could go back in time and forget everything about the candlesticks. I wished I'd never gone to the estate sale. I wished I'd stayed in the city, where we had predictable crimes, like muggings and corner store hold-ups and hit-and-runs. But no, I'd come to suburbia for the weekend and was now neck deep in a crime because of a giant misunderstanding.

I stood from the bed. When I crossed the room to close the curtains, ready to attempt sleep, I froze in my tracks. My bedroom window faced Anthony's living-room window, among many others. He stood in his living room, staring up at my window and sipping something in a glass tumbler. When he saw me eyeing him, he didn't even flinch. He stood there, calmly sipping and watching me.

I steeled myself and tried to stare back, but I only lasted a few seconds before I yanked the curtains closed and turned off the light.

CHAPTER 4

I planned to leave early Sunday morning to make it to the city and back before nightfall. Libby's unease about the new neighbor increased exponentially after dark, as if Anthony Pierce wasn't capable of doing anything untoward in the daylight. I bit back the urge to remind her the body-in-the-closet incident had occurred midmorning, because I also felt a prickle at the back of my neck at the thought of what had happened in the dark last night.

As I filled my to-go coffee mug in the kitchen, I noted the old green Cadillac parked in the driveway next door. It had been there all night, sitting like a docked barge every time I'd looked out the bedroom window. I'd woken three times: One was from a strange dream about a woman missing in the woods; again because Ada had decided that 2:00 a.m. was a good time for a cry; and a third time for no reason I could gather other than that a sound outside must have startled me. I saw nothing, however, other than the Cadillac when I looked.

I finished filling my mug with an extra splash of caffeine to compensate for my disrupted sleep and snapped the lid, ready to head for the door. Libby was upstairs with the kids still, shoving tiny feet into socks and policing teeth brushing.

When I opened the front door, I gasped in surprise at the sight of someone standing there poised to knock.

Anthony Pierce, looking fresh and damp and flushed in the face, as if he'd just finished showering after a jog. His spicy, heady scent welcomed itself in the door, like it had come over for a visit.

"What are you doing here?" My voice snapped harder than I meant. I wondered if I was subconsciously annoyed with him for being so attractive and simultaneously unsettling. I wanted to run away from him *the exact same amount* that I wanted to stay and talk to him.

He held up his hands like he sensed my discomfort. "I just want to talk to you."

I glanced over my shoulder at the stairs. No sign of Libby or the kids, but they could descend at any second, and Libby would lose her shit if she saw me talking to him. I turned back around to tell him it wasn't a good time and froze with my mouth open.

A news van had pulled to the curb in front of the house. ACTION8 was splashed on the side in vibrant blue-and-gold lettering. A young, eager-looking man climbed out of the passenger seat wearing a blazer and button-down. His tie flapped in the motion, and he held a notepad in his hand.

"Nope," I said plainly. In a move identical to last night, aside from the reversed roles, I grabbed Anthony's arm and yanked him inside. My fingers hardly closed around his thick wrist, and tugging on him was like trying to move a boulder, but the urgency of my grip and the sharpest yank I could muster got the job done.

He stumbled across the threshold like I had done last night and landed in my sister's pristine entryway like a black UFO crash-landed on a white planet.

I shoved the door shut and threw the dead bolt. I turned around and pressed my back into it and found Anthony blinking at me in surprise.

"What are you doing?" he asked.

"Shhh!" I hissed, mostly to keep Libby from hearing him,

but also because I felt the need to hide from the reporter on the other side of the door. "They can't see us together!"

"Why not?" he whispered. He looked confused and slightly amused by the situation.

I flapped my hand in exasperation. I somehow had managed not to spill my coffee in my other hand. "Because! They think we're a couple, and you're a . . . *criminal,* and I'm just trying to make tenure!" I barked at him in a harsh whisper.

He notably ignored the criminal comment. "You're a professor?"

"Yes."

"Of what?"

"Computer sciences. Why is that relevant?"

He shrugged. "I was curious about what kind of doctor when you introduced yourself to my lawyer yesterday."

I threw a glance at the staircase again right as the doorbell rang. The sound jolted me like a cattle prod. "Well, now you know. You need to leave. My sister will murder both of us if she catches you in here. Go out the back door."

"Okay. I'll go. I just came over here to ask you something."

"Ask it."

I was grinding my teeth into dust, and praying the reporter would go away, when Libby called down the stairs. "Penny? Are you still here? Who's at the door?"

My heart trilled in my throat. I was a rabbit in a trap in multiple ways. No matter which way I turned, I faced trouble: the wrath of my sister, the criminal next door, or a reporter who wanted details on all of it.

Anthony watched me in anticipation. All I had to do was scream and all hell would break loose. Libby had told me to stay away from him, and here he was *inside her house* because of me.

I knocked my head back against the door, wishing I could rewind and make it all go away.

"Pen?" Libby called again.

"It's . . . a reporter," I managed to call. My voice sounded strangled.

"A reporter? Why would—Max! Don't do that."

I sent silent thanks to my nephew for distracting her. Then I snapped my fingers at Anthony and pointed toward the kitchen. "Out the back door. Go!"

He held up his hands in surrender and started that way. I followed right on his heels and, with a rush of relief, noted the absence of a gun sticking from his waistband. He stopped when we made it to the dining room and turned to me. "Did you happen to find anything in my house yesterday?"

I flinched at his abrupt movement and the reminder he'd said he had come over to ask me something. "What, you mean other than a dead body?"

His face flattened into a frown. "Yes, other than that. I saw your nephew running around, and he's . . . well, he's a little grabby, what with the closet incident and all, so I'm wondering if he picked it up. It's a small key, and I really need it back." The vulnerable desperation in his voice put an odd pang in my chest at the same time I realized I was right about Max swiping the key at the estate sale.

I thought back to the safe and the crowbar I'd seen in his office last night. "What does it open?"

He eyed me like he knew I already knew the answer. "Something important."

The sound of hurried but light footsteps overhead reminded me we were on borrowed time, but I realized I had a serious bargaining chip.

"Suppose I do have it. I might be willing to negotiate its exchange." I did my best to sound confident. When his eyes darted to my tote and then my pockets, like he might try to search me for the key, it took all my strength not to flinch.

He was looking in the wrong place anyway. I'd stashed the key upstairs under my bedside lamp.

He stepped closer and I got dizzy off his scent. He radiated heat and an unnerving but enticing energy. His voice came out a low growl that nearly liquified me on the spot. "In return for what?"

The doorbell rang again, as if on cue. I sucked in another sharp breath like I'd been electrocuted. "First and foremost, for clearing up this ridiculous misunderstanding that I'm your girlfriend and any way involved in this."

He bobbed his head in agreement. "And what else?"

I tightened my grip on my tote and summoned the courage to demand something I wasn't entirely sure I wanted to possess. "And you have to tell me what all this has to do with Portia Slate."

Clearly, he was not expecting this. All his brooding swagger drained from him; it was as if I'd pulled the plug on a bathtub. His mouth fell open in shock. His eyes went desperately wide. "What do you know about Portia?"

"I—"

I couldn't get another word out before Max's tiny voice came singing down the stairs. "Aunt Penny! There's someone at the door!"

My lungs seized in panic. I shoved Anthony toward the French doors. "You have to leave. *Now.*"

He stumbled a few steps and turned to me as he walked backward. "Penny, I need that key."

In that moment, the threat of getting caught talking to him was greater than whatever handing over the key might lead to. I just needed him gone.

"Okay! I'll bring it to you tonight. I'm on my way out of town right now. Now *go.* The gate leads to your yard." I pointed and nervously looked over my shoulder.

"Thank you." He reached for the nearest handle in the line of doors and slipped outside.

I turned right in time to see Max appear from the kitchen, dressed for the day in his favorite T-shirt covered in cartoon bugs. "Who were you talking to, Aunt Penny?" he asked with an innocent tilt of his head. His curls were still mashed on one side from sleep.

I marched across the room and ruffled his hair to fluff it into shape. "No one, bud. I've got to get going."

I headed for the front door, finally ready to leave. I was sure the reporter would have given up after two rings and no answer, but he was still standing on the porch.

"Penny Collins?" he asked when I opened the door.

I cringed at the realization they knew my name, but naturally they did. How else would they have known to show up at the house? And on that note, I preemptively braced myself to be prepared for more reporters waiting at my apartment in the city.

I saw another car had pulled up on the street in the time since I'd been talking to Anthony. A man in a tweed jacket leaned against the passenger door staring at the house like he was waiting to see how the first reporter fared before giving it a go himself.

Feeling trapped and wanting to get to my car, I stepped outside and closed the front door behind me. "Yes?" I reluctantly said to the first reporter on the porch.

"I'm wondering if I can ask you a few questions about your relationship with Anthony Pierce and yesterday's incident."

I gave him nothing but a flat stare. "I don't have a relationship with Anthony Pierce, and I have no comment on yesterday's incident. If you have questions, I suggest you go talk to him." I pointed at the old Victorian. I stepped around the reporter and headed for my car in the driveway.

The other man parked at the curb watched me without comment. Something about his gaze put an unsettling stir in my gut. I couldn't identify it other than as being uncomfortable, and I found myself thankful when I heard Anthony's voice call out from his porch.

"Hey, I'm the one you want to talk to," he said, and both men looked over at him.

I silently thanked him for the diversion as I climbed in my car with a sense of hopeful relief he was going to hold up his end of the deal and make this go away.

By the time I drove all the way up to campus, packed up my office, went home and filled two suitcases with clothes, filled a tote bag with books, boxed up my potted plants, crammed it all into my compact EV, and battled south-bound traffic all the way back down the peninsula, night had fallen.

Libby was already cleaning up dinner when I came through the front door.

"There you are," she said over a sip of wine. "I was starting to worry."

"Sorry. Traffic was brutal." I hoisted one of my book bags up onto the island.

She poured me a glass of wine. "I made you a plate if you're hungry. I'm going to head up for bath time."

I took a sip of the luscious red wine and let the flavor flood my mouth. "I'm starving, thank you. I'll be unpacking for the rest of the night, so I'll be out of your way."

I internally cringed at lying to her, but she would lock me up and throw away the key if I told her I was going over to see Anthony. I still had to figure out how I was going to sneak out, and was banking on her being distracted with the kids all night.

"You know where to find me," she said with a wave and headed toward the stairs.

I was, in fact, starving, so I rummaged in the fridge for the leftovers and found a container of pasta with a meaty sauce. Among her many skills, my sister's cooking ranked at the top. I stood over the sink and forked a few mouthfuls, washing it down with wine, and nearly choked when I looked up to see Anthony staring at me from his living-room window.

He waved, at first like he was saying hi, and then in a motion that said *come here.*

He'd been waiting for me to get home, clearly. And watching.

A tingle shot up my spine at both facts. I set the pasta down, but kept the wine. I took another gulp to quell my fear over willingly returning to his house. For all intents and purposes, it was not a good idea, especially going over there without telling Libby where I was.

I could simply hurl the key over the fence and never talk to him again, but, especially after my emails with Dr. Benson, I wanted confirmation he'd told all the relevant parties I was not tied to him in any way. And I also desperately wanted to know what had happened to Portia Slate.

The latter perhaps went most against my better judgment. The true danger lay down that road, I was certain. The look on Anthony's face this morning when I'd mentioned Portia's name, coupled with her dead bodyguard, said I should leave it all alone. But my curiosity went beyond simply that. I was concerned. I may have only met her for a fleeting moment, but too many women disappeared at the hands of powerful men.

If I had to be wrapped up in this mess, I was at least going to find out what happened to her.

I waved back at Anthony. I held up one finger to tell him he'd have to wait a little longer, and then pointed toward his back door. There was no way I could walk out my sister's front door and into his if I was hoping not to get caught, even if Libby was the one encouraging me to be more adventurous.

I killed an hour unpacking and waiting for Libby to settle in front of the TV. Once she got there, it would be mere minutes before she was asleep.

Now I was sitting on the bed, scrolling the news on my laptop and waiting for the sound of a laugh track to start from downstairs. The headlines on Portia Slate had only continued to multiply:

BILLIONAIRE'S WIFE STILL MISSING
SILICON VALLEY TRAGEDY: WHEREABOUTS OF PORTIA SLATE
REMAIN UNKNOWN
LOCAL AUTHORITIES INCREASE SEARCH EFFORTS IN MISSING
SOCIALITE CASE

I'd met Portia Slate only briefly that day on campus. I was often outsourced as the department welcome wagon, not because I was particularly welcoming, but because I was young, female, and, despite my sister's opinions, possessed a higher-than-average degree of social skills for someone in my field. It occurred to me as Portia and I had sipped coffee that she'd been outsourced too. In her case, as the public face of her husband's foundation. When she asked me about work and I quipped about my unofficial job description including having to entertain guests, we found ourselves bonding over our shared annoyance with the relationship maintenance that was often forced on women. While we chatted, her bodyguard remained close enough for me to remember his face. Portia was as beautiful in person as she was in all the photos, surprisingly nice, a little distant, but the one characteristic that caught me off guard was a melancholy sadness that seemed to hover around her like a faint mist.

That day, I couldn't think of what she, a woman living in the lap of obscene luxury, could possibly have to be sad about. But now the memory of it took on new meaning.

Though it would be years before they met and married, at the time her husband, Connor Slate, had founded EnViSage, a now multibillion-dollar cloud computing company, Portia had been in high school. Granted, he'd been young at the time too, but their twelve-year age difference, his imposing status near the top of all the world's wealthiest lists, and her stunning beauty made their marriage an easy target for criticism. The public narrative on Portia had been prepackaged for easy consumption. She was the trophy wife. The accessory. One of the many objects that belonged to Connor Slate.

Until we'd heard it on the news last night, I'd forgotten EnViSage's deal with StarCloud had fallen through. I kept a vague eye on Silicon Valley politics—which company was swallowing which—mainly as a barometer for what kind of job market my students would be entering. I hadn't thought much about another multibillion-dollar handshake going bust. But I briefly wondered now if the failed deal and Portia's disappearance were at all connected.

I followed a few of the news links reporting on her case. The social media masses had opinions. Some had started campaigning that she'd been murdered; others offered thoughts and prayers for her safe return. I thought back to the woman I'd had coffee with that day and sincerely hoped she was all right, despite my growing certainty she wasn't.

I was scrolling an armchair detective's account of "What Happened to Portia" when the sound I'd been waiting for gently tinkled up the stairs like a tinny bell: a canned laugh track telling me my sister had made it to the living room.

Finally I had my cue to head next door and get some answers.

CHAPTER 5

The warm evening embraced me in a thick hug when I made it outside. I was still wearing the jeans I'd worn up to the city and had put on a tank top to combat the heat. I'd stowed the key in my bra, in case something went amiss, and I needed to keep it hidden somewhere less obvious than a pocket. By the time I'd cut through the side gate and into Anthony's yard, sticky sweat had sprung up beneath my arms and at the nape of my neck.

My heart thrummed wildly as I approached the house. I almost immediately regretted my decision to be more adventurous. I threw a glance over my shoulder at Libby's house, for fear I might find her spying on me from a window. The coast was clear, but the vantage point made me realize what a direct shot into my bedroom window Anthony had from his backyard. I flushed at the thought and made mental note to keep my curtains closed.

Before I could stop myself and fully consider that what I was doing was a terrible idea, I climbed the back steps and headed for the door.

It opened before I even reached it. Of course it did; Anthony had been waiting all day for my arrival.

"Hi," he said. "Thank you for coming." His voice was as smooth and velvety as the night.

"My sister knows I'm here and she'll come looking for me if I don't come back," I burst by way of greeting. The first part was a lie, and the latter only true if Libby woke up from the couch and found the note that I'd stuck to the alarm clock in my bedroom set to go off at midnight: *I'm next door. If I'm not home by midnight, call the police.*

Anthony's mouth tugged up on one side. "Okay," he said, and sounded like he was trying not to laugh. "Please come in."

A draft curled around my ankles as soon as I stepped inside, as if the house had reached out to grab me. Anthony had the air conditioner on, but the chill felt like more than simply re-frigerated air being pumped through vents. Something sinister hid in the walls, and its presence made me shiver.

I wondered fleetingly if Portia was somehow stashed in this very house.

When I entered, I intentionally stepped out of the hall and into the office where I'd seen the safe. If there was a chance Anthony was going to open it in my presence, then I wanted to see what was inside. The painting, a ship on a stormy sea in swirls of blue, gray, and black, had been swung back over the hole in the wall.

He followed me into the room and stopped in the doorway, notably blocking it.

My heart kicked up into my throat. I fought to keep my voice steady. "So, did you fix the issue of people thinking I'm your girlfriend?"

He shoved one hand into his back pocket and combed the other through his hair. "I told the police, yes. And that re-porter from this morning."

"You think that's enough?"

"It's the most I can do."

I glared at him. "Well, that's a defeatist answer if I've ever heard one. I'll have you know the chair of my tenure commit-tee asked me about it because he saw it on the news. He said there better not be any distractions that could compromise my case." I narrowed my glare even sharper and pointed a finger at him. "I swear, I am *this* close to the finish line after breaking my back for five years, and I can't give them any reason to doubt me. If you do anything to mess it up . . ."

He stepped back from the threat in my voice. "Penny, I—" He couldn't say another word before the sound of shattering glass cut him off.

We both flinched, and Anthony strode across the room and grabbed my arm so quickly, I got dizzy. Before I could blink, he was yanking open the closet door and shoving both of us inside.

"What—?"

"Shhh!" He clamped a hand down over my mouth and pulled the door shut. He pressed his back to the wall and held me flush against the front of his body. My nose hovered an inch from the closed door. The small space swallowed the light, save a tiny line near our feet. Dangling coat arms brushed against me in scratchy wool, and I felt the hard corner of a filing cabinet digging into my thigh. The closet hardly had room enough for storage, let alone two adults.

"Don't make a sound," he said on a nearly silent breath right beside my ear.

I nodded as much as I could in his grip, having no idea what was going on, but trusting the fear in his voice. His hand was warm and hard over my mouth. Small, rough calluses dotted the otherwise-soft skin that smelled like clean soap. He squeezed me like a vise. My heart thrashed in my chest. I was sure he could feel it pounding against his arm where it was fastened over me. His other arm wrapped around my waist. I couldn't have moved even if I had the space.

I strained to hear over the sound of my own panic. I held my breath, aside from tiny sips of air, taking them in through my nose as quietly as I could. Somewhere in the distance, on the other side of the door and my raw terror, I heard the sounds of voices, the crunch of a boot on broken glass.

"Is he home?" someone said. The closed door muffled the man's deep voice.

I tensed in fear and felt Anthony's grip tighten. His chin pressed into my temple. Never had I been held so tightly. The dizzying power of it made me wonder if he was protecting me or desperately trying not to get caught. Or maybe both.

"Should we wait for him to come back?" a second voice asked from out in the room, closer this time.

I heard Anthony suck in a breath. I couldn't see a thing, but felt his lips inches from my ear.

Heavy footsteps approached the door. I glanced down at the line of light near our feet to see a shadow cut through it. I squeezed my eyes shut, silently begging whoever was on the other side not to reach for the knob. The way Anthony was holding me like our lives depended on not getting caught had me burning in silent terror.

The footsteps stopped, and I sensed someone large and dangerous on the other side of the door. A wolf outside our tiny house. I couldn't tell if I was feeling my own heart beating erratically or if that second *wha-whomp* every other time was Anthony's heart pounding into my back.

Please leave, please leave, please leave! I screamed inside my head.

One second expanded into ten, thirty, a thousand, an eternity.

Finally the footsteps resumed and moved away from the door.

"No. He'll get the message," the first man said. Another crunch of glass underfoot, and then silence.

The tension in Anthony's body didn't release for a solid minute. When he loosened his arms, I felt like a balloon that had been let go—weightless and buoyant. He reached around me for the doorknob and leaned both of us forward to open the door slowly. The light crept back in, bit by bit. I didn't fully exhale until I saw the room was empty.

Anthony let out a breath and stepped around me. "Stay here." The look in his dark eyes was deadly serious.

I couldn't do anything but nod.

He marched to the office doorway and looked side to side in the hall before disappearing around the corner.

I listened to him walk toward the back door, the crunch of glass again, and realized only then my legs were shaking.

I wobbled to the desk chair and sank into it, the worn-in leather gently hissing under my weight. I held my head in my hands and took deep breaths. The room spun. I jumped at the sight of someone passing by the door, but realized it was only Anthony heading to the front of the house in his sweep. After five of the deepest breaths I could manage, he reappeared at the door.

"What the hell was that?" I asked.

His face was flushed and the unsettled jump in his eyes telling, but he tried to play it cool. "A couple of visitors."

"What did they want?"

His full lips pressed into a line, instead of answering. He only then seemed to take in the sight of me slumped in the chair with my forehead in my hand and elbows on the desk. "Are you all right?"

I glared at him in response. "Are you serious? What *was* that?"

He huffed a breath and dragged a hand through his mussed hair in a move I'd nearly memorized by now. "That was . . . a thing." He pivoted back into the hall.

I pushed up out of the chair, my legs less wobbly now, and followed. "A *thing?* Two people just broke into your house!" I sucked in a sharp breath. "Wait, is *that* who you expected when I rang the doorbell last night?"

I noticed then he had no gun stashed in his pants, which was perhaps the reason he'd shoved us in the closet.

He didn't answer me, but instead swung open a narrow

door at the end of the hall and pulled out a broom. Broken glass glittered on the polished floor. Those men had punched in the back door's window. Anthony silently set about sweeping up the glass. The plastic dustpan looked like a toy in his big hands.

"Anthony? Can you hear me? What's going on?"

He turned, still bent over, and held up a hand. "Give me a second, please."

"A second for what?"

He stood to face me, suddenly towering over me. "To think." He then bent back over and scraped the pile of broken glass into the dustpan and carried it out the back door, which still stood wide open.

I followed him with needles in my gut at fear those men were waiting in the backyard. The night felt thick and close. The only light in the dark yard was what spilled out from the house and the moon above. He crossed to the trash bin sitting outside the detached garage and tilted the dustpan, dumping in the pile of glass. Then he opened the garage door, the hinges groaning in greeting, and he stepped inside. "Come here, I could use a hand."

Once more, I followed.

The inside of the garage wasn't entirely the horror show of rusty bone saws and bear traps dangling from the ceiling, like the twisted nightmare I'd imagined, but it wasn't totally innocent either. A roll of plastic sheeting stood like a statue in one corner, piles of rope coiled in snakes of different thickness: thin enough to bite through skin and thick enough to tie up a boat. Spools of fishing line, but no poles. An axe. A hard black case with a heavy clamp sat atop a workbench next to a pair of pliers stained with something dark. A clear bag of zip ties spilled over. The crowbar hung from a hook on the wall beside a hammer.

"Umm . . ." I muttered as Anthony went to a dark corner

where an assortment of different-sized panels of wood leaned against the wall. He looked through them as someone might a bin of vinyl records before he found the one he wanted.

"Grab that hammer, will you?" He nodded at the workbench while he hoisted the piece of plywood out of the pile. "And nails."

I hesitated, wondering if I should touch anything in the garage in case it implicated me in a crime. "What exactly are we doing?"

"Fixing the window. The nails are right there." He moved past me with the board and flicked his chin at a set of drawers beneath the workbench.

I glanced around and found a rag stained in what I hoped was oil and used it to pull open the drawer. I grabbed a handful of nails out of a jar, their thin shape a fistful of icy spikes in my palm, and found the hammer hanging on the wall. I followed Anthony back out into the night. He already stood on the back porch, holding the board up to the broken window.

"Come here and help me hold this." He moved to the inside of the door and beckoned me with a hand.

I did as instructed and followed him back inside. He closed the door and held the board up to cover where the window used to be. "Nails?"

I presented a handful. He took four and stuck them between his teeth like a row of metal toothpicks. "Hold this in place." I shoved the rest of the nails in my pocket and handed him the hammer, understanding how I would be assisting. I gripped the board, its splintered edges biting my palms, and held it in place. "Don't let it slip," he said around the nails, and pulled one out. He reached to the board's top corner and pounded the first nail in, with a series of loud whacks. I flinched at each one while I did my best to hold the board steady.

With his arms up over his head, and me beneath, sandwiched between him and the door, and not unlike how we'd been in the closet, the heat of him encompassed me once more.

He finished the first nail and leaned over to do the second in the opposite corner. I watched his hands as he pounded it in, one holding it with surgical precision, a point between his thumb and index finger, and the other, strong and laced with veins as he wielded the hammer.

"You can move now," he said behind me when he finished, still talking around the nails.

I slipped out from between him and the door and watched him pound in a bottom corner. I hadn't thought I was attracted to manual labor, but I had never seen Anthony Pierce use a hammer before. "Why are you so good with your hands?"

He paused and looked at me, the final nail still sticking out of his lips. He pulled it free and set about securing the final corner. "We're covering a hole; it's not rocket science. More nails, please." He held out his hand.

I fished the remaining nails out of my pocket and watched him hammer them along the sides of the board, further securing it in place. "Well, sure. But you still didn't answer my question."

He stayed silent and finished the job. Once the last nail was in place, he stood back and assessed his work with a nod. Then he reached out and locked the door.

I thought he was doing it for safety purposes; his house had just been broken into, but when he turned to me and held out his hand, the locked door took on a whole new meaning.

"I'm going to need that key now." His steady, low voice put the tiniest jump in my nerves.

It occurred to me then—locked inside his cavernous house, standing in front of him as he held a hammer—that I actually wasn't afraid of him. If he intended to hurt me, he would have left me to face the intruders, instead of stowing me away in the closet. Not only that, but I had all the leverage, seeing I had the key, and he'd clearly gone to desperate measures to open the safe with a crowbar in its absence.

I took a step back in the hall, which once again felt narrow and cramped. "No. You can't have it. Not until you answer some questions."

His eyes narrowed. I felt them dart to my pockets, like he might try to search me. Little did he know, he wouldn't find anything there but lint. I felt the key burning my skin inside my bra like an invisible flare.

My face flushed at the thought of him searching thoroughly enough to find it.

His gaze softened and he sighed. He tried for patience. "Can I please have the key?"

"No." I pivoted on my heel and marched down the hall toward the front of the house. I knew a three-year-old who could play keep away like a champ, so I was ready for a battle. "We had a deal: the key for information."

He followed, the size of him apparent and looming behind me. "It's not information you want, trust me."

I spun around to glare at him. He almost ran into me. "I beg to differ. You just shoved me into a closet and held your hand over my mouth like we were going to die if we got caught, and I think I deserve to know why."

A bolt of guilt shot through his eyes. His lips tightened, and he shook his head with a quick, remorseful angst. "Fine. Three questions."

"How about ten?"

"You really have ten things you want to ask me?"

"At least."

"Well, that's too many."

"Fine. Five."

He glared down at me. We'd made it to the edge of the foyer. The sweeping staircase spilled into the room to our left; the giant chandelier dangled from above, throwing dim sparkles of light. I saw his jaw working as a silent battle played out in his eyes.

"Fine. Five, but I get veto power over what to answer."

I knew it was as good as I was going to get. "Deal. Who were those guys?"

"Veto," he said plainly, and stepped around me into the foyer.

"What? You can't veto the first question." I followed on his heels.

"I can veto anything I want; that's how a veto works. It's better if you don't know. Next question."

We rounded into the kitchen. Remnants of whatever he'd had for dinner littered the butcher-block island. From the looks of it, something meaty and juicy with a salad.

"Fine," I said. "What does this have to do with Portia Slate?"

"Veto."

"Oh, come on!"

"Also better if you don't know," he said, and pulled a bottle of scotch out of a cabinet. He grabbed two crystal glasses and set them on the island. I didn't like scotch, but after what had just happened, I wasn't opposed.

"Well, this is going nowhere fast. How about you volunteer some information I'm allowed to know, then. Tell me a fact."

He filled each glass with two fingers of caramel-colored liquid and spoke without looking up. "Okay. You look great in a bathing suit."

My face caught fire; I could feel it scorching like the surface of the sun. Surely, I was ten shades of scarlet.

He sipped his scotch while sliding the other glass across the island toward me. When he eventually looked up, his eyes raked over my body like he was reliving a memory of seeing me in a swimsuit. He must have seen me in the backyard with the kids. He shrugged with a sly grin. "You said you wanted a fact."

My tongue tripped over itself. "I, um, yes. I did say that." I picked up the glass, for lack of a better idea for what to do with myself, and sipped the harsh liquor. It went down in a smooth, fiery gulp, like someone had selected the bottle with great care and paid a large sum for it.

Anthony rounded to my side of the island and leaned back against it. The heat and smell of him seemed to mix with the liquor. I didn't know which ingredient was making me drunk. "Here's another fact, a few more, actually. You're not a very good spy; I've seen you watching me, I find you exasperating yet fascinating, and I wonder what it is you find so interesting about me, because you're obviously intrigued enough to be here."

I looked up at him and studied the planes of his handsome face. Memory of his body squeezing mine in the pitch-black closet sent a warm rush through me as I noticed the ochre-colored flecks in his dark eyes. In the right light, they could have been gold.

"You seriously don't know?" I asked. My voice came out low and breathy. Transfixed. "Why I find you interesting?"

He held my gaze like it was something alive and precious between us. His lips parted, and a soft, oaky breath spilled out before he spoke. "I would imagine it has something to do with the body in the closet, but other than that, no."

He was right; the body in the closet was the primary factor. But strip that away, and he was still an enigma. Brooding, curt, surprisingly polite when he wanted to be. Not to mention gorgeous, smart, and good with a hammer. Despite everything else, gazing into his eyes had me wanting to know something personal about him. Anything.

"Tell me something about yourself, Anthony."

He kept staring at me, slowly blinking his thick lashes. The hard edge in his eyes melted away and a welcoming vulnerability replaced it. His voice came out in a soft, raspy murmur. "My friends call me Tony."

I was so lost in the heavy haze of his voice and his stare, the warm liquor pooling in my blood, that I didn't think of the words coming out of my mouth. "You have friends?"

He snorted an amused, awkward laugh. "I've got a couple, yeah."

I wanted to drown in my glass of brown booze. "Sorry. That sounded so rude. I didn't mean it like that. It's just, you seem like a lone wolf."

He polished off his drink and set the glass on the island. "That's fair. Uncle Lou was really the only person I had; no one else in the family talks to us. I can guarantee I'll be the only family member at his funeral on Tuesday. But besides that, people like me can't really afford to get close to others. It creates leverage, and that's a dangerous thing in my line of work."

The statement left a lot to unpack, but one question was obvious. "And what does your line of work involve exactly?"

He folded his bulky arms and tapped his thumbs against his biceps. His lips pursed out like he was debating what to disclose, and I wondered if I was going to get another annoyingly vague answer. "Technically, I'm a financial consultant. It's just that some of the stuff I consult on isn't exactly on the books. I'm basically the suit side of Uncle Lou's business."

I blinked in shock to have learned anything at all. "And he was, what, a hit man?"

"No!" he said with an affronted laugh, even though I wasn't kidding. All evidence pointed to the obvious.

"Okay, then what was he?"

He sighed with another pass through his hair. I wondered if he'd go bald early because of all the tugging, but based on the thickness of the wavy mane, the chances seemed slim. "Look, sometimes people get into bad stuff, and they need someone to make it go away. That's what Uncle Lou did. He made bad stuff go away for people." He watched me as I put the pieces together. I felt his eyes outlining my face, my lips, dipping down to my throat and back up again.

I knew what he meant; I just didn't think such people actually existed in real life. "So he was a fixer."

He silently held my gaze for a few telling beats. "And all of this"—he gestured to our general surroundings, and I took it to mean everything from the house to the body to the break-in—"was part of a job he was working on. That's why I'm here, and why I need that key."

I felt it vibrating like a tuning fork, where it was buried in my bra. Anthony's eyes dipped to my hip again, my pocket, and I tried not to give myself away that he was looking in the wrong place. "What's in that safe?" I asked.

He watched my lips through hooded lids as I spoke, as if he wanted to bite them. "Something important."

I fought to keep my voice steady while I tingled all over. "And what happens when you get it open? Are you going to finish the job and leave?"

"That's the plan," he said in a tone so close to a growl, I gripped the island for support. "So," he said, leaning in even closer, "I really need you to give me that key."

I was under his spell. Completely hypnotized. I would have done anything he asked. And judging by the size his eyes grew to when I dug my hand into my bra, I had as much power over him too.

I removed the key and held it between us.

He took it from me, and a sincere smile spread across his face. If I expected him to invite me back into the office to see what was in the safe, I was sorely mistaken. "Thank you. I'll walk you home now, if you'd like."

I blinked at him. "That's it?"

"Yes."

I folded my arms and frowned. "You didn't hold up your end of the deal, pal. I still don't know what this has to do with Portia Slate."

He released a breath that sounded painfully weary. "I really shouldn't answer that question, but I have one for you: What do you know about her?"

I held his gaze, glad to be getting somewhere. "I met her

once. She came to campus when the Slate Foundation donated a computer lab. We had coffee together . . ." I paused to emphasize the next thing I said. "Her *bodyguard* was with her." I could tell from the look on his face that he understood my implication. "How did he end up in your closet, Anthony?"

His jaw was working so hard, he hardly opened his mouth to speak. "I really can't tell you that."

"*Can't* or *won't*?"

"Shouldn't. For your safety."

The word *safety* landed like a stone dropped in my belly. I suddenly felt cold.

He let out a stiff breath. He stood very close and rested a hand on my shoulder. His eyes melted into a sincere plea. "Penny, I'm very sorry you're involved in this. But the more you know, the worse this will end up. The best thing you can do is stay away from me."

"Gladly. But do I need to be worried?"

He weighed his response for longer than was comfortable, and looked like summoning the answer was causing him distress. "I'll keep an eye on things."

"'Keep an eye on things'? What does that even mean?"

"Exactly what it sounds like. Now I need you to go home." He hooked his hand behind my elbow and started leading me out of the kitchen.

I tried to dig in my feet, but the floor was slick, and his grip was firm. "Wait!" I wormed my way out of his hold and faced him with my hands up. "I'm not going anywhere until you tell me about Portia."

"Well, I'm not going to, so maybe you should make yourself comfortable in one of the bedrooms upstairs. That would make it easier to keep an eye on you anyway." He tugged at his collar like he was uncomfortable and frustrated. It was the first I'd seen him truly flustered, other than the closet incident— which, somehow, there were two of now.

I defiantly held my ground and crossed my arms. I was quickly running out of bargaining chips and still didn't have what I'd come for. "Well, what if I go to the police and tell them I know who was in the closet?"

"Go ahead. They already know."

I flinched. "What? How?"

"Because I told them."

It was the last thing I expected him to say. My face folded in a frown of confusion. "Then why isn't it all over the news?"

He gave me a hard stare, which sent a shiver prickling my skin. "Because someone doesn't want it to be, Penny."

The silence that followed his statement might as well have been a scream. It echoed through my mind like a banshee telling me to run.

Several pieces clicked sharply into place.

"Right. Okay, then," I said, and started to back away. I needed to get out of the house, but I didn't want to turn my back on him. "I'm going to head home now. Thank you for the chat. I hope you have a nice night." Words kept falling out of my mouth like books from a broken bag.

Anthony watched me go with his lips hinting at a smug, little grin as if he'd finally found the right button to press to get me to leave. "Do you want me to walk you home?"

"Oh no. I'm fine," I said with a wave of my hands and a confidence I didn't feel. I was going to sprint, hop the fence if I had to, and hide under the covers all night.

"Okay, Penny. Have a good night," he said with a little wave as I disappeared around the corner into the foyer.

"Good night." As soon as he was out of sight, I dashed for the front door. I tore it open and ran down the front steps, not even bothering to close the door behind me. I skirted the side of the house, glancing over my shoulder to make sure he hadn't followed, and made my way back to Libby's gate, which I'd propped open. I didn't fully breathe until I was on the other side of it.

Inside, Libby slept on the couch in front of a glowing TV, as expected. I left her there and hurried up the stairs.

It wasn't until I was in pajamas, tucked into bed with the curtains drawn that I let myself fully process what I had learned.

Anthony said his uncle Lou *made bad things go away for people* and he'd stepped in to finish the job. Portia Slate was missing; her bodyguard was dead. The first was widespread news; the latter had been covered up, perhaps because it would have exposed the truth about the former.

I squeezed my eyes shut and let the pieces fall into the most logical pattern. A terrifying, chilling mosaic exploded behind my lids, and I was almost certain of one thing.

Portia Slate was dead, and Anthony and his uncle had covered it up.

They were a family of fixers, and they'd fixed her murder.

CHAPTER 6

If there was a threshold for the amount of caffeine that could be safely consumed in a single morning, I'd surpassed it hours ago. My eyeballs were vibrating. I didn't sleep. I tossed and turned all night, thinking of Anthony and Portia, and then tried to compensate with my sister's stash of organic fair trade dark roast.

Searching everything I could about Portia Slate and her bodyguard, I'd been to infinity and back. Nearly anything I could want to know about Portia, from her birthplace (New York) to her height (five-seven), from her favorite dessert (chocolate mousse) to her favorite vacation spot (Mykonos), waited online like a catalogue spread of oversharing. Despite a hefty social media presence (1.5 million Instagram followers), it wasn't all coming direct from her; she'd been interviewed, quoted, photographed. There was no shortage of interest in her.

But her bodyguard, I couldn't even find a name. He was nothing more than a blurred figure in the background of every photo. Surely, he had a family. Parents, if nothing else. But truly, I had no idea the kind of person who went into private security. Maybe he had no one to notice or mourn his death.

There was also the break-in at Anthony's house last night. I had no idea what to make of it, but it couldn't have been anything good.

It was a complex problem, but I solved complex problems all the time. *It's just a puzzle.* As I sorted through the pieces, I realized something that usually helped with the hardest problems was going back to the beginning. So that's what I did.

Portia's disappearance might have been the true origin of it all, since it happened the furthest in the past, but as far as my involvement went, the catalyst had been Lou Griotti's death. That's what brought Anthony to town and moved him in next door. Without that, there never would have been an estate sale or a body in the closet. I would have spent Saturday splashing in Libby's pool and lounging in the sun rather than being interrogated as an accomplice.

I shouldn't have been surprised I couldn't find an obituary for Lou online, but somehow I was. I still didn't even know how he'd died.

Libby found me in the kitchen, guzzling coffee and rapidly blinking out the window, staring at his house in a trance. As per usual morning routine, she turned on the TV to a local news show and set about preparing breakfast.

"What's up with you?" she asked.

My jitteriness must have been obvious. Perhaps it was my tapping foot or the mug of coffee threatening to spill in my shaky hand. "Nothing. I couldn't sleep."

She secured Ada in her high chair and deposited a small pile of Cheerios for her to immediately club with a fist and send scattering. "Well, maybe if you stop staring at the *m-u-r-d-e-r-e-r* next door, you could relax." She glanced at Max as she spelled out the word.

He was too busy driving a small toy truck through the Cheerios obstacle course, which his sister had provided on the tabletop, to notice.

I took another sip of coffee I most certainly did not need, rather than respond. I'd come to a conclusion, and had been trying to figure out how best to approach telling Libby, because she would surely try to stop me. Unfortunately, the caffeine had robbed my brain of tact, and the words just fell out.

"I want to go to his funeral."

She paused filling a sippy cup with orange juice and looked up. "What? Whose funeral?"

"Who do you think?" I said, and nodded toward the neighbor's house.

She secured the cup's lid and tipped it twice to make sure it wasn't leaking before she handed it to Max's outstretched hands. "They're having a funeral? I thought Anthony was the only relative in contact with him."

"He is . . . Wait. How do you know that?"

When my sister blushed, it was at a fraction of the intensity my face burned, but still. I saw a pink wave unfurl into her cheeks. "I may have asked Nicole what she knows about the case," she said sheepishly.

"You did what?!" I squawked. "You talked to the detective's wife and didn't tell me?"

"Don't yell at me! I'm not the one going over to his house late at night and getting snatched. My information gathering is much safer."

My stomach bottomed out. I thought for a second she meant last night when I'd snuck out, but quickly realized she was referring to the night before when I confronted Anthony about the news story.

I poked my finger into a Cheerio and traced a figure eight on the tabletop, trying to sound casual. "What did you learn from Nicole?"

She cast a glance over her shoulder toward the neighboring house, as if Anthony might overhear, and then leaned in with a telltale glint in her eye. She was ripe with gossip and looking only the slightest bit guilty about it. "He's a financial consultant from Manhattan. Single. No spouse, no kids. He and Lou were estranged from the family. Lou left him everything."

I digested the information and realized Anthony had told me things he hadn't told the cops. Or at least Detective Warner hadn't told his wife, who then hadn't told my sister. I wasn't about to tell Libby the financial consultant part was a cover and Anthony and his uncle were a tag team of fixers who covered up crimes for other people, because the only way I could have known that was by sneaking into his house the night before and hearing it straight from his mouth.

"Did you happen to find out how Mr. Griotti died?"

Libby frowned, perhaps realizing that was still a hole in the story. "No. I'd heard it through the grapevine he'd passed, but never the reason why. Nicole said Daryl is really stressed. Especially with all this Portia Slate stuff happening so close. At least he's not on that case too."

Right then, and as if on cue, the morning news show returned from commercial break. The bubbly anchor, who was ten shades of perky blond, somberly narrated a headline that caught my attention.

"A new development in the Portia Slate missing person case this morning has authorities reconsidering what may have happened to the tech billionaire's wife."

My stomach dropped to my toes once more. I stopped breathing. I dove on the remote Libby had left on the island and turned up the volume.

"Authorities recombed the area around the Slates' estate in Woodside," the anchor continued. "After several hours, they found what they are calling the first big break in the case."

My breath lodged in my throat again. Surely, they could not have found Portia's body. The story would have been framed differently from the start if that was the case. Instead of dragging us along for mystery theater, they would have gotten to the point in the first sentence: *Billionaire's wife found dead.*

I waited an excruciating few seconds for the reveal.

"Mrs. Slate was reported to have been wearing a pair of blue running shoes when she went missing last week. One of those shoes has now been found in the woods outside her home."

The image cut to an interview with a hardened-looking, middle-aged man in a beige police uniform. *Alan Prescott, San Mateo County Sheriff's Office* popped up in the bottom of the screen. He stood outside, under a copse of shady oak trees near the end of a gated driveway, and spoke into an invisible microphone.

"We combed these woods multiple times, but this is a large area. Even with our resources working around the clock, it's entirely possible the evidence was overlooked until now."

I could only imagine what Portia was doing in those woods that caused her to lose a shoe. Running from her husband? Running for her life? Maybe she tripped and there was a struggle, and her shoe came off. Maybe she took it off on purpose and left it behind as evidence because she knew she was going to die. Maybe she never made it out of those woods alive.

"At this point, we can't be certain what the shoe means," Prescott said onscreen. "But it does confirm that Mrs. Slate was, in fact, in these woods before she went missing."

The image cut back to the news anchor. Her mouth set in a solemn line. "We will continue to report on this story as it unfolds. Of course we are all still hoping for the safe return of Mrs. Slate." She looked down for two seconds, as if to cleanse her palate, before moving on to the next story.

"I wish they'd stop calling her *Mrs. Slate,*" I said bitterly. "Or *the billionaire's wife.* She was a person."

"*Is* a person," I heard Libby say.

"What?" I turned to see her spreading Nutella on a piece of toast for Max.

"Portia Slate *is* a person. You said *was.* They don't know if she's dead yet."

I bit back the urge to tell her I was almost certain Portia Slate was dead, her husband had killed her, and our new neighbor helped his uncle make it disappear. I glanced at Anthony's house and felt a rage boil up inside me. I could go to Detective Warner and tell him everything. I could drive up to Woodside and knock on Prescott's door until he listened to me. I could kick in Anthony's door and demand he tell me the whole truth.

But none of that seemed likely to achieve anything.

Or . . .

I had another thought. One that suddenly made me feel alive with brazen power and terrified at once—both of which could have been caused by the caffeine.

I could do it. I could figure out what happened to Portia Slate and gather enough evidence for an irrefutable story someone would have to listen to. I could take it to the blond news anchor still narrating the day's stories on TV. I could take it to someone at the *Chronicle.*

If no one else was going to stand up for Portia Slate, I could.

But I had to have more than a theory and a few anecdotes. I needed proof of something.

Movement out the kitchen window caught my eye. Anthony exiting his front door and heading for the Cadillac.

Surely, there was evidence of the cover-up inside his house. The thought of breaking in swam like a tempting little fish through my veins. But I knew that was a bad idea. There'd been a dead body in that house, and I knew he owned at least one gun. Not exactly the optimal candidate for my first breaking and entering. No. I would have to be patient. I would have to be smart. I would have to wait for an opportunity.

And the perfect opportunity was one day away.

"I am going to go to the funeral tomorrow," I said definitively. I was banking on the fact there would be a reception at the house after.

Libby managed to sound completely judgmental in her silence.

I busied myself scooping up the Cheerios mess Ada had made. I started babbling in defense of myself. "I, for one, think it would be horribly sad to have no one show up to your funeral. If he was estranged from his family, it might only be Anthony there." I didn't let on Anthony had told me this would likely be true.

I risked a glance at her and could see the flicker of interest in her eyes. *She* was the one always pushing me to take more risks, be more adventurous. She didn't know what I was up to, of course, but still. Saying no would be counter to her efforts. She rested her hands on her hips and sighed as she surveyed the chaos of breakfast with small children. It wasn't too bad, all things considered. Ada was sticky with slobber and mushed Cheerios, but confined to her chair. Max's hair was tangled in a nest, and he had Nutella and toast crumbs smeared cheek to cheek, but he was happily kicking his legs under the table and sipping his juice.

Libby turned to me with a resigned look on her face. "Well, I'd be remiss to let you go alone, so we'll have to find a babysitter. And something black to wear."

The next day, I borrowed heels from Libby; we had the same size feet, despite me being three inches taller. I'd dashed to a local department store for a tasteful black shift dress, because I didn't have anything readily funeral appropriate in what I'd packed from home. I put in a pair of pearl earrings and painted my lips red.

Libby wore ballet flats with bows on the toes and a black A-line dress with cap sleeves. As we approached the church, she dabbed at the bodice of her dress with a tissue pulled from her enormous purse, trying to blot out a stain bequeathed by one of her children, but only succeeding in adhering tiny shreds of tissue to herself.

The old mission-style church and its accompanying courtyard took up a whole block on the outskirts of the trendy downtown area. A black iron fence marked its perimeter with slats crowded enough to look like pinstripes. A tall palm tree near the front steps swayed in the light summer breeze.

"Lib, come on. We're late," I said, and hurried up the sidewalk. The handoff with the babysitter had not gone as smoothly as hoped, hence the stain on Libby's dress and our tardiness.

Libby scuffled along behind the hard clicks of my heels. "With all due respect, Pen, he's dead and won't know the difference."

I cast her a glare and reached for the iron handrail bisecting the steps. We were two minutes late, and I hoped the absolute dearth of people outside meant the service had already started— and not that we were, in fact, the only guests to show up.

Sadness stung my chest at the thought of the latter. My throat tightened. A vision of Anthony sitting inside, alone on a pew, with his head solemnly bowed, made me ache.

I arrived at the front doors and reached for the old iron handle on one of the wooden panels. When I pulled it open, the distinct aroma of wood, leather, and candle smoke hit me in the face. The density of the air said the church was not empty and the warmth was due to a crowd of bodies huddled into the narrow space and not any kind of heating system.

I stopped at the edge of the vestibule and my mouth fell open.

"Holy sh—" Libby cut herself off right in time. She quietly cleared her throat. "I mean, *wow.*"

Packed was an understatement. At least fifteen pews lined each side of an aisle, and each one was brimming with guests. Shoulder to shoulder, rows of bodies in black sat; some wore delicate fascinators, veils, or sunglasses. A few heads discreetly turned to see my sister and me arriving unfashionably late, and I swore I recognized the nighttime anchor from the local news station. Two rows behind him, unless my eyes were deceiving me, was a pro basketball player and his wife.

"Is that . . . ?" Libby said, pointing at someone nearby, as a priest in flowing white robes walked to the pulpit at the front of the room.

"Come on," I said, and grabbed her arm. Midway up the church, I spotted open space at the end of a pew near the wall. I walked on my toes to stop my heels from clicking on the tile floor. Libby crept along behind me, gawking at the crowd, and mindlessly dusting the flakes from the tissue off her front.

"Excuse me," I said to the man nearest the empty seats when we climbed in and sat down. He cast me a glance and did a brief double take, like he might recognize me, and I realized I'd forgotten to account for the fact everyone still thought I was Anthony's girlfriend.

Damn it.

"Okay, I swear I just saw a celebrity chef and at least two influencers," Libby gushed in what was hardly a whisper. She sat halfway on my lap as she tried to squeeze in next to me. She gasped. "Oh! And that's—"

"Shhh!" I hissed, and batted down her hand she'd lifted to point at whomever she'd recognized.

She glared at me and leaned in close enough so her lips brushed my ear. "Okay, but please tell me you are aware we walked into a church full of famous people."

An uncomfortable heat pushed up into my face. Most people were looking at us, given our late arrival and less than silent entrance. Covertly staring back at them to get a read on the room was no small feat. But Libby was right: Three out of every five faces I saw, I recognized. Nearly all of them were obscured behind a hat or sunglasses or a tall collar, as if they were trying to hide in plain sight. I wondered if there was some kind of code of silence for celebrities, and they were all sworn to secrecy that they were in attendance, simply by the nature of their fame.

Anthony had told me his uncle made bad things go away for people, and the types of people who got into the kind of trouble that needed to be fixed, and could afford the level of fixing Lou provided, were of a select demographic.

We were sitting not only in a church full of famous people, but a church full of Lou Griotti's clients.

In a daze, I scanned the crowd for Anthony. From my current vantage point, all I could see were the backs of heads, but even from afar, I made out the set of his broad shoulders, the disheveled tumble of his dark hair. He sat in the front row nearest the aisle. It was an obvious place to look for him, but even if I hadn't known where to find him, I would have known him by the outline of his shape. His normally rigid posture slightly dipped today; his head drooped. Despite everything else, he'd lost a family member—one of his closest, based on all accounts. And that was sad.

Libby suddenly clawed at my arm. "Oh, my God. What is *he* doing here?" she hissed, and nodded across the aisle. I followed her gaze to find a face that did not surprise me in the least.

And yet, I still stiffened at the sight of Connor Slate. He wasn't in disguise. He wasn't trying to hide, like anyone else in the room. He confidently sat between two men in black suits, and while most everyone else in the crowd leaned on a partner for support, the space beside him that should have been occupied by Portia Slate was most notably not.

The priest moved into reading a Bible passage, which I tuned out, as I stared a hole into Connor Slate. He sat, eyes forward, unfazed. I glanced at Anthony, also eyes forward and listening to the priest, and then up at the blown-up photo of Lou Griotti surrounded by billowing flowers and a shiny black urn on a pedestal.

Any doubt I had that it was all connected vanished. Portia, her bodyguard, Connor, Lou, and Anthony.

I swallowed a thick lump at the thought of what it all meant, when the sound of Anthony's name drew my ears to the front of the church.

"And now, Anthony Pierce, Lou's nephew, would like to share a few words."

Anthony rose from his pew and buttoned his suit jacket. He nodded at the priest before he walked up to the pulpit and faced the crowd.

I sucked in a sharp breath at the sight of him in his suit and tie. He was striking. It was the first time I'd seen him wear anything other than all black, and the white shirt beneath his jacket brought out a rosy flush to his cheeks. His dark eyes roved over the audience, landing nowhere, until they found me. He'd opened his mouth to speak, but stopped as if he'd stumbled. For a second that lasted a lifetime, he stared at me with a vulnerability I hadn't seen before. It was plain and raw on his face, and the sympathetic urge to run to the front of the church and hug him hit me with enough force that I had to re-cross my legs and remind myself he was involved in a murder cover-up.

The moment passed, and he gazed out at a distant point in the back of the room as he began speaking.

"Thank you all for coming today." His voice came out rough and thick. Like gravel in a tumbler. He cleared his throat and started over. "Thank you all for coming today. My uncle Lou would have appreciated it, though he would have died before admitting it." He softly laughed at his own pun, which sounded unplanned, as a few chuckles tittered around the room. The flush in his cheeks grew deeper. "Sorry." He smoothed a hand over his jaw, as if trying to wipe the smile from it. "No, Lou was never one for much outward affection. He kept his heart close. He and I are a lot alike in that regard. And if it weren't for him, I wouldn't have had much of anyone in this world. He was the kind of guy who showed you what you meant to him through actions. I don't think any of you would be here today if you didn't know that." Another titter and some nods of agreement.

"Listen, I'm not a man of many words, but I will say this: My uncle Lou was there for me when I didn't really have anyone else, and that kind of loyalty leaves an impression. I would have done anything for him." He paused for a brief second as he looked out over the room. If I wasn't mistaken, his eyes landed directly on Connor Slate. "And I still will."

Several members of the crowd stirred, adjusting their posture and clearing throats. I couldn't tell if it was his delivery or their reaction, but the words landed like a threat.

Anthony turned to the photo of his uncle and pressed his fingertips to his lips. He then touched the photo and muttered, "Love you, Uncle Lou" before he walked down from the pulpit.

He returned to his seat, and the priest asked everyone to stand and turn to a page in the hymnal to join in a song.

I soundlessly mouthed the words and then listened to a few prayers. At the end, the priest announced there'd be a private burial of the ashes back in New York at a later date, but a reception would be held at Mr. Griotti's house immediately following today's service, and all were invited. I silently celebrated the victory and realized my plan would work out better than I'd hoped if even half of the people in the church showed up to the house. The distractions would be overflowing.

As soon as the service ended, Anthony moved like a black flash and hurried out a side door to disappear.

"Okay, who the hell *was* this guy?" Libby whispered, still swiveling her head around the room. "I mean, no family, but a funeral full of famous people and billionaires?"

"Yeah, it's strange," I muttered in a serious understatement, and to shield the fact I had the answer to her question. "How long do we have the babysitter for?"

Libby checked her smartwatch with a flick of her wrist. "Two more hours."

"Great. Plenty of time," I said, and headed toward the doors in the throng of people.

"Plenty of time for what?" Libby called after me, but I didn't answer.

The old Victorian bustled with guests. It was ten times as crowded as the estate sale had been. People floated in and out from the kitchen and dining room, which were littered with food and drinks. They perched on the sofas in the living and sitting rooms. Conversations bubbled; reserved laughter burst out. It felt like half funeral reception and half Hollywood party. I was grossly mistaken about no one showing up to Lou Griotti's service.

And I was also mistaken in my hope Anthony had cleared up the rumor we were a pair. More than one stranger squeezed my arm and muttered condolences, thinking I was an extension of the grieving nephew. Several others eyed me from a distance, as if staring at me would help them understand how someone like me would end up with Anthony Pierce. I did my best to ignore all of it.

To my despair, the gathering remained contained to the ground floor. No one had ventured upstairs, and though my curiosity to snoop kept tugging me toward the staircase with the force of gravity, I didn't want to be the one to commit the faux pas.

By the time my sister had had two glasses of champagne and was bonding with an A-list actress over the rare chance to be away from their children, I saw an opportunity to escape down the hall. The crowd remained concentrated to the front of the house in the rooms designed for company. I doubted anyone would be hanging out in the back corner room, unless it was Anthony vying for a moment of peace, but I made sure he was deep in conversation with a handsome woman, who looked like a local mayor, before I snuck off into the caverns of his house.

On reflex, I shuddered when I passed the closet with the green doorknob. The door at the end of the hall leading onto the back porch was still boarded up from the break-in, a second memory that made me shudder. I shook off the bad energy from both and turned to the last door on the left of the hall.

The office was an obvious place to start. Surely, the safe had been emptied of whatever it had held, but the rest of the room might have still contained useful information.

I was thankful to find the door unlocked, even though it was shut. When I entered, I closed the door behind me and glanced around. I bypassed the desk, which held only a set of gold pens, a glass paperweight, and last month's issue of *Forbes* on top of it, and crossed the room to the painting. Behind it, the safe was closed—of course it was—and up close, I could see scratch marks from where Anthony must have tried to open it with the crowbar.

"What were you hiding?" I whispered. I poked the keyhole and wished I hadn't surrendered the key.

With a sigh, I turned back to the desk. Inside the top drawer, I found an assortment of pens, a roll of stamps, paperclips, a bankbook. I picked up the bankbook and flipped it open.

"Whoa!" I blinked at the figures I saw inked into the grid of boxes. Forget selling the house. Anthony was set for life if he, alone, had inherited his uncle's money. I scanned a few pages, in case there was a deposit from Connor Slate in a sum worth fixing his wife's murder, but nothing obvious jumped out.

I replaced the book and opened another drawer. This one held a hole punch, an old computer mouse, and a box of envelopes. As I shuffled through the flotsam and jetsam of boring office products, I realized anything incriminating would likely

be locked up. Based on the clientele in the living room, I figured Lou Griotti probably had an encrypted hard drive full of
information that could sink the careers of every person out
there—if not land them in jail too. I doubted he tended toward
carelessness in his line of work.

"Damn it," I muttered, and closed the drawer.

The only other place in the room to look was the closet,
where Anthony and I had hidden.

I turned the old brass handle to open the door as I shivered
at the memory of being crammed inside it.

The space was very small, as I knew from experience. Other
than the hanging suit jackets, it held a row of shoeboxes on a
shelf and the filing cabinet that had dug into my thigh when we
were hiding.

"Bingo," I said, and knelt in front of it.

I pulled open a drawer and scanned the labeled tabs sticking
up like tiny flags.

Tax returns. House maintenance. Car info. Utilities.

Lou Griotti did keep meticulous files, but about mundane
things. Even if there was some secret code in his notes on land-
scaping or a cryptic money trail in his tax returns, it would take
me days—weeks, even—to find it.

I shoved the drawer shut and stood with a huff.

Feeling like my plan may have been in vain, I reached for the
shelf above the coats and grabbed a shoebox.

Shoes. A pair of men's loafers, which looked like they'd been
worn maybe once.

I put it back on the shelf and reached for the next one, right
as I heard the office door open.

I jerked in surprise, both at getting caught and at what I saw
in the box.

A single blue running shoe. Women's size 8.

The ground felt like it shifted beneath my feet. The world
stood on end. I hardly had time to register I was holding Portia

Slate's other shoe, and had found the evidence I'd come for, before someone spoke.

"Are you lost, Dr. Collins?"

I whipped around at the sound of the voice.

A vaguely familiar-looking man stood in the office doorway with a sinister grin on his face. An uncomfortable sensation at the sight of him, some unconscious knowing, made me take a step back closer to the open closet.

I clutched the shoe, like it somehow might protect me. "I . . . um . . . no," I muttered, trying and failing not to sound nervous.

He stepped farther into the room and kept grinning.

"You aren't?" he said in an unsettling purr. "The gathering is out in the front of the house."

Seeing him against the backdrop of the old Victorian, the darkly paneled walls, the shiny wood floor, I suddenly knew where I recognized him from.

"You were there that day. The day of the estate sale," I said as the pieces slid into place. He was the man with the tweed jacket in the foyer examining the table when Libby and I walked in—and the man leaning on the car outside Libby's house the day the reporter showed up.

"Indeed," he said.

I took another uncertain step back as I tried to reason why he'd been at the estate sale, outside Libby's house, and was now here, at the reception, calling me by my name. The pieces were oddly shaped, and the thread running through them sounded an alarm deep in the most primitive part of my brain.

He must have read the confusion on my face. "I work for Mr. Slate," he said.

My entire body turned to ice in an instant. He knew what I was doing. He knew I knew what his boss had done and was here to stop me. An instinct told me to run, but he was blocking the door, and I had nowhere to go.

I shifted my weight onto my back foot, trying to look casual. I was still wearing Libby's borrowed heels and would very much have liked to swap them for the running shoe in my hand. If only I had its mate. "What do you do for Mr. Slate?" I asked.

He smiled at me again, a chilling and sinister grin, with only his lips, that made me take another step back. There was hardly anywhere to go, unless I climbed back into the closet, and I didn't have a large man as a shield this time.

"Tie up loose ends. Mostly," he said.

My body froze over again. Standing there with Portia's shoe in my hand, I couldn't have been more of a loose end if the words were tattooed on my forehead. Desperate, I said the only thing I could think of.

"Anthony knows I'm back here."

This put a pause in his approach toward me. "Does he?"

I fought to sound brave again. "Yes. He's going to come looking for me."

To my equal-parts confusion and despair, this only seemed to make him happier. "I'm counting on it."

Then he lunged at me.

He was large enough that I couldn't easily get around him. With the desk on one side of me, and the open closet on the other, my options were limited.

His hand closed around my wrist, and in a reactive move of equal force, I swung the shoe at his head.

"Let go of me!" I shouted as the rubber heel bounced off his temple.

He reeled back, but only slightly, as if he was used to taking blows to the head. "You're going to put up a fight, aren't you," he growled.

I swung at him again, but he blocked my attack while still holding my other wrist. In a flash, he swung his own arm around to his back and pulled a gun out from under his jacket.

I instantly stopped struggling and stared at the black beady eye of the barrel pointed at me. My heart was beating so hard that it had nearly stopped.

"You can either walk out of here with me, or I can carry you out, but either way, you're coming with me. Now."

My brain tried to calculate the steps to the door; a pattern of moves to get around him; the correct words to scream for help—*something* to save myself. But with a gun pointed in my face, the best my brain could summon was standing frozen and gaping in disbelief.

"Good girl," he said at my apparent acquiescence. He tugged on my arm to get me to walk, and it snapped me back to life.

A primitive roar ripped out of me as I swung for his head again in one last desperate attempt.

He ducked with a huff, dodging it, and then gave me an annoyed look. "I guess we're going with option two, then."

The gun came flying at my head before I even blinked. It whacked my temple with a sickening crack.

And then everything went dark.

CHAPTER 7

When I was six, my sister tied me to the swing set in our backyard. We were playing pirates, and I'd been captured and bound to the ship's mast while she stowed my stolen treasure belowdecks. The mast was a metal pole; my bindings, a jump rope; my treasure, a plastic tiara and a slingshot; and belowdecks, the far end of the yard in the shade of the gardening shed. Libby had lost interest in our game and left me there, laced to the icy pole, until I began to cry.

My father heard me from over in the shed, where he was tinkering with our lawn mower, which he'd taken apart simply to study how it worked. When he approached me, wiping his hands on a greasy towel, I expected him to untie me and punish Libby with a lifetime of the worst-possible chores. But instead he examined the pink sparkly rope wound around my body, from ankles to shoulders, and nodded. He leaned in and wiped the tears from my cheeks with a callused thumb, which smelled like grease and grass, and said, "It's just a puzzle, Penny. And you're smart enough to solve anything." He ruffled my hair with his big hand and went back to the shed.

I gaped at him in disbelief as I squirmed against my bindings. *How dare he!* I raged inside my little head. More tears boiled up and I thought of shouting for Mom, but decided trying to rescue myself would be less of a hassle. Once my vision cleared, I got to work assessing the situation and made a plan.

Libby had intentionally or carelessly, I'd never been sure, left my ankles looser than my arms. The pink rope bit into my shins, which already had plenty of scabs from the trips and falls customary of my childhood, but I managed to work one foot free and then the other. Once I had my knees free, I could shimmy down the pole to free my shoulders and eventually turn around to untie my hands.

Once I was loose, I ran across the yard, beaming, and triumphantly presented the tangled rope to my father. I got a tacit nod of approval in return—which was high praise from him.

He told me years later he'd never taken his eyes off me and had the pruning shears at the ready, but he knew I would find my way out.

That day in the backyard, in what had been a child's game, my father imparted lasting wisdom to me. His voice became a refrain through my studies and career, through life in general. *It's just a puzzle, Penny. And you're smart enough to solve anything.* I'd heard it in the most trying times, and the sound of it always brought me back to the basics of that day: assess the situation; make a plan.

Little did my father or sister know, but that formative sunny day in the backyard would one day play out again in a much less innocent and edifying way. If only they'd prepared me for a head injury and shadowy isolated location, in addition to being bound, as part of my childhood lesson.

Now I tensed against my bindings. A far less friendly set of zip ties cinched my ankles to the legs of an uncomfortable chair and bound my wrists behind my back, making me long for a sparkly jump rope. A gag filled my mouth and was tied behind my head. An axe had been driven into my temple, surely. The place where I'd been hit throbbed furiously. The vision in my left eye had only now recovered.

The gap between Lou's office and wherever I was now was a gray blur, with the mental visibility of a blizzard. I'd come to as I was being pulled out of a car, but only long enough to blink at unfamiliar surroundings, desperately struggle in a panic, and be whacked in the head again. The second whack must have been harder than the first because a full lifetime could have passed between then and now. I'd lost all sense of space and time. The only way I knew we were in the same century? I was still wearing the same dress and heels I'd worn to the funeral, and my head injury was fresh enough to ache.

"Ouch," I muttered against the gag, and winced all over again. Lifting my hands to check was out of the question, but I knew if I could reach for my forehead, a large lump would be there to greet me.

I took a breath to curb the panic licking at me like flames.

I was somewhere underground. The claustrophobic feeling I always got in parking garages squeezed in on me. The air hung colder and thinner, as if in a reminder I was someplace I wasn't supposed to be able to breathe, and everything above could crumble and bury me alive. I shivered at the thought. The walls and floor were a continuous shade of concrete. One boxy pillar stood guard in the middle of the floor, holding up the ceiling. A staircase cascaded from the top right corner of the room. A stack of chairs similar to the one I was sitting in stood in the opposite corner.

I considered shouting for help, but even without a gag in my mouth, I wasn't sure anyone would hear me, and if anyone could, they likely were not the type of visitor I wanted.

I struggled against my bindings again, feeling the zip ties bite into my skin. My ankles stung already. My arms ached from the angle.

It's just a puzzle, Penny.

I wiggled my feet, thinking if I could kick off my heels, I could slip my feet free, but it was no use. Whoever had tied me up knew what they were doing. My wrists were chafed. I'd have to dislocate a shoulder to get an arm free. That, or tip the chair over and hope it landed at the right angle to snap one of its legs. In all likelihood, tipping would only succeed in hurting me.

I closed my eyes and listened as hard as I could, but the concrete walls may well have been soundproofed. All I heard was my own heartbeat, which I was struggling to keep calm.

Think.

A plan for escape felt futile. I didn't even know where I was. The blip of memory from before being whacked in the head for a second time only contained flashes of a car's interior and what could have been a garage. I'd been driven inside, possibly already underground, and then carried deeper underground.

Was I in a house? An office building? A secret compound? On a boat?

The last option was the only thing I was sure could not be true. Wherever I was, it was most certainly on land.

A door opened in the distance, shooting a shaft of light down the stairs. I tensed as footsteps carried down the concrete with soft scrapes. Given the shape of the room, it took half the staircase for me to be able to see the person's legs, and the whole thing for me to recognize the man in the tweed jacket.

"Hi, Dr. Collins," he said as he approached me. "Glad to see you're awake." He held a tablet in his hands and tapped his fingers across it before locking the screen and holding it behind his back. He leaned over and spoke to me as if I were a child. "Before I remove your gag, I want you to understand no one can hear you if you scream, so there is no use. Also, if you try to bite me, I will be forced to knock you out again. Understand?"

Bite him? I silently wondered if I might have attempted that during one of the blank spots in my memory.

"Do you understand?" he repeated, slower and louder.

I glared at him, insulted, and nodded.

"Good girl," he said with the same sinister purr from when he grabbed me in the office. He set the tablet on the floor a short distance away from me and slowly reached for the rag tied around my mouth.

The cottony cloth had absorbed all the moisture from my tongue. I coughed and smacked my lips, trying to bring it back. "Can I have some water?"

He considered me with a tilt of his head. "That depends."

"On what?"

He placed his arms behind his back again and began to pace in front of me. Once more, I felt like defenseless prey trapped in a cage with a predator—except this time, it was literal. "On how useful you are."

I tensed against my bindings again. "What does that mean?"

"It means you're here for a reason, and now it's only a matter of time."

I frowned at his cryptic response. "A matter of time until what?"

"I think you know."

"I promise you, I truly do not."

He sighed and reached for the tablet. He poked at it to find something that must have already been saved on it, because I couldn't imagine a Wi-Fi signal penetrating these concrete walls. And on that thought, I realized I had no idea where my phone was. I'd had a clutch at the funeral and could not say what had happened to it once we left the office. In all likelihood, my phone was smashed to pieces on the side of the road somewhere and my ID burned.

I ached at the thought of my sister. She must have been terrified and worried sick.

The tweed man found what he was looking for and flipped the tablet around to face me.

The photo of me and Anthony from the news, the one of him catching me on the curb outside the police station, stared back at me.

I groaned and rolled my eyes. "*Seriously?* For the hundredth time, *I am not his girlfriend.* I'm just a professor! I teach undergrads how to code! I'm only trying to make tenure!" I struggled against my bindings like a prisoner raging in their cell. "I don't even know him!"

"No? Then why did he tell me he'd kill me if I hurt you?"

"Because he—what?" My heart thudded in my ears as the gravity of what he said took hold.

He leaned closer with another smug smile. "Yes. That morning I was outside his house, he told me if I so much as spoke to you, he'd hunt me down, and if I laid a finger on you, then he would have no choice but to kill me. Now, why would someone be so fiercely protective of someone they didn't know?"

My jaw had fallen off its hinges. My mouth popped shut and back open a few times, but no sound came out. I was a dummy with no ventriloquist.

The tweed man's voice dropped to a low purr as he leaned in even closer. "I knew from the moment I saw you two the day of the estate sale, the spark that went off like a firecracker there in the foyer, that you would become a key piece in this little game we're playing."

I was reeling from so many things, but one realization hit me over the head like a falling star. "It was you. *You* told the cops I was his girlfriend that day."

He straightened his posture and quietly laughed again. "I never talked to the police that day, but glad to hear my impression was corroborated."

My mind was a complete haze—not simply from being hit in the head multiple times in the recent past.

Anthony had threatened to kill this man? Over *me?*

What game were they playing?

And for the love of all that was holy, what goddamned *spark* was everyone talking about?

A vision of Anthony hiding me in his closet flashed in my mind; his arms circled around me, holding me. Then there was the way he held a hammer, the sweaty J, that night in his pajamas, the way he looked in a suit at the funeral.

A warmth unfurled in my belly. I got the urge to cross my legs, but my feet were tied so my knees were spread, which only made the ache burn deeper.

It was all complicated. The thoughts felt like dozens of puzzle pieces that refused to fit together. I shook my head, trying to make sense of something, but that only made my wounded temple throb.

"Look, I don't know why Anthony said those things to you. We are not a couple. As far as I know, he's wrapped up in murdering Portia with the rest of you psychos. Please, I just want to go home."

Uttering Portia's name shifted the air, as if someone had opened a window and pumped in a cold blast. The tweed man's demeanor completely changed. His face grew serious, almost studious.

"What do you know about Portia?"

Here we go again, I thought. This woman held such power over all of them. Like they were ready to lie down and die for information on her.

"Only what I've seen online and on TV," I said vaguely.

The answer did not sit well with him. His eyes narrowed into pinpricks, and he leaned in. "Where is she?"

I flinched from his sudden invasion of my space. I had nowhere to go, but I leaned back as much as possible. "I assume in a shallow grave or at the bottom of the bay by now, but I should be asking *you* that question."

He chewed on his lip and mulled my answer. His tablet *dinged* from his hand. When he looked at it, his face lit up. "Ah, well. Looks like our guest of honor has finally arrived. It's

about time. This should be fun to watch." In a swift and unnerving move, he circled behind me and looped his arms over
my head to hold the tablet so I could see the screen.

A black-and-white security image played out, and revealed
Anthony.

I sucked in a sharp breath.

He wore his customary all black and crept along what appeared to be the outside of a wall. Based on the dim light, night
had fallen.

Another wave of worry rolled through me. If it was dark
outside, I'd been gone for at least seven hours. Poor Libby
must have been out of her mind worried.

The tweed man poked the screen to enlarge the image. His
breath slid down my neck, as if a pitcher of warm water had
been poured. We watched as Anthony scaled a stone wall with
the ease of a cat. Where I would have needed a boost, only to
get high-centered with a leg on either side and then fall into a
heap of broken bones, he jumped up and grabbed the top of it
to pull himself over like it was nothing.

"Ha!" the tweed man chuckled, impressed.

I had to admit, it was impressive.

But the daring athletics aside, I realized we were watching a
video of Anthony breaking into the place where I was being
kept. And the tweed man had been expecting him.

He circled back in front of me and gave me a serious look.
"This place is surrounded, but everyone has instructions not to
interfere until he gets to you," he said while he tapped at his
tablet. "You aren't going to do anything foolish when he comes
down here to find you, are you?"

I blinked at him as it struck me with a startling realization
what role I was playing in all this.

Bait.

They didn't want me; they wanted him. And I was the leverage to get to him.

People like me can't really afford to get close to others. It cre-

ates leverage. Anthony had said those words to me that night in his kitchen. When we had crossed the line into close enough for him to come rescue me, I couldn't be sure, but here we were.

I stared up at the tweed man, wanting to scream. For help, in fury, to warn Anthony. He was about to walk into a trap, and I had no idea the tweed man's intentions, once he was caught in it, but they couldn't have been good.

I decided it was in my best interest to cooperate until further notice.

I nodded.

"Good girl," he said with a wink. He wedged the tablet between his knees so he could reach for my gag and shove it back up into my mouth.

My heart thrummed with the enthusiasm of a hummingbird's wings. The tweed man moved to the corner to watch his tablet, and I could only assume to monitor Anthony's progress in locating me. I tried to count. Why? I didn't know, but numbers often soothed me, and I thought perhaps knowing how long it took Anthony to get to me would somehow help us escape on the other end of whatever was going to happen.

I got to fifty-five when the tweed man locked the tablet's screen and stepped back completely into the shadow. Given where he stood, flat against the far wall opposite me and adjacent to the staircase, there was no way Anthony would see him when he came down the stairs.

I was bait in a pool of light, a slab of meat in a cage with an open door, and I hoped Anthony had the sense to recognize the scene for what it was.

Another thirty seconds passed before the door at the top of the stairs opened again. The beam of light spilled down so gradually that he must have been opening the door inches at a time. I heard the first cautious footstep, and then another. His shadow tumbled over the steps, long and broad from the light behind him.

At the sound of his voice, deep and secret and soft, my whole body went tingly with simultaneous fear and relief. "Penny?"

I tensed, wishing I could warn him about the monster in the shadow.

His legs came into view first. Then his outstretched arms, holding a gun in his hands. I flinched at the sight of it. By the time I could see his chest and shoulders, he'd reached the bottom of the stairs. When he saw me, he sagged with visible relief.

"Penny!" My name was a lyric on his lips. He shoved his gun into his waistband and strode over to me.

I shook my head and threw my eyes at the tweed man in warning, but he was too busy hurrying to my side. He lifted an intimidating knife from his jeans and snapped it open while he squatted at my feet.

"I'm so glad I found you. I'm so sorry." He reached for my ankle, his hands a hot flash on my skin, as the tweed man crept out of the shadow behind him.

I jerked and kicked against my bindings; I screamed at the gag, but only succeeded in garbled nonsense.

Anthony looked up at me with a vulnerable empathy in his eyes. "It's okay. You're safe now."

The words weren't even out of his mouth before the tweed man clubbed him in the back of the head, and he collapsed at my feet.

CHAPTER 8

Watching the tweed man struggle to position an unconscious Anthony in a chair beside me gave me an appreciation for the man's size all over again. He grunted and cursed, and by the time he had outfitted Anthony with a set of zip ties to match mine, hands bound and feet shackled to his chair, he was wiping his brow and declaring the need for a drink.

"Don't go anywhere," he said to me with a sick chuckle, obviously proud of his twisted joke.

He marched up the stairs and left us alone.

The space suddenly felt suffocatingly tiny. I was no longer by myself, but the fact Anthony sat beside me, equally as defenseless, was a source of terror more than comfort.

His shoulders drooped forward and his chin nearly rested on his chest. He was out cold, and I still had a gag in my mouth, so the best I could do was grunt at him and try not to cry.

He'd walked straight into the trap—the big, sexy, reckless oaf. It was like he'd seen me, and all sense of reason and precaution abandoned him—I didn't really want to unpack what *that* meant, though the thoughts were dancing through my mind like a chorus line.

How had *I* become leverage over *him*? We'd known each

other for barely three days, and here we were tied up together like some bizarre couple's retreat gone wrong.

From my position beside him, I studied the architecture of his body. Even drooped over and slack, he was all muscle. His hair fell forward, nearly covering his face, but I could still make out his long lashes and the way they fanned over his impossibly high cheekbones. His lips pursed out in a loose swell, slightly parted and relaxed like a pair of pillows. He was unfairly beautiful, and I hated how attractive I found his attempted rescue—how attractive I found *him.*

What a mess we were in, all because someone saw us arguing over a pair of candlesticks and got the wrong impression.

He suddenly stirred and inhaled a sharp breath.

I jumped at the sound and felt tears blur my eyes in relief.

A gravelly grumble escaped his mouth as he sat up and blinked a few times. It took him several seconds to gain his bearings. I watched as it happened, knowing the feeling for having gone through it myself not long before. He winced, the same as I had done, when the pain in the back of his head reminded him of what had happened.

I waited for him to turn and see me. When he did, his face lifted and then fell.

"Penny!" He leaned like he meant to reach out for me before the restraints held him back. He said my name in the same reverent tone he'd used when he came down the stairs. It stirred a confusing warmth in my chest.

My eyes welled up again. It was all too much. Being snatched and hit and tied up, all to end up with Anthony Pierce gazing at me like the missing piece that completed a puzzle.

"No! Please don't cry," he said with a shake of his head.

But I couldn't help it. The tears were coming in a flood of relief and pain and anger at him for putting me in this situation.

He leaned in again, and I saw the muscles in his arms straining against the ties. He looked like he could Hulk out of them, but they wouldn't give. "Penny, you can't cry," he said desperately. "Not with that thing in your mouth. You won't be able to breathe if your nose gets stuffed up."

As soon as he said it, I noticed the limited air flow battling the clog of tears, and it only made me cry harder, more desperately. Messy, wet, panicky tears.

"No, no, no!" he pled. He jerked his body so his chair moved an inch toward me. His knee and elbow pressed into mine. "You have to stop. Here, I'm going to help you."

I flinched when he leaned in farther. A strangled yelp garbled from my mouth.

"I'm not going to hurt you! Relax. I'm going to take your gag out."

I turned to look at him with a question on my face. *How?* Because the last I checked, his hands were bound behind his back too.

He understood my silent query and answered by way of snapping his teeth together.

His mouth?

I gaped at him in disbelief, but based on the determined yet soft look in his eyes, and the way he was leaning in as if to kiss me, he was serious.

His chest and arms strained against his bindings and his T-shirt. I leaned in, still crying, and let him come close. When he was an inch away, he looked me in the eye and nodded, silently asking for consent for his strange and wildly desperate plan. I nodded back, just as desperate, and felt my heart pound my ribs like a drum.

In a move that ended up being absurdly tender, he brought his face against mine and bit at the gag. His nose pressed into my cheek, and I felt his lips brushing my skin as he searched for purchase with his teeth. A tear rolled from my eye and followed the curve of his nose. It was all so obscenely intimate, I would have collapsed if I hadn't already been sitting down and tied to a chair.

"Almost," he said in a muffled burst of warm breath. The motion of the word pressed his tongue to my cheek for a split second, which made me gasp. I shut my eyes at the dizzy spell that came over me in a wave. His hair brushed my temple, and I reflexively leaned into him. There may have been a moment of involuntary nuzzling. "Turn your head," he said softly.

I followed his command, under a spell, and felt his mouth move closer to mine until they overlapped at the corner. I'd never touched lips with someone I wasn't kissing. What an odd situation to have one event occur without the other.

Anthony's lips were soft, so incredibly soft, where they touched mine. I wanted to melt into them and stay there forever. I'd lost sense of what we were even doing, until I felt him bite down and tug. He grunted at me and tilted his chin up, indicating I should do the same. He had a solid grip on the gag; all I had to do was move my jaw back and tilt my head up. I did as much and felt it slide off over my chin.

I exhaled in relief. He lingered with his face in the crook between my chin and neck, buried in my hair, and deeply inhaled.

"Thank you," I muttered. My mouth was already parched again. My voice still strangled with tears.

"No problem," he said in a deep rasp, and sat back against his chair.

The longing I felt for him to return burned in my veins. Whether it was from fear, desperation, or pure desire, I couldn't tell, but the confusion pushed a fresh set of tears up into my eyes. I sniffled.

"Hey," he said. "No more crying. We'll figure this out."

"What are you even doing here?" I said, a blubbery mess.

"What?"

"I said, what are you even doing here? You're one of the bad guys!"

He reeled back as far as he could go. "*Bad guys?* Penny, have you been paying any attention?"

I swallowed a sob and nodded. "Yes! They murdered Portia, and you and your uncle covered it up for them."

"What? Penny, that's not true."

My voice continued to get higher pitched and more waterlogged. "Yes, it is! I found her other shoe in your closet! I know she's dead, and I know—"

"She's not dead."

"What?"

He turned to me with a serious yet guarded look in his eyes. "Portia is not dead."

I blinked at him in confusion. He said it with such certainty, I could only assume he knew the rest of the story. "Then where is she?"

He clenched his jaw tight enough that I could see his muscle twitch. "Gone."

The word didn't ring with a finality to indicate he was using a euphemism, but I still didn't understand.

"What does that mean?"

He glanced at the staircase and lowered his voice to a near whisper. "It means Portia wanted to disappear, so we made it happen. But things got . . . complicated."

I gaped at him in shock. The pieces I'd been turning over and over for days suddenly fell into a new pattern that made a whole different kind of sense.

"Wait," I said, still piecing it together. "Her husband didn't kill her?"

He shot me a sideways glance. "No. He's looking for her. Hence all this." He gestured at the room with his chin. "He wants her back," he said, sounding like he was spitting out a bitter seed.

"Oh, my God," I muttered. My head was spinning fast enough to make me feel like I'd taken an ill-advised turn on a carnival ride. The cast of characters I'd had listed in my mind shuffled and reorganized into a whole new reality.

Portia was missing, but on purpose. And Anthony and Lou had set it up.

"So, then, where is she?" I repeated my question right as the door at the top of the stairs opened.

Anthony sucked in a sharp breath, and I flinched.

"Don't say anything," he whispered.

I nodded in agreement. My whole body vibrated with tension. I fought to steady my breath.

The tweed man appeared at the bottom of the stairs with a grin on his face. "Mr. Pierce, nice of you to finally join us. Dr. Collins and I have been anxiously awaiting your arrival." He nodded his head at me and took note of the gag hanging around my neck, instead of firmly stuffed in my mouth. "What happened here?" He stepped toward me, and Anthony tensed.

"Leave her alone. She has nothing to do with this," he growled. The sound of it sent a shiver through me.

The tweed man stopped his approach toward me midstep and pivoted to face him. He tilted his head with the grin I'd come to recognize as his signature look. "Oh, but she has everything to do with this, because without her, we never would have gotten your attention, Mr. Pierce." Anthony shifted uncomfortably as he came closer and leaned in. The tweed man's voice dropped to an icy hiss. They were nearly nose to nose. "We killed your uncle, and you didn't get the message. We dumped that two-faced piece-of-shit bodyguard on your doorstep, and you didn't get the message. We broke into your house, and you didn't get the message. I was starting to wonder what it would take. And then, like a godsend, the girl next door shows up, and all we have to do is snatch her, and you come running. Makes my job a lot easier."

The tweed man turned his head to wink at me and found a look of shocked horror on my face.

They killed his uncle? And *the bodyguard?*

I suddenly saw the past days' events in a new light. The tweed man had been outside Libby's house the day with the reporter to keep tabs on me. He had broken into Anthony's house that night we hid in the closet. And, surely, Connor was at the funeral earlier to intimidate Anthony, or at least let him know he was watching. And the tweed man had come to the reception to snatch me, because none of the other things had had the intended effect.

The revelations crashed over me in pounding waves. I was drowning; I didn't know which way was up. The sensation left me both spinning and aching with sorrow for Anthony's loss. Not to mention, petrified I was wrapped up in something far more sinister than I'd realized.

"Now that we have your attention, Mr. Pierce, I have a simple question for you: Where is Portia?" the tweed man asked.

"Go fuck yourself," Anthony spat out without a second's hesitation.

A dark chuckle popped from the tweed man's mouth as he stood up straight. "I figured you'd say as much." With a wind-up quicker than a blink, he pulled his arm back and threw his fist at Anthony's face.

I shrieked in fright and flinched. The sound of knuckles against cheekbone made a sick, hard crack, not the pumped-up sound effect of a movie. It made me realize I'd never witnessed someone get punched in the face in real life.

Anthony took the hit like he *had,* in fact, been previously punched in the face in real life. He shook his head with a rough breath and worked his jaw. Clearly, the hit had been intended to hurt him, not knock him out again. An angry red welt bloomed out over his cheek, like he'd stepped out into a cold morning, but he only looked a little fazed.

"Any idea where she is now?" the tweed man asked as he flexed his hand.

Anthony glared at him with a silent fury while I held my breath.

The tweed man released a frustrated sigh. His voice took on a cold, taunting edge. "You know, your uncle didn't even beg. Most guys plead and cry; I've seen grown men piss themselves. But the only thing he said before I shot him was: 'Anthony will take care of this.'"

A tear rolled down my cheek at the anguish on Anthony's face. He tried to hide it, but I saw it in the corners of his mouth, the set of his jaw, the sheen that glossed his eyes.

The tweed man huffed a tiny, dark laugh. "At first, I thought he was simply being stubborn and putting on a show. A real tough guy. But then I realized he didn't beg because he had nothing to beg for. No family—except you—no wife, no real friends. What was the man even living for in the end? It felt like a waste, actually. To take a life no one cared about."

"Fuck you," Anthony barked, and fought against his restraints again. Veins throbbed in the side of his neck. The muscles in his arms looked fit to burst through his shirt.

The tweed man laughed again. "So you *do* care. Then why wasn't it enough? Why didn't you give us what we wanted then? Because of you, we had to keep going, and now here we are."

He stepped over in front of me and reached out to smooth my hair like I was a pet. I flinched and turned my head, but he kept his callused palm pressed against my cheek. Another tear spilled out from my eye. "What's it going to take, Mr. Pierce? How many people have to die before you tell us what we want to know?"

"Leave her alone," Anthony demanded.

The tweed man pivoted with a scrape of his shoes. "Gladly. Just tell me what I need to know."

Anthony silently glared at him, as if he was trying to melt him with his eyes. The pause seemed to stretch forever.

My heart had lodged in my throat like it planned to never leave.

Eventually the tweed man got tired of waiting. He sighed. "Mr. Slate told me to handle you by whatever means necessary. If you're not going to cooperate, then you leave me no choice." He reached into his waistband and pulled out a gun. Whether it had been there all along, or was Anthony's gun he nabbed after he knocked him out, I wasn't sure, but he used it to smash into the side of Anthony's face and then pummel him in the abdomen with two sharp blows. The series of hits left the room echoing with cracked bones and scented with blood. The tangy bite almost made me gag. A large gash had split open over Anthony's left eye and began streaking his face red. He sat hunched over as far as he could bend, struggling for breath and wheezing.

"Stop!" I wailed. "Please!" Tears strangled my voice. I felt them streaming down my face in hot rivers.

The tweed man grabbed Anthony's hair and tilted his head up. I saw his Adam's apple bob as he struggled to swallow. Blood colored his cheek red, from his temple to his chin. His brow had begun to swell. The gun was inches from his face. "I'll ask again: Where is Portia?"

"Anthony, tell him!" I begged. I fought against my own restraints, as if I stood a chance of intervening. The ties bit into my skin in reminder that I didn't.

Anthony licked a trickle of blood, which had found its way to his mouth, and exhaled a tight breath out of his nose. His lips parted to speak, and my pounding heart surged in the hope he would put an end to this before he got himself killed.

"She's nowhere," he said.

The tweed man snarled and released his hair with a sharp shove. "Fine. You want to do this the hard way? We will." He stepped back and cocked the gun, loading a bullet into the chamber with a sharp click, and then pointed it at me.

I flinched with a frantic yelp.

"Where is Portia?" he asked again, directing the question at Anthony.

My vision swam with tears. The whole room narrowed to that beady little black eye. I couldn't form words to beg, to plead, to try and talk my way out of an impossible situation.

He moved his finger to the trigger, and I winced—as if it was enough to prepare me to die.

"Stop!" Anthony shouted. His breathing was labored. His voice cracked and broke. "Stop. I'll tell you."

The tweed man relaxed his elbow, but didn't lower the gun all the way. He turned to look at Anthony. "Go on, then. Tell me."

Anthony heaved a painful-sounding breath. It looked like it took all his strength to lift his head to speak. "She's in Iceland. There's an isolated fishing village on the east coast. You'll find her at the Glacier Point Bed and Breakfast."

A small smile broke out over the tweed man's face. He moved to stand in front of Anthony and bent over so they were face-to-face. He pressed the gun barrel into Anthony's knee. "You better be telling me the truth. I'm going to go confirm. If I find out you're lying, I *will* come back, and I *will* hurt her." He nodded toward me.

I shriveled at the sincerity in his voice.

He headed for the stairs and left us alone again.

Anthony immediately sagged forward and closed his eyes. Blood continued to drip from his temple, now landing on his pants.

I knew he'd bought us time and I hoped it would be enough to come up with a plan.

It's just a puzzle, Penny.

I forced a deep breath to fill my lungs. *Think.* We were both tied up; he was seriously injured, perhaps on the verge of losing consciousness again; and I had nothing more to work with than I had before he'd arrived, other than the knowledge he'd go to desperate measures to save me.

Except for one thing. One thing that the tweed man didn't account for. I'd willed him not to notice the whole time he was tying Anthony up. I found it a small miracle he overlooked it again when he came back to question him. It might have been our only shot. But getting to it would be risky. And painful.

I weighed the risk and decided it was worth not dying in this basement.

"Anthony!" I whispered.

He grunted in acknowledgment, but didn't lift his head. His chin pointed at his chest. A stream of blood still trickled down his temple. I ached at the sight. It made me all the more determined to get us out of here.

"Psst! Anthony!" I hissed again, this time rocking sideways to bump him with my elbow as much as I could.

His head bobbed. He angled his face at me a half turn. Blood dripped into his eye and caught on his lashes like red dewdrops. "Hmm?"

"How much time do we have?"

"What?"

"I know you lied to him about where Portia is, so how much time until he figures it out and comes back for another round?"

He blinked away more blood as a small smile twitched his lips. "How do you know I lied?"

"Because Portia hates the cold. She would never go to Iceland."

"How do you know that?"

"Because I've read her entire life's history on the internet. Now, I have a plan. How long until he comes back?"

He cast an appreciative glance at me before he tried for a deep breath. He didn't get far and winced. "Hopefully, long enough for my ribs to heal. I think he broke them. What are you doing?"

As he spoke, I did my best to hop over closer to him. With a good upward bounce—never mind the zip ties slicing into my skin each time—I could move a few centimeters. I stopped, once my shoulder was flush against his.

"My plan. I want you to bump me."

"What?"

"Knock me over."

"What?"

"Look, I know you've taken a few hits to the head, but this really isn't that complicated. If we get enough momentum going, you can tip me sideways and my chair will fall over."

"Are you nuts? That'll break your arm when you hit the floor."

"Perhaps, but your knife is behind me, and I think I can reach it."

"I—" A breath caught in his throat, and he paused the next argument on his tongue. He shifted his head to glance behind me. "My knife?"

"Yes. It went flying when the tweed man attacked you. He didn't notice. It's been there the whole time."

"The tweed man?" he asked with a curious tilt of his head.

"Yes. I don't know his name, and he's always wearing tweed. Do you see the knife? If I land right, I think I can grab it."

I could feel him calculating: He was weighing *the risk of my injury to set us free, potentially* versus *the beating we both might take when the tweed man discovered his lie and came back downstairs to express his discontent.*

"Penny, that's really going to hurt. How about you knock me over?"

I scooted a centimeter closer again, ready to get to work. "That's very noble of you, but you're already injured—"

"Exactly. What's one more hit?"

"—and you're twice my size. There's no way I can knock you over. It's simple physics: I'm smaller. Now hit me!"

"I'm not going to hit you."

"Not like that. You know what I mean. Come on. *Bump* me. *Scoot* me. *Nudge* me—Ah!" I yelped when he rocked to his right and then slammed into me from his left. My chair rose up on two legs, but not quite far enough. I landed with a soft thud.

"Good! Do that again, but let me get ready this time." I braced for impact as he winced. A fleck of blood had escaped from his brow and landed on my thigh in a little crimson dot. The visceral reality of our situation hit me like a gut punch. I took a deep breath. "Okay, ready," I said.

This time, when he rocked over and slammed into me, I threw all my momentum with it. My chair lifted again, teetering on two legs, and teasing us with a promise.

"Come on, come on, come on!" I begged. I was a domino about to crash. All I needed was a breath of air, a hair to fall into place, a dust mote to land. But the chair wouldn't cooperate.

"Shit," I spat when I landed on all four feet again.

Anthony groaned, clearly in pain and now frustrated too.

My skin was raw beneath my zip ties. I'd nearly lost sensation in my hands and feet. But a determined fury burned in my belly.

"Okay, one more time. Give me all you've got."

"Penny, I—"

"Just do it!" My voice cracked in a desperate wail. I felt

tears prick my eyes, but I would not let them fall again. Hope wasn't lost yet.

Anthony glanced over at the fraught sound I made.

"Please," I begged.

The same last-ditch desperation burned in his eyes. He nodded. And then he came in like a wrecking ball.

I gasped when he slammed into me and I threw everything I had into leaning sideways. The chair went up, up, up, on two legs, and I held my breath.

"Yes, yes, yes! Go, go, keep going!" Anthony pled.

"I'm going! I'm going!" I squeaked. My whole body tensed. I tottered on the precipice, hoping to fall and fearing it at the same time. With one final inch, I passed the point of no return, and the cold, hard floor was all too eager to greet me.

I slammed into it with ten times the force I'd expected. My teeth rattled in my jaw. The chair smashed into my arm like a club. No bones snapped, but surely my arm would be ten shades of purple. My body sagged against the bindings, tearing my skin in at least three places, but we'd done it. I was on the floor.

"Penny?" Anthony asked. His voice hovered above me, cautious and full of desperate concern. "Are you all right?"

The wind had left my lungs and taken my voice with it. "Yeah," I croaked. "You were right: That hurt like hell. Don't look up my skirt." I could feel my dress flipped up around my thighs and exposing my crotch, a consequence I'd overlooked in my plan. At least I had put on nice underwear this morning.

"It's kind of impossible, given your position, but I promise I'm not looking on purpose," Anthony said. I detected a hint of a smile in his voice.

I'd worry about my dignity later; there were more important matters to tend to. I moved my hands as much as I could, feeling around for the knife behind me. "Am I close? Where is it?"

I'd lost sight of him completely, but the sound of his voice fell over me like a raspy, warm blanket.

"To the left and about six inches back."

"*Inches?* I hoped you pushed me right on top of it."

"Sorry. Next time we're kidnapped and tied up, I'll be sure to have better aim."

I thrust my hips back into the chair as hard as I could, ignoring the pain shooting through my left arm pinned beneath me, and managed to move back an inch. "I mean, it's really not too much to ask when you think about it. I'm trying to come to your rescue. The least you could do is shoot for accuracy." I thrust again and moved another inch.

"There you go. Do that again," he encouraged.

I did it again, sure my left arm was losing a layer of skin against the cold floor. I felt the chair grinding against my bruised bone. "You never answered my question," I said for distraction.

"Which one?"

Once more, I scooted. "The one about how much time we have."

He paused as I scooted a final time and felt the icy edge of the blade kiss my fingertips. "Hopefully, enough. There! You've got it."

My hands were half numb and I felt something warm and wet when I gripped the knife's handle. The zip tie had cut into my skin; I was bleeding. "How sharp is this thing?" I asked as I maneuvered the handle into my palm and the blade beneath the plastic band holding my hands in place.

"Sharp enough," Anthony said. "Flip it around; the blade is the wrong way. You're going to cut yourself."

"Judging by the blood I can feel, I think that ship has sailed."

"Well, yes. But there's a difference between a ligature laceration and a blade."

"Spoken like someone with experience. I thought you weren't

one of the bad guys." I grunted as I locked the knife into position and began to saw. In that moment, I didn't know if accidentally sinking the blade into my skin would have been worse than the pain I was already in from the zip ties. It was a true toss-up.

He ignored my sarcastic comments. "You've almost got it. Just push down and pull up."

"Push down and pull up?"

"Push down with the knife and pull up with your arms at the same time."

"What's that going to do?" I asked as I did it, somewhat annoyed he was micromanaging my escape attempt.

"It will create leverage. There! Like that. Keep going!"

A high-pitched whine spilled from my lips as I pressed the knife down and lifted my elbows as much as they could go. My hands were either going to fall off, or I was going to pass out from the pain.

"Almost! *Almost,*" Anthony cheered me on.

Sweat broke out on my brow. I bit my lip and squeezed my eyes shut. I was seconds from giving up, from surrendering and dissolving into a puddle of defeated, bloody tears, when three things happened at the same instant.

The pressure around my wrists released with a snap, Anthony desperately whispered, *"Yes!"* on a broken breath, and the door at the top of the stairs opened.

I didn't have time to cut my feet free before the tweed man came stomping down the stairs.

"I told you that you'd regret lying to me," he boomed in an angry voice while we could still only see his feet. "And now—" He stopped at the foot of the stairs, one hand on the rail, and surveyed the scene.

I was still on the floor, hands behind my back, but head angled enough to see him, and Anthony was still bound to his chair, bloodied and bruised.

"What happened here?" the man asked.

Anthony didn't speak, but I could feel him silently willing me to do something. What, I wasn't sure.

I thought as quickly as I could. Flailing my arms at the man would only prompt him to tie me up again, so I played the part of still-helpless victim.

"I had an accident," I said.

The sound of his shoes scraping the concrete floor came closer. "An accident?" he purred. His voice took on a completely different tone when he spoke to me. Something dark and indulgent, like a big cat playing with its food before he ate it.

My hands twitched with urge to pull my skirt down, but I kept them behind my back. "Yes. I tipped over," I said.

He leaned down to meet my eyes, and I felt his gaze slowly travel over my bare thighs and upturned skirt. The smell of cigarettes wafted off him in noxious clouds. Checking Anthony's information on Portia wasn't the only thing he'd done while he was gone. "Well, I bet that didn't feel very good, did it," he said in a low hum. He placed his palm on my thigh and slid it upward. I tensed at the contact, my stomach turning over, and fought to hold still. He grinned and kept sliding his hand higher toward the exposed lace of my underwear as Anthony made sounds of protest I couldn't make out. My hearing had gone offline. I seethed in rage and fear while a primal instinct buried in the most basal part of my brain took over.

I quietly mumbled.

"What was that?" he asked, and leaned in closer, leering and choking me with the scent of stale smoke.

I lifted my head to meet his eyes and made sure he heard me the second time. "I said, *Don't touch me.*" While he was still bent over with his hand on my thigh, I swung my right arm around and drove the knife into his torso. It sank between his ribs with a sensation I couldn't describe, and never wanted to feel again. Anthony was right about his knife: It was certainly sharp enough.

The man gasped. His eyes went wide in shock before he stood and stumbled back. The knife slipped out, but stayed in my hand and was now dripping blood. I blinked at it in horror, stunned at what I had done. The white noise of shock filled my mind with a buzzing that drowned out everything. I couldn't be sure how long he'd been calling me, but Anthony's voice eventually penetrated the haze and broke through.

"Penny! Penny, cut me loose!" he demanded.

I was still staring at the knife in my hand, which had begun to tremble. The man lay on the floor in a heap, moaning and swearing. "Holy shit," I muttered. "I stabbed him."

"Yes. Yes, you did," Anthony said. "Now cut yourself loose so you can cut me loose before he gets back up."

He's not dead, I convinced myself based on what Anthony said. He wasn't going to get back up if he was dead.

"Penny! We're on borrowed time here!"

The urgency in his voice snapped me back to reality. I twisted to push myself up with my right hand and free my left arm. I yelped in pain, once the pressure of the chair was released from on top of it. The bruise inside my elbow already bloomed like a small flower bed beneath my skin. The limb dangled like a useless noodle. My wrists were bloodied, as were my ankles. I finally took a moment to smooth my skirt as I sat up to free my feet.

"I didn't mean to stab him," I muttered, mostly to myself. "I didn't plan on that."

"That's okay," Anthony said. "You did what you had to do to save us."

"To save us," I parroted as I sliced my right foot free.

The man continued groaning. I averted my eyes from the pool of blood leaking onto the floor. The tablet sat on the concrete beside him, where he'd dropped it.

I got my left foot free and struggled to stand on wobbly legs. Vertigo hit me as I stumbled a few steps. How long had I been tied up? I had no idea, but the blood in my body looped around in disorienting ways. I yanked the gag off and threw it on the ground.

The man muttered something that sounded like *you bitch* as he tried to sit up. I took a step toward the sound as Anthony called again.

"Penny! My hands! Cut my hands free!"

"Yes! I'm coming," I said as I fled the man rising from a pool of his own blood like a scene from a nightmare. I ran around behind Anthony and sliced through his plastic handcuffs. He immediately grabbed the knife from me and cut his feet free. When he stood, he instantly doubled over in pain, wincing and cursing.

"Yeah, ribs are definitely broken," he muttered at the floor.

Any hope of him carrying my bruised body to safety was out of the question. He could hardly stand up.

I slithered under his dangling arm and threw my arm around his back. "Come on, big guy. Let's go."

We stood, both of us wincing, right as the man on the floor sputtered at us, "Y-you're not g-going . . . anywhere." Blood trickled from the corner of his mouth in a syrupy line, and I wondered for a stomach-churning second what I'd hit with the knife. I expected to see him reaching for a gun, but instead he was reaching for the tablet.

"No!" I said, and lunged for it, shrugging off Anthony in the process.

"What are you doing?" Anthony said, and clutched his injured side.

I kicked the tablet out of the tweed man's reach and then grabbed it. "He was using this to monitor you finding me; we were watching security feed. He said this place is surrounded and everyone had been instructed not to interfere until you got to me. He's going to tell them we escaped!"

"Give me that!" the tweed man groaned, and then coughed up blood.

"Oh, God," I said, realizing I was right, and horrified for multiple reasons.

Anthony took the cue and marched over to him with new-found strength. He stepped on his hand that had been reaching for the tablet, and then reached around his back to free the gun he somehow knew was stashed there. Then he took the gun and used it to strike him in the temple.

"*You're* not going anywhere," he said, and shoved the gun into his waistband. He stood for several seconds over the man, knocked out cold in a pool of his own blood, as if contemplating what to do with him. Then he turned to me. "Come on."

I poked at the tablet, deciding it might offer a handy escape map. I still didn't even know where we were. "I assume we'll need this to help us get out of here."

"Good idea," Anthony said with a nod. "Let's go."

We hobbled toward the stairs, and after he winced on the first few steps, I shoved myself under his arm as a crutch again, for fear that otherwise we weren't going to make it.

"Thank you," he muttered, and sounded only a little embarrassed.

"Mmm-hmm. Think of me as a flotation device. A water wing, if you will."

He huffed a tiny, painful sound. "Don't make me laugh."

"Sorry. But can I ask you a question?"

"Yes."

"Why didn't you shoot him?"

We were halfway up the stairs now. The flight seemed endless—with my battered body and a two-hundred-pound man draped over me like a shawl. Sisyphus had nothing on this.

"Because someone would have heard it," he said.

My heart sank at the realization of what he meant. "So, this place really is surrounded? Where are we?"

"The Slates' estate."

"What?!"

"Shhh!"

"Sorry." I lowered my voice. "But *what*? We've been at Connor Slate's house this whole time?"

"Not exactly the vision you had in mind?"

We were so close to the top now. The door stood three steps away. I was sweating and shaking under his weight, but determined to make it, though I feared what was on the other side. "I mean, I can't say I'm shocked a billionaire genius has a secret torture basement, but I thought it would be a little more posh."

"That's the rest of the house, don't worry."

"You've been here before?"

We reached the landing. He delicately lifted his arm from my shoulders with a wince. "Yes. Now stay close and keep quiet."

I opted to follow directions when he reached for the gun and checked it was loaded.

He opened the door very slowly and peeked into the hall before motioning for me to follow him.

"Anthony, wait," I whispered after a few steps. I paused to look at the tablet. The screen had lit up, and on it, I saw video of us. From the angle, I knew the camera was in the ceiling behind us. I grabbed his arm and pulled him around a corner, hoping there wasn't another camera there waiting for us.

"What is it?" he whispered.

I tapped the tablet screen in an effort to figure out what program was running. It was not an app I recognized. Given our location, I surmised it was probably a bespoke smart system designed by Connor Slate. "We're on camera right now," I muttered, and tapped through a few screens. Black-and-white images flashed by: exterior shots, a kitchen, an office, a bedroom. "This thing pinged earlier, and the tweed man showed me a video of you climbing a wall. It's a motion-activated security system. It looks like it covers the whole—" I cut off with a gasp when I saw a figure move through one of the images.

"Shit," Anthony hissed, looking over my shoulder. The person in the video, another burly-henchman type, was watching his own tablet. "We've got a long way to go to get out of here without getting caught. Can you turn it off?"

I glanced up at the hopeful look on his bloody face. "The security system?"

He nodded like it was a simple request.

"Um . . . maybe," I said, and went back to tapping the screen. I spent most of my time teaching JavaScript, Web building, and database management to undergrads. Sure, I might have known my way around the Dark Web or how to bypass a firewall in a pinch, but I'd never tried to override the security system in a billionaire's mansion before. I chewed my lip and followed a few screens into the settings menu.

"Well?" Anthony said impatiently. "Can you?"

"I'm a professor, not a hacker," I said, and shot him a glare before I went back to tapping the tablet. When I got to the screen I wanted, my heart sank at the confirmation of what I feared. "No, I can't. It's biosecurity protected."

"What does that mean?"

I flipped the screen around to show him the prompt. "It means we need Connor Slate's retina scan to turn it off. Does he happen to be home at the moment?" I was joking, but he answered me seriously.

"No."

"How do you know?"

"Because he would have killed us by now."

I seized in fear and felt as if I'd walked through a sheet of ice. "I get the sense he *is* one of the bad guys?"

"The baddest."

I swallowed and flipped the screen around to navigate back to the security footage. A second person had come into view somewhere in the house. The grid of images with thugs moving in and out of view made me feel like we were Mr. and Mrs. Pac-Man trying to evade ghosts.

I suddenly had an idea.

"Maybe we don't need to turn it off. Maybe we need to use it to navigate our way out. As far as these other guys know, we're still tied up in that basement." I pointed at the second person who'd sat in front of a TV. "Where is this room?"

Anthony squinted at the screen. "Not on the way out."

"Great. One down then. Where's this guy?" I pointed to the roving henchman. He paced a hallway full of windows.

"Looks like the east wing," Anthony said with a tiny upward lift of his lips. "Also not on the way out."

"Perfect."

"Let's go," he said. "If you see anyone start to move fast, let me know."

I nodded and followed like a shadow as he led us down a concrete hall underlit with little spotlights, like it was an artsy gallery rather than a creepy basement. Only the sound of our footsteps, his labored breathing, and my pounding heart filled the long corridor. I kept one eye on the tablet at all times. Our friend in the TV room remained committed to the screen. The one patrolling the east wing had paused to gaze out at the yard.

When we reached the end of the hall, we turned up another staircase, shorter this time, which led to a wide landing with an overstuffed couch and a pool table. A full bar nestled in the corner, complete with taps and a mirrored wall of bottled booze. A TV the size of a small theater screen filled the opposite wall.

"Nice home theater," I bitterly muttered.

"This isn't the theater," Anthony muttered back, and led me away from the man cave.

We turned up another short staircase, and I wondered how many levels subterranean we'd been. We entered another hallway, this one gleaming white with vibrant art splashed on the walls like graffiti. Anthony turned to me and pressed his finger to his lips in another reminder, perhaps because we were getting closer to the inhabited parts of the house.

I kept quiet for half the hall, until we passed an open archway, and it gave way to lanes of glossy wood and a telltale smell.

"Is that a *bowling alley*?" I said, still whispering, but unable to stop myself.

Anthony took my elbow and pulled me along from where I'd stopped to gaze in wonder. His grip was looser than I'd ever felt it, perhaps because he was holding the gun in his right hand and had to grab me with his left, and that was the side where his ribs were broken.

I silently vowed to behave so I wouldn't cause him any more injury.

We emerged from the hall into a soaring room—the likes of an *Architectural Digest* feature, and much more in line with what I expected for a billionaire's home, though the secret basement, man cave, supermax prison security system, and bowling alley were on par as well.

A literal tree stood in one corner, potted in a small vat. Sectional sofas surrounded an island-sized coffee table. Large, original, and imposing art filled the walls. The entire back wall of floor-to-ceiling glass shimmered from the swimming pool's reflection on the other side of it. The single room put Libby's entire house to shame—it made Lou Griotti's Victorian look pitiful.

"Wow!" I said in awe.

Anthony turned us toward another hall, and I wondered how many times he'd been inside the Slates' compound to be able to navigate what seemed like an endless maze. We passed doors to an office, a guest room, a bathroom, a full-on gym. When we got to the end of the hall, he held up his hand, and I came to a stop behind him. He peered side to side around the corner and then turned to me. He used his T-shirt to swipe at the blood on his face, which really only succeeded in smearing it around. The wound still glistened, fresh and open above his eye. He would need stitches.

His voice came out so softly, I leaned in to hear him. "There are doors into the backyard at the end of this hall. We just need to make it there, and we can get outside." He glanced down at my feet. "Can you run?"

I still wore the heels from the funeral. I'd been walking on my toes to keep them from clicking during our escape. But footwear was the least of our worries at this point.

"Can *you* run? You're the one with the busted ribs."

He pressed his palm to his left side, as if trying to stop his bones from poking out. "It'll be rough, but yes."

I'd expected him to say no and was now second-guessing my footwear. Running in heels was a surefire way to snap an ankle. "Wait!" A thought struck me as I backtracked into the hall.

"Penny, where are you going?" he whispered.

I held up a finger and slipped into the doorway leading to the gym. I knew from the shoe I'd found in the closet that Portia and I wore the same size. I could only hope she kept her workout shoes in her home gym.

Like in the rest of the house, expensive things filled the glossy space. In this case, exercise equipment. I didn't waste any time appreciating the collection of cardio and weight machines. I beelined for the small rack on the floor that held neatly stored pairs of athletic shoes.

"Thank you," I breathed in relief for the first break in what felt like ages. I kicked off my sister's heels and stepped into a pair of squishy pink sneakers that felt like little clouds in comparison.

"What are you doing?" Anthony said from the doorway when he caught me lacing them up.

"Getting ready to run." I stood and smoothed my skirt, debating if I had time to find Portia's closet and borrow a change of clothes as well. Judging by the look on Anthony's face, I suspected the answer was no.

"Come on," he said, and tilted his head.

I abandoned the tablet, seeing that we were a few feet from freedom. We reentered the hallway, him with gun in hand, and me with Libby's shoes in hand—which could have served as a close-contact weapon if needed, given the spiked heels. Thankfully, we made it to the end of the second hall without needing either. We stopped in front of a set of French doors, which led onto the pool deck. The Slates' swimming pool glowed a deep emerald and turned the light wobbling through the glass an otherworldly green.

Anthony paused again and gave me another serious look. "Opening this door is probably going to trip an alarm. If they've got the inside of the house rigged, we can only assume the exits are monitored too. So, when I say go, you run, okay? I'll be right behind you."

I nodded as nerves gripped my body like fists. "Where am I running?"

"Across the yard. Cross the pool deck and head for the lawn. Then go straight."

It sounded simple enough. "Okay."

"Ready?"

"Yes." It was a flat lie. I was trembling.

He nodded once and turned the door handle. Where I expected a blaring bullhorn, the alarm was merely a soft beeping. A set of staccato bursts, like a repetitive, robotic songbird. I imagined all the tablets lighting up in a much more aggressive warning. The urgency of Anthony's hand in my back and the sound of his voice told me the threat was indeed real.

"Go!"

I threw myself through the door and into the warm night. My skin tingled at fresh air after so many hours underground. I inhaled deeply, drinking it in and replenishing my lungs. My ankles throbbed with each step. I felt the cuts from the zip ties on my legs and wrists stinging. But I ran. I ran as fast as I could across the pool deck, around the glistening green puddle sunken into the center of it, and onto the lawn.

It stretched for what seemed like miles, but was probably a good fifty yards. Still, who needed a yard this big? What were the Slates doing in their backyard, playing polo? Halfway across the lush stretch, floodlights flashed on behind us. I knew Anthony was a few paces behind, both by the sound of his strenuous breathing and the long shadow suddenly thrown out like a black ribbon beside me.

Clearly, he'd been right. We'd set off an alert.

I turned to look over my shoulder and nearly tripped at the sight of the estate lit up in all its glory. *Massive* was an understatement. It was a hotel. A cruise ship. A compound with more space than any two people could ever possibly need. In the second before I turned back, I swore I saw the outline of a helicopter perched like a bird of prey atop the east wing.

"Keep going!" Anthony shouted behind me. There was no longer a point in keeping quiet.

I kept running as we quickly closed in on a stone wall. The smooth expanse that stood at least eight feet tall unfurled in each direction, with no gaps or gates I could see.

"Anthony!" I screamed, and pointed at it as if we were about to drive off a cliff.

"I know! Keep going!"

"Going where?!"

"Over that wall! My car is on the other side!"

I slowed to a stop with my arms in front of me so I didn't crash into it and dropped Libby's shoes, which I was still holding. My momentum pushed me up against the cool, smooth stone anyway. Its earthy scent pressed into my nose as I felt its grittiness beneath my fingertips. I could sense Anthony rushing up behind me. The heavy thuds of his steps closed in fast, and I had a vision of him scaling the wall like a cat on the way in.

"Okay, but you have to understand when you say *over that wall,* that doesn't just happen for me, like it does for you. I'm not—" I cut off with a squeal as I felt his hands grip my rib cage on either side.

"Jump!"

I jumped and flailed my arms above me, desperately reaching into the night sky like I might grab onto a star. He'd thrown me a solid foot into the air, but it wasn't high enough. My palms slapped at the wall, my left arm screaming in protest from the chair injury. Gravity eagerly pulled me back down, until I felt a second thrust. This time, his hands were beneath my feet, like he was the base in a cheerleading squad, and I was the flyer ready to touch my toes midair.

He let out a groan of pure agony, like his body was splitting in two—which it may have been, given the broken ribs—as he used all his strength to hoist me up on top of the wall.

I flung myself at it, ass in the air, throwing my arms over it like a barrel, and landing on my belly. It was thick and at least a foot wide.

"Don't look up my skirt!" I wailed.

"Penny, just go!" he commanded. His voice shrank away as I realized he was backing up for a running start to launch himself over the wall as well.

In the time it took him to run three steps, plant a foot, and pull himself up like a cat, with maybe eight lives now, but still a cat, I'd managed to fling one leg over the wall. I lay parallel atop it, holding on for dear life. Anthony pulled himself to sit, then agilely spun around to face the other way.

I simply gaped at him. "Didn't that hurt?"

"Very much," he said on a tight breath. He clutched his ribs and pushed off the wall to fall eight feet and land like a cat, with seven lives, on the other side. "Kick your leg over and come down. I'll catch you."

I moved with the grace of a beached whale, gingerly bringing my other leg up, and turning on my belly so my legs hung over the other side. I gripped the top and slowly slid my feet down against the stone. "That's really not necessary. It's not that far, and you're hurt. I'll lower myself far enough to—"

The sound of a gunshot split the air in two. I flinched so hard, I let go of the wall and fell. Luckily, he was right there to catch me.

"They're shooting at us now?!" I screeched.

He recovered from the force of my body hitting his—despite the circumstances, a warm and stirring sensation—and reached for my hand. "It appears so, yes. Time to go." He pivoted and ran two steps, dragging me behind him, and then stopped.

"What?" I asked, breathless and trembling in anticipation of the next gunshot.

"My car's gone."

"Gone?" I said, too shocked to register what it meant not to see the old green Cadillac in front of us.

"Yeah. It was right here." He let go of my hand and swiped his hair. In spite of our dangerous situation, the familiar move brought me an odd sense of comfort.

I took a moment to look around and realized we stood at the edge of a heavily wooded area. The gravel beneath our feet must have been a back entrance driveway to the Slates' estate. Aside from the house glowing in the distance, and the stars and moon overhead, it was dark. I saw the wet shine of Anthony's eyes and the glint of his teeth when he winced and palmed his ribs again.

"So, what do we do?"

The question was hardly out of my mouth before another gunshot rang out, this one much closer. I flinched and covered my ears, but it had been too close and too loud. The ringing nearly muted Anthony's voice when he reached for my hand and shouted: "Run!"

I thanked every star in the sky that I'd put on Portia's shoes as we disappeared into the woods.

CHAPTER 9

I'd never been a runner. My preferred form of physical activity was yoga and the only marathons I participated in were of the Netflix variety. But running for my life lit a different kind of fire than a perfunctory resolution to get more exercise ever could.

Anthony led the way as we crashed through the woods. The lack of a clear path made for branches and sticks and pointy little rocks ready and waiting to lash out in a reminder we were disrupting their territory. I ran with my arms out in front of me for safety, one eye on Anthony's back and one on the uneven forest floor. The fact we were both in all black—me still from the funeral, and him because he didn't own anything else—was both a blessing and a curse. Other than my pink shoes, we'd be hard to spot, but I kept losing sight of him in the dark too.

The moon cut through the thick trees in silvery streaks. Given all the branches and our speed, it set off a strobe light effect that had me blinking away dizziness.

Or maybe that was from the head injuries. Or the cumulative blood loss from all my various cuts. Or the fact we were being chased and shot at.

"Anthony!" I pled, once we were deep enough into the dark to have lost all sense of direction. "Can we stop for a minute?"

My breath sawed in and out of my lungs. I doubled over with a cramp. "I don't hear anything anymore. I don't think they're chasing us."

I heard him slow to a stop ahead of me. He wasn't nearly as winded, but the breaths he was taking were jagged and shallow. He paused to listen for half a minute. Only silence called back. He walked to meet me in a small pool of moonlight between two trees. He leaned an arm against one and put a hand on his hip.

Sweat dampened my brow. It took me three gulps of air to be able to speak. "You're still bleeding." I raised a shaky hand to point at the gash on his forehead.

He touched his fingertips to it and pulled away blood. "Shit." He used the hem of his shirt to swipe at it again, flashing his bare abdomen and half of his chest. I gasped at the purple-and-black stain already spanning his ribs like an abstract oil painting. "That bad, huh?" he said with a small huff, which made him wince.

"We need to get you to a hospital."

He shook his head. "No. We need to get out of here."

I approached him with my hands raised in a sign I planned to touch him. "Yes, out of here and to a hospital."

"Penny, we can't. Ouch!" he responded, hissing, when I pressed my thumbs to his forehead.

"Sorry. At least let me help you, then. You're bleeding all over the place."

He waved a dismissive hand. "Head wounds bleed a lot. I'm fine."

I glanced around, almost as if I'd find an opportune first aid kit stashed in the middle of the woods; then I realized I'd obviously have to improvise. "Sure, and it's a good thing blood doesn't make me woozy, because you look like Carrie on prom night." I bent over and reached for the hem of my skirt, suddenly finding inspiration.

"What are you doing?" he asked over the sound of a loud rip.

"Improvising." Thankfully, my dress was a cotton polyester blend, which meant tearing the fabric was pretty simple. I tore up two inches and then followed a path all the way around the skirt, ripping off a makeshift bandage as I went. When I finished, it was markedly shorter and looked more suited for a rock concert than a funeral.

"Come here," I told Anthony, and beckoned him to lean down.

He cooperated, wincing at the motion, and let me fashion him a bandage. Given the size of my skirt and the size of his head, I wrapped it three times, making sure to cover the wound before I knotted it. Then I took what remained of my skirt, which was much cleaner than his shirt, and wiped the blood off his face in gentle strokes.

"Better," I said. "Although now you look like Rambo."

"Between a telekinetic murderous prom queen and an action hero, I'll take the latter."

"I have faith you could pull off the former with the right dress."

Our banter served as temporary distraction from the serious matter at hand. Namely, that I had just stabbed someone so we could escape. I could still feel the knife going in, and I wasn't sure I'd ever be able to *un*feel it. I truly hoped I'd only incapacitated him and had not done worse.

"So, now what?" I asked after several moments of silence. After what had happened, I knew we wouldn't be going home.

He shifted against the tree, clearly in severe pain. He must have been running on adrenaline back at the house, and it was now catching up to him. "We need to get to Daly City."

"What's in Daly City?"

"A backup plan."

I frowned at yet another cryptic answer. "Why don't we go to the police?"

He shook his head. "No. Involving the police would be a mistake. They are not my biggest fans right now."

I tugged at a thread dangling from the bottom of my skirt. "Well, then, can *I* go to the police? I mean, I *was* kidnapped."

Even in the dark, I could see the guilt on his face for putting me in that position. "No. You are safer with me until we figure this out. I'm not letting you out of my sight."

The ferocity in his voice stopped me from arguing. I chewed my lip in thought. The last several hours had changed everything. "My sister is probably worried sick."

"She called your mom for support. She'll be fine."

"She—what? She called our mom? How do you know that?"

"She told me. When you disappeared from the reception, she came and threatened to kill me with a bamboo shrimp skewer, and then said she was calling the police and your mom. I talked her out of the first, but not the second."

"Oh, *God.* If she called our mom, she is not okay." Guilt washed over me with enough force that I weighed the risk of fleeing on foot back to her house.

Anthony must have seen the struggle in my eyes.

He sighed a weary breath, which made him sound a hundred years old. "Penny, I'm sorry for all this, but we can't go home. My uncle is dead because of me. Portia is trapped because of me. You're in danger because of me. I'm not putting anyone else even more at risk." The sincere sorrow in his voice sang out into the night like a requiem. I ached for him, this bruised and broken man held together with grit and a torn funeral skirt. The pain in my chest pulled me toward him.

"Did they really kill your uncle?" My voice was soft. Gentle.

He met my eyes, and even in the dark, I could see the ocean of pain in his. He nodded. "Yeah. Shot him in a parking garage and left him there."

There was obviously much more to the story, but in that moment, my only thought was to take away even an ounce of his pain. I placed my hand on his arm, as if I could absorb it through his skin. "I'm sorry."

He shook his head with a haunted look in his eyes. "At least I got them to keep it out of the news, but it's my fault. I put this whole thing in motion. It was my idea, and now everything is a disaster. Well, I guess not *everything*." He looked up at me with a shy flutter of his lashes and then quickly back down at the ground.

A deep flush curled into my face with the heat of a bonfire. I was glad it was too dark for him to see it. I thought back to what the tweed man had said about him running to my rescue. My hand was still on his arm. I moved it, for fear he'd feel the sudden nerves coursing through it.

"How did you know where to find me?"

"I knew they'd take you somewhere isolated and secure. The Slates' house is basically a prison compound, as you saw." He huffed a dark laugh, which sounded cryptic and layers deep.

"And if you knew they would take me here, why didn't you expect it to be a trap?"

He closed his eyes and quietly hummed another laugh, this one warmer and light. "Humbling me again, Dr. Collins." He opened his eyes and gave me a tiny half smile. "I told you, I'm the suit side of things. I'm not exactly a field expert here."

My lips twitched with a mirroring smile. "Is that why you shoved the bodyguard in your closet right before you had an estate sale?"

He grimaced in embarrassment and laughed at the same time. "They dumped him on the back porch *literally ten minutes* before the sale started! What was I supposed to do?"

I shrugged. "Put him in the garage?"

Despite all his blood loss, he still managed to blush.

"You seriously didn't think of that?" I asked with a grin.

"I panicked!"

The sound of our laughter felt out of place in the dark pit of this night, but my heart still fluttered at it.

"So," I asked, once we had quieted, "what's your plan?"

He tilted his head up toward the sky, either in thought or pain, I couldn't be sure, but I traced the line of his jaw with my eyes. A smear of blood had run beneath his chin and dried there. "We have to get to Portia."

"And where is she?" I asked the million-dollar question once more.

He gave me a look like he was closer to sharing the truth, but still not willing. "Not Iceland."

"No, really?" I said sarcastically. "Don't tell me she's in Daly City and has been right under their noses this whole time."

He leveled me with a flat stare. "No, she's not. But we do need to get there. How far is it from here?"

"Way too far to walk."

"Really?"

"Yes. I drive this peninsula all the time. It's at least twenty-five miles."

"Shit. Why is everything so spread out here?"

"Welcome to California. What's in Daly City?"

My question hadn't dissolved on the air before a branch snapped in the distance. We both turned toward it. I stopped breathing and felt Anthony's hand protectively circle my wrist. His thumb rested directly on my pulse, which had sped up considerably.

I gazed off into the dark, straining my eyes in search of whoever was out there. As my heart pounded, I silently hoped it was a forest creature, a deer or even a mountain lion, and not a deranged human with a gun. I'd happily take my chances against either of the former.

Another snap cracked, and then a gunshot sliced the air. The bullet splintered the tree, mere feet from us, opposite the one Anthony was leaning on. Before the shattered wood even hit the ground, he was yanking on my arm and pulling us away.

In that moment, I didn't care what was in Daly City as long as going there got us the hell out of the woods.

We ran until we found a road. We followed it, turning in toward the trees and shielding ourselves whenever a car passed. We definitely wanted to avoid getting hit, but also didn't want anyone to call the cops on us—a man and a woman traipsing through one of the most affluent areas in America, looking like they either had escaped or were serial killers.

It must have taken two or three miles before we wound down out of the hills and came to flat land in a residential area. We stopped under a streetlight to catch our breath. The street was wide and empty; all the luxury vehicles were in their driveways or tucked into garages for the night, with the exception of a little blue Honda Civic parked on the curb outside of a towering Colonial, with a rose border.

"We need a cab," Anthony murmured.

"There are no cabs; this is Woodside," I said as I kept my eyes on the blue Honda. It was clearly out of place, and I wondered if it might be an opportunity. A plan started to take root in my head.

He huffed in annoyance. "Train?"

"Not this far south."

"What is with the serious dearth of public transportation around here?"

"Again, welcome to California. You don't have your phone, right?"

"Of course not. He took it back at the house."

"Figured. Just checking. What about your wallet?"

He patted his pockets, as if it had only now occurred to him to check. "Yes."

"How much money do you have?" My eyes were still on the house and the Honda.

He opened his wallet and thumbed through the bills. "A few hundred bucks."

The house's front door swung open, and I couldn't believe our luck when a pretty blond girl stepped out. She wore jeans and a Stanford hoodie, with a tote slung over her shoulder. She had *nanny* practically emblazoned on her forehead.

"Perfect. Give it to me," I said, and held out my hand.

"Give what to you, the money? Why?"

Clearly, he hadn't been paying attention. I pointed at the girl approaching her car. She didn't think to look across the street for any suspicious characters, because she was in a very safe area.

"Because I'm getting us a ride," I said. "See her? She's nineteen, twenty, tops. If she goes to Stanford and is working a side hustle over the summer, she's a financial-aid student. She'll be interested in a bribe."

"How could you possibly know that?" he asked with a heavy dose of skepticism, but notably didn't put his wallet away.

"Because my life is college kids, Anthony. Kids who go to Stanford and drive old Hondas and work part-time jobs are not the spawn of millionaires. This girl will happily take a few hundred bucks to drive us up the peninsula if it means she can skip a week with whatever hell brats live inside that house she just came out of."

He silently blinked at me like he didn't understand or believe the words coming out of my mouth.

I tsked and snatched the money out of his wallet. "Watch, I'll show you." I stepped out into the street with my arms raised, money clutched in one hand, and slowly approached her. "Excuse me? Miss?"

She turned, and the second she saw us, she pressed her back

to her car door and instantly brandished her keys between her fingers in a jagged claw.

"Whoa! It's okay. We're not going to hurt you," I said, and cursed the world that required women to be so afraid in public. I well knew the fit of my own keys between my fingers. "We need help." I waved the money at her and aimed for a smile that would land closer to *desperate victim* than *stranger on the street trying to trick you.*

She cautiously eyed me, taking in my ripped dress, bloody ankles and wrists, and the swollen bruise at my temple. Her eyes flashed to Anthony, still some distance behind me, and her gaze hardened. Her jaw clenched and she jutted out her chin toward him. "Did he do that to you?"

I glanced back at him to see he'd taken a few steps closer and wondered if lying would at least get *me* a ride. But that wouldn't solve anything, given the fact there were people still chasing us, and I did honestly feel safer by his side.

"No, not at all," I answered with a shake of my head. "We've had a rough night."

She continued to eye him, unsure. But she hadn't run away or pulled out her phone or screamed for help, so I figured I'd keep going.

"See, I actually got kidnapped earlier today, and he rescued me. Kind of."

"Kind of?" Anthony blurted from behind me. The sound of his voice came closer, and he appeared at my side.

"Okay. It was a team effort. But I did most of the heavy lifting."

"I threw you over a wall with broken ribs!" he sputtered.

"Anthony, please!" I held up my hand to quiet him.

The girl's eyes bounced back and forth between us. We had her interest, but I couldn't tell if she was swaying. She leaned back when she took in the full size of Anthony, now that he'd come closer. In that moment, I was thankful for the dim light and his black shirt disguising the fact he was soaked in blood. From the corner of my eye, I clocked the bulge of his gun still tucked into his waistband, and I thought for a second we could approach this situation very differently. But then I decided this poor girl would already be traumatized enough from bloody Bonnie and Clyde asking for a ride; she certainly didn't need us stealing her car at gunpoint too.

"How much money?" she asked, and my heart soared.

I looked at the wad of cash in my hand and wondered why Anthony carried so much with him—all my money was plastic—and then I remembered the estate sale. I almost laughed when I realized I was probably holding the candlestick money.

"Two hundred dollars," I said.

She nodded and pulled out her phone. The little screen lit up her face in a blue glow. "Look, I'm not going to give you a ride. I'm smarter than that. But I will call Dave for you."

A swell of pride hit me at the recognition this girl had been raised to be so aware, but at the same time, I hated the reasons she needed to be. But my criticism of society's shortcomings was for another time.

"Dave?" I asked.

She nodded and continued to tap her phone. "Yeah. Designated Dave. He was in my stats class. He'll drive anyone anywhere. He's cheaper than Uber and stops for food at no extra charge. He usually only takes payment through his app, but he'll probably make an exception for the price." She held her phone to her ear as an outbound call started to ring.

I smiled in hope, not at all surprised we'd stumbled upon an entrepreneur so suited to our needs, given the locale.

"This kid has his own app?" Anthony muttered.

"Of course he does. Did you forget where you are? Half the kids at Stanford only go there so they can drop out, found the next unicorn company from their garage, and become a billionaire before they're twenty-five."

"Huh," he said right as Dave answered.

"Hey, Dave. It's Sadie," the girl said. "I ran into some people who need a ride. They seem like they might be a little un-
hinged, and maybe running from the cops or something, but
they've got two hundred dollars in cash." She listened while
Dave spoke. I strained to hear what he was saying, but even in
the quiet night, the volume was too low. "I'll ask," she said,
and then looked over at us. "He wants to know where you're
going."

"Daly City," Anthony said. "East Side Self-Storage."

I turned to him in surprise. *A storage facility?* What kind of
backup plan was in a storage facility?

Sadie repeated the information to Dave and listened again.
"Yeah, I'm leaving work. They're here on the corner. I don't
know, they appeared out of nowhere. This man and woman.
He's tall and has a weird headband, and she's wearing pink
running shoes. Otherwise, they look like they escaped a funeral."

I glanced down at our appearance and ironically smiled that
she had no idea how correct she was.

She listened again, and I hoped she was friendly enough
with Dave to convince him of this favor if the two hundred
bucks alone didn't do the job. I imagined she was, considering
he knew where she worked without her needing to tell him an
address. Maybe they were in a financial-aid-kids side-hustle
club. "Okay," she said, and lowered her phone. "He said he'll
do it. He's finishing a run nearby, but he'll be here in five minutes."

I squeezed my fists in victory and heard Anthony let out a
breath of relief. "Thank you!"

"Yep. Please don't murder him. Dave is a cool guy." And
with that, she slipped inside her car, slammed the door, and
sped off.

Anthony and I were left alone again. This time, not completely in the dark, but still dark enough to blend in with our clothing. Which was good, because we didn't need the neighborhood watch sounding the alarm on us.

"What time do you think it is?" I asked while I stared up at the sky. We were far enough from any big city to see the stars. They twinkled in the warm night, immune to the trivialities of human existence below them.

"Probably nine or ten."

"Hmm," I hummed inconsequentially and mostly out of exhaustion. The funeral felt like a thousand years ago, when it had only been hours. "How are you feeling?"

"I've been better."

"You know, there's probably an urgent care within walking distance. Actually, Stanford is one of the best hospitals on the West Coast, we could—"

"Penny, no."

I knew he'd refuse, even before I made the suggestion. "But you're hurt."

He turned to me with a gravely serious look in his eyes. The streetlight highlighted a blotch of dried blood on his neck. "I know, but the people who are on our tail are never going to stop. So, if *we* stop, that will only slow us down and let them catch up. We have to keep moving. At least until we are somewhere safer."

A frightened lump pushed its way up into my throat at his tone. I forced it down with a swallow. The fact he didn't even consider Woodside safe told me enough about trusting his judgment. I took a breath and braved a question I'd been fearing all day. "What about my sister and her kids? If they've been following me, they know they are your neighbors."

Sincerity painted his dark eyes, and he gave me an assuring nod. "They'll be fine. I called a friend to keep an eye on them."

"A cop?"

"No."

I paused and considered my words. "A *not* bad guy?"

He looked over at me with the same silent acknowledgment—he was saying yes without saying yes—that he'd given me when I surmised his uncle was a fixer.

"So, is there like a network of you all, or something?"

His mouth twitched at the corner like he was considering smiling. "Something like that."

"Interesting. Well, when we get wherever we are going, can I call Libby to at least tell her I'm alive?"

The way he eyed me, with an uncertain combination of guilt and worry, replaced the nervous lump in my throat, like it had never gone away. "Sure."

"Thank you." My voice shook only slightly. I looked back up at the sky. "So, what's at this storage facility?"

"You'll see when we get there."

The smooth, calm sound of his voice, like the concern was minimal, broke something loose inside me.

"You know what? No. I want you to tell me right now. After the day I've had—the past few days since you came along, actually—I think I deserve some answers." My voice snapped louder than I meant.

He flinched at the sound and dragged me a few paces away from the streetlight. "Keep it down!"

"Okay! I will, sorry. But you owe me information." I realized the words were the same ones I'd said the night I'd taken him the key. He'd been frustratingly vague then, and I wasn't going to allow him to be now. Not anymore.

I could tell by the look on his face he was reliving the same memory and realizing how unfairly elusive he'd been this whole time. "You're right. Five questions," he said.

I snorted. "How about as many questions as I want?"

"Is that one of the questions?"

I glared at him and punched my hands into my hips. "Okay, first question. Where's Portia?"

He folded his arms with a frown and a wince. "You know I'm not going to answer that one."

"Why not?"

He leaned in, and his voice became a gravelly growl. "Because if they somehow catch you and you have that information, I don't know what they will do to get it out of you, and I can't risk that. So it's better if you don't know." A vein pulsed in the side of his neck. His eyes burned like black coals.

"Oh," I whispered, thoroughly intimidated and oddly turned on by the intensity in his voice. I cleared my throat to regain my bearings and tried another approach. "Okay, here's a better question, then. How do *you* know Portia?"

He cocked a brow at me.

"You said she wanted to disappear, and this was all your idea. The look on your face when I first asked about her that day you came over was nothing short of desperate panic. And you let the tweed man hit you like a punching bag, instead of telling him where she is. Also, you clearly know your way around her house. So that makes me think this all started as more than a 1-800-find-a-fixer situation. I think you *know* her. From before all this." I waited for his response, hands still on my hips. I even tapped my foot.

When he decided to tell me the truth, I saw it in his whole body. His posture changed from the rigid, firm wall I'd grown accustomed to and turned soft at the edges. His shoulders loosened; his jaw relaxed. He exhaled in a way that sounded like one would exhale at a homecoming. The pure relief of comfort and family after being away.

"We grew up together. In Queens. Her brother was my best friend."

As unsubtle as his shift in demeanor had been, my dawn of realization could have lit up the entire night sky in a blaze of light. The keystone of the whole puzzle fell into place. The motivation behind it all.

He cared about her.

"So you *really* know her."

"Yeah."

As I let the revelation settle, a detail I'd read when I was mining the Web for information on Portia came back to me. "Portia's brother died when she was thirteen."

"I know," Anthony said solemnly. "We were in high school. They didn't have the best home life—none of us did—and I promised Jake I'd always look out for her. After he died, I kind of took over in his place." He stepped toward me with a plea in his eyes, as if he wanted me to absolve him of some sin. "I tried to talk her out of marrying Connor, but she didn't listen to me. He's a monster, Penny. I knew it from the very start, but Portia only saw a way out from a life she hated. It was a huge mistake. I could see it on her face every time she visited—*literally.* She tries to hide it all with her online image, but she's miserable and not safe."

His words were coming faster and faster, as if he'd been holding his breath and waiting to tell someone this story for ages and had to get it all out before he ran out of air again. "A few weeks ago, she visited me in New York, and . . . something bad happened. Something worse than anything before. I had to help her. So we made a plan."

I was floundering for what to say. He'd just confessed that the billionaire's missing wife was essentially his little sister and they'd made a plan to make her disappear on purpose. And now we were fleeing from said billionaire and his henchmen in an effort to get to Portia and, I assumed, finish the job.

Anthony desperately searched my face, as if I held the answer to an unspoken question. Or perhaps the solution to all our problems.

"I—" I started, but didn't know where to go. I felt like I needed a diagram to keep straight all the information I'd learned in the past few hours. "What was the plan?" I managed to ask.

He gave me a hard look. "I'll tell you the whole story when we're someplace safer."

I opened my mouth to protest right as a silver minivan turned the corner blaring pop-punk out the windows at far too loud a volume for this neighborhood and time of night. The driver, a twentysomething kid, with buzzed hair minus his topknot, leaned out the window.

"Yo! Tall dude with headband and girl in pink shoes, your chariot has arrived!" He thumped his palm against the outside of the door twice as if to say *saddle up!*

"This is Dave?" Anthony muttered.

"What were you expecting, a tinted limo?"

Dave whistled along to the song pumping from his speakers and drummed his fingers on the door.

I gave him a friendly wave as I approached.

He tipped an invisible hat, still whistling, and pushed a button to automatically slide open the side door.

The smell of artificial fruit came billowing out of the van in a cloud thick enough to make me cough.

"Hi, Dave," I said as my eyes watered. I climbed in and moved to the far middle seat to allow Anthony to climb in behind me. "Thanks for the ride, I'm P—"

"Pamela," Anthony cut me off.

I turned and glared at him as I sank into my seat. He shook his head with a scolding frown and mouthed, *No names,* like it should have been obvious.

I realized with a flare in my cheeks it should have been. "Right," I said. "I'm Pam. And this is Tommy."

Anthony rolled his eyes and buckled his seat belt.

"Right on. Pam and Tommy," Dave said, bless his oblivious little Gen Z heart. "Nice to meet you. Where are we headed?"

Anthony gave him the name of the storage facility, and he punched it into the phone mounted on his dash.

I noticed then the cluster of fruit-shaped air fresheners dangling from the rearview mirror like a bunch of rainbow-colored grapes. Every air vent had a clip-on freshener too, giving the van the fruity, cotton-candy odor reminiscent of a middle-school locker room.

I coughed again.

"Don't mind the smell," Dave said, and flipped a U-turn. "All part of the experience when you ride with Designated D. People puke in here a lot. Gotta keep it fresh."

I instantly yanked my hands off the seat's armrest and pointed my feet up on my toes as if he'd said there was a mouse on the floor. Out of the corner of my eye, I saw Anthony frown and noticed not only were our seats fashioned with rubbery upholstery, but the floor was rubber too.

"That's the difference between me and other rideshares," Dave said. "I don't charge you for puking in my car. I know what I'm signing up for when I accept the job. Plus, my uncle owns a power wash in Menlo Park. I take old Starla there and hose her out whenever I need to." He lovingly patted the dashboard above the wheel. Then he whipped around in his seat and pulled a business card out of his shirt pocket. "You guys don't look like my normal clientele, but I'm expanding my fleet next semester. I'm trying to take on a few new drivers. Hit us up if you need another ride sometime."

I took the card from between his fingers, fully convinced we'd just met the friendliest person on the planet. "Thanks, Dave." The card was clean and simple. DESIGNATED DAVE, with a QR code I was sure linked to his app. If I'd had my phone, I would have scanned it and assessed his work. But if I'd had my phone, we wouldn't have been in the backseat of a college puke trolly, to begin with.

"No problem, Pam. Hey, are you guys hungry?" he asked as we cruised past a Taco Bell near the freeway on-ramp. "I'm happy to stop."

"Yes, please," I said; right as Anthony said, "No, thanks."

I shot him a glare and mouthed, *I'm starving.*

He glared back and mouthed, *Later.*

"Sooo no?" Dave said, slowing with his turn signal on.

"No," Anthony confirmed.

"Right on, boss."

I folded my arms like a petulant child and pouted. Until he'd offered, I hadn't realized how hungry I was. The last thing I'd eaten was a mini quiche at the funeral reception. No wonder I was so lightheaded and cranky.

Dave chattered like a happy little squirrel nearly the whole drive. Anthony stayed mute, brooding like a vampire in the shadow, while I did my best to engage without disclosing any personal information that would earn me another glare from my accomplice. Luckily, the drive was relatively short, so late on a weeknight. We flew up 280 without interruption, and soon Dave was slowing outside East Side Self-Storage in Daly City.

"Here's fine," Anthony said at the gate. He presented the wad of cash to Dave from over his seat.

"Ah, right on, man," Dave said, sounding like he'd forgotten he was getting paid for our trip, and maybe was simply doing a friendly favor. "You guys have a nice night."

"Thanks, Dave. You too!" I sang as I climbed out the door and heaved a breath of non-fruit-scented air. A headache poked at my temples from the ride.

The crisp night hung gritty with fog farther north. The stars were gone now, lost to the hazy dome of light pollution and marine layer. I shivered at the slight chill in the air. Daly City sat directly south of San Francisco on the narrowest part of the peninsula. I couldn't recall a time I'd intentionally made a trip to the city; I only ever passed through.

"That kid lives on another planet," Anthony muttered once Dave drove away.

"The smart ones usually do. I'm excited to check out his app."
I flicked his card with a smile. "Will you hold this for me?"

He took it with a frown. "Your dress doesn't have any
pockets?"

I laughed. "Your naivety is adorable. Now, what are we
doing here?"

He pocketed the business card and headed for the slatted
black gate guarding the entrance. It was a set of gates, I realized: one big enough to drive through and one to walk through
flanking its side. Anthony pushed a button inside a metal box
mounted on a skinny pole, and the smaller gate opened with a
buzz. "Getting supplies. Come on."

"What kind of supplies?" I asked and followed him
through.

"The necessary kind."

"You know, if you're more forthcoming to start, I won't
have to ask so many questions."

"And if you trust me and do what I say, all the answers will
become clear."

I kept quiet and followed him along the ends of several
aisles of storage units. Overhead lights buzzed, casting yellow
pools on the concrete. The night was quiet, save the distant
rush of the highway and our footsteps. I got the sense we were
the only ones at the facility.

We eventually turned down one of the aisles and passed several orange garage doors pulled taut in their stucco walls. Each
had a padlock, combination lock, or large chain securing it shut.
I could only imagine what was behind each—and most important, what was behind the one Anthony stopped in front of.

With a sharp breath and a grunt, he sank to a knee and lifted
the dial lock.

"You know the combination to that, right?"

"Thankfully, yes. The combo to this was inside the safe at
the house."

"Ah," I said, nodding. "A safe inside a safe. So that would make whatever is in here pretty important, then."

"Yes," he said as he finished the combo and yanked the lock free. He grabbed the handle at the door's base and shoved it up. Then he stood with another grunt and wiped the grit off his hands. "Like I told you, it's the backup plan."

We stood back as the door rolled all the way open.

I blinked at what I saw inside, not exactly surprised, but not sure how it was supposed to help us.

CHAPTER 10

"A car?" I said once we'd stepped inside the unit, and Anthony had pulled the door shut behind us. He found a switch on the wall that powered on a buzzing fluorescent light dangling from the ceiling.

I looked around as if there might be something else in the unit—a bed, some snacks—things that seemed infinitely more helpful than a car in the moment—but saw nothing other than the hunk of metal on wheels shrouded under a giant gray sheet.

Anthony pulled off the sheet with a flourish, sending dust tickling my nose and exposing a glossy black muscle car straight out of a 1970s action movie.

"That's discreet," I said.

He walked its perimeter, gathering the sheet in his hands and checking the tires. "What can I say, Uncle Lou had style."

I slid my fingers along the shiny hood and felt the power underneath even while it sat at rest. The hulky, two-door, black-on-black bullet, with silver accents and a low profile, had *Camaro* curled in metallic script outside the fender. "While I can agree with you on that point, I'm wondering how an old sports car is supposed to help us. When was the last time this thing was driven? Will it even start?"

Anthony fished the key out of one of its tailpipes and unlocked the driver's door. "Yes, it will start. And it's not just an old sports car." He rounded to the trunk and unlocked it. "Come here."

I walked to the back, thinking I'd only be happy if there was a foot-long sandwich in there, but quickly realized my needs went beyond hunger at the sight of what it held.

"Whoa."

"Backup plan," Anthony said with a proud smile.

Two suitcases, a duffel bag, and—the thing we both reached for first—a case of bottled water.

Anthony ripped open the plastic and handed me one. I was halfway done with it, shocked by my own ravenous thirst, by the time he tore the lid from his bottle and drank with the same zeal.

"What's in the suitcases?" I asked, and wiped a dribble from my chin. The water was so refreshing, I wanted to backstroke in it.

He finished his bottle before tossing it aside and reaching for the nearest suitcase. The red hard-shell case came from the same era as the car. He squeezed two silver tabs with his thumbs, and it opened with a pop.

"No way," I said with a gasp. "That's a pretty solid backup plan."

Stacks of neatly bound cash lined the case in rows of green. Anthony grabbed one and flipped through it, as if to make sure it was real. "Uncle Lou was always prepared." He plucked a small stack from the bundle and replaced it in his wallet.

"This is why you let me take all your money for Dave earlier, isn't it?" I said. "You knew there was more here."

"Yes. The rest is for later," he said, and snapped the case shut. "What we really want is in here." He reached for the other suitcase, the larger green hard-shell, and popped the clasps.

Billows of brightly colored clothes burst free, as if they'd been waiting spring-loaded for decades: silky shirts in loud floral patterns, color-blocked button-downs, khakis, hats, a pair of vintage aviators. It was a Halloween costume goldmine.

I reached for the aviators and put them on. "What happened to Uncle Lou's style? I thought he was more of a somber-suit kind of guy."

Anthony was digging around in the pouch that lined the top flap of the suitcase. "If he ever needed this backup plan, it would have been to change his appearance. That's why all this stuff is so—"

"Colorful?" I asked, and held up a truly hideous mustard-yellow button-down with a flared collar.

"Yes."

I pawed through more of the clothing, wondering if there was anything in my size so I could change out of my torn dress. "And he never thought to, I don't know, *modernize* over the years?"

Anthony pulled a zipped pouch from the suitcase's pocket and set it on the trunk. Then an old flip phone that miraculously turned on when he powered it up. "Here's something modern for you."

"Burner phone?" I asked and could hardly believe I'd spoken the words out loud.

"Yep."

"Can I use it to call my sister?"

He frowned at the phone as he pressed the clicky plastic buttons, maybe entering a passcode. "Not yet, but soon." He set the phone down and reached back into the suitcase's pouch. This time, he pulled out a small first aid kit in an old, dented tin.

"Hey, that's handy," I said, and reached for the kit. I quickly found the Band-Aids inside were crinkled and had lost their adhesion. "Or not. Also old."

Anthony was still digging in the bottomless suitcase with one hand. "The fact nearly everything in here is old goes to show he never needed his backup plan. This car used to be stored in New York, but he brought it out here with him basically untouched. Yes!" he victoriously hissed, and pulled a rattling pill bottle out of the suitcase. "Bless you, Uncle Lou." He uncapped it and dumped two white pills into his hand.

"Painkillers?"

"Mmm-hmm." He popped them in his mouth and opened another water bottle to wash them down. "He was prepared for all scenarios."

"How old are these?" I asked as I examined the bottle. However they'd ended up in the trunk, it was not by way of legitimate prescription.

"Either old enough to have lost their potency or double it. We'll find out. Want one?"

"I think I'll pass. What's in this one?" I asked, and reached for the duffel bag.

He snapped out his hand and grabbed my wrist. "Don't open that one."

I cautiously held my hand steady, suddenly nervous. "Why not?"

"Because it's exactly what you think, and I don't want you to freak out."

A tingle trotted up my spine. My palms began to sweat. "It's a bag of guns?"

"Among other things."

He was right. Knowing there was a gun in his waistband was enough to put me on edge. The thought of *other things* only made me want to run away.

I relaxed my arm and he let it fall from his grip. "What about this?" I asked, and reached for the zipped pouch he'd set on the trunk's floor.

"IDs."

I unzipped it and out slid a small stack of driver's licenses and a few passports. They all contained Lou's picture—at various ages—at least one thing other than the phone had been updated—but with different names: Jonathan Walker, Christopher Kirk, Nicholas Miller.

All generic names, all from different states. The passports were Canadian, French, and Italian.

"How do you even get one of these?" I asked, and held the Canadian passport up to the light, searching for a watermark that would indicate fraud. I nearly dropped it with a yelp when I saw Anthony had taken his pants off.

"What are you doing?" I said, and clumsily tried to throw a hand over my eyes. I hit myself in the face with the fake passport and only made matters more awkward. I'd been too distracted to notice him stripping down right in front of me.

"Changing out of my bloody clothes. Feel free to do the same. I'm sure there's a belt in there somewhere you can use."

He was so casual about standing there in his tight, short underwear. Black, of course. I'd caught him stepping into a pair of khakis with his muscular thighs on display and felt a hot sweat instantly break out over my skin. He'd taken off his shoes and set the gun in the trunk. His black jeans sat in a pile on the floor. I had to turn away from the adjusting of various body parts he was doing as he struggled to pull on pants with one arm. His left arm—the one nearest his broken ribs—hung nearly slack at his side.

"Sure. Yeah. That's a good idea. I'll change too," I said, and reached into the suitcase for distraction.

"I'm going to need help with my shirt," he said with a pained grunt. "I don't think I can lift my arm over my head anymore."

I turned to him with my mouth hanging open, trying and failing to keep my composure as I flushed a deep shade of crimson. Good thing he was too distracted by his broken bones to notice. "You want me to . . . help you take off your shirt?"

"Yes. You know what? Get the knife out of my pocket; we'll cut it off." He spoke like a man simply trying to be pragmatic, and not one with any clue he was making the situation progressively sexier.

"Okay," I said in a dizzy haze. I squatted to reach for the pants he'd abandoned and found the knife in the back pocket. I pulled out the blade and nearly dropped it with a gasp when I saw it was still stained with blood. The tweed man's blood from when I'd stabbed him.

"Don't look at it," Anthony instructed, realizing what had happened. "Here, let me." He closed his warm hand over mine and took it. "Hold my shirt."

I shook away my memory of sinking the knife into flesh and took a deep breath. I did as instructed and held his shirt out away from him.

He plunged the knife through the fabric and dragged it up. I followed the path, tugging at the separating sides until it hung open over his bare chest.

The hot sweat returned to my skin at the sight of his toned muscles and the dusting of dark hair trailing faintly all the way to his waistband. He was a sculpture, and I desperately wanted to touch him, but all my lecherous feelings cooled at the sight of the bruises flowering his left side.

"Oh, Anthony," I said on a breath. I couldn't help but press my palm to the injury, hoping my touch would somehow soothe it.

He sucked in a pained breath, but slowly let it out, as if I did in fact have some effect on him. "It's really not that bad. I've had worse."

"Are those expired trunk pills kicking in, or are you trying to impress me?"

"Both?" he said with a soft laugh.

I gave him a sincere smile and leaned in conspiratorially. "I was already impressed when you threw me over the wall."

This seemed to put an ounce of wind in his broken sails. His lips pulled into a soft smile. "Help me out of this, will you?"

I nodded and bit my lip to keep from smiling at the opportunity to undress him. As gently as I could, I peeled the shirt over his right shoulder and then his left. I slid my fingers into the pocket between the short sleeve and his skin to push it farther off his right arm. His shoulder muscles flexed as he tugged his arm free, putting the rounded contours right in my face. I moved around to his left side to repeat the process much more gingerly.

"You know you're, like, cut, right?" I said, unable to keep the commentary inside my head silent.

He shyly laughed. "Do you mean literally? Because yes, I am aware I have multiple open wounds at the moment."

"No. I mean, how often do you work out? Do you *own* a gym back in New York? Look at you!"

"Penny, stop it. You're embarrassing me." He was sincerely blushing, and it was adorable.

"Hey, man. You're the one who asked me to undress you. I'm simply stating objective facts here. How many abs do you have? *Eight?* Is that *eight?* I thought those things only came in six-packs, max."

Now naked from the waist up, he threw his arms over his torso. "Please don't make me laugh. It hurts too much."

I poked him in the right shoulder, as far from his injured ribs as I could go. "Not so tough now, huh? You can throw me over a wall like I'm a garden gnome, but you can't handle a laugh?"

"Seriously, please stop. You're going to kill me," he said, still laughing.

"Maybe you should pop some more expired trunk pills. That might help take the edge off."

"*Penny.* Pick out a shirt for me. Make sure it's hideous."

"Well, that's an easy order." I bent over into the trunk to shop for the ugliest thing I could find while he gathered his destroyed clothes into a pile. "Good thing you and your uncle were the same size. Well, I guess good thing you are the same size he was a few decades ago. Perfect." I landed on a purple button-down with an atrocious pink floral pattern.

"Not exactly," Anthony said when I turned around. He tugged on his khakis to show they hung too short by about three inches.

I shrugged. "High-waters are in now. Arms out."

We put on the new shirt as carefully as we'd taken off the old one. He buttoned it himself and rolled the sleeves to his elbows. Of course he managed to make it look good.

"How do I look?"

"Like Rambo went to church in the eighties."

"Excellent."

I tugged at my dress in a hint I wanted to change as well, but I wasn't about to do it in front of him. He set about reorganizing the trunk and still didn't get the hint when I cleared my throat a second time.

"Anthony? Do you mind?"

He straightened up and looked at me. "Do I mind what?"

I let out a dramatic sigh and waved my hand in a motion for him to turn around. "Could you look away while I change, please? Not all of us are centerfold-worthy and ready to strip down in front of strangers."

A soft flush curled into his cheeks, and he gave me a devilish grin. "Are we still strangers?"

"Well, no. I guess not. But I'd still rather maintain whatever dignity I have left. So, if you don't mind." I circled my hand again to shoo him away.

He folded his arms with a smug grin. "Fine, but so you know, I've already seen up your skirt three times today." He spun around and faced the wall as I gasped.

"You *were* looking!"

"I was not! The situation kept presenting itself."

"*Twice!* There was the chair and the wall. But you said three times. That means you looked on purpose! What was the third time?"

He stalled, and I could feel the guilt radiating off him. "Okay, fine. In the van. With Dave. When you climbed in before me. You'd ripped your dress to make me this headband, which was very kind and helpful of you, so your skirt was shorter. And then you bent over, and it was just *there,* right in front of me. The situation wasn't as desperate as the others had been, so I *could* have looked away, but at the same time, I couldn't. I mean, have you *seen* yourself from behind? And I—"

I tapped him on the shoulder to stop his babbling.

He turned around to find me changed into the repulsive yellow button-down and a pair of linen pants I'd tugged up to my boobs and rolled three times at the ankles. I'd latched a belt around the middle of it all to hold it in place.

"How do I look?"

He eyed me up and down with his mouth still open from his apology tour about my skirt. When he snapped it shut, I expected something charming and smooth, but instead he said, "Like a banana."

"A *banana*?" I cried. "I liken you to one of the greatest action heroes in cinematic history, and you call me a *banana?*"

"A sexy banana?"

I held up my hands in protest. "No. Too late. Get in the car. I assume whatever comes next involves driving this beastly closet on wheels out of here, so let's go."

He grabbed another water bottle and shut the trunk as I headed for the passenger door. "A *very* sexy banana?" he tried again.

I cast him a glare, with my middle finger in the air, while I secretly swooned he'd called me sexy. Twice.

We might have made less of a disturbance if we'd shot off all the guns in the trunk at the same time than when Anthony started the engine and pulled out of the unit. The car roared like a beast with a fire burning in its belly. It was deafening inside the unit, slightly less earsplitting as we rolled down the aisle to the gate, and almost a normal level of obnoxious when we finally pulled onto a street.

I demanded we stop for food before we got on the road, and he even let me run in to pee as he sat in the drive-through of an In-N-Out. For once, I welcomed the chaos inside of the always-busy burger joint. I pulled my hair forward to hide my bruises, but no one even looked up from their fries and milkshakes.

Once we had our food, I devoured the best cheeseburger of my life—Anthony ate two—and sucked down a giant soda. I could feel the caffeine feebly trying to kick-start my nervous system, but I was basically a dead battery. The only juice that was going to bring me back to life was sleep.

I'd nabbed a lumpy sweater from the trunk and folded it into a pillow as Anthony drove east. We'd crossed the Bay Bridge and headed northeast toward the valley cities between the Bay and Sacramento. We were in a gap between two of them now. The highway stretched deep into the night ahead of us. I knew from traveling this route many times that sweeping fields filled the space on either side of us as we cut across California's agricultural spine.

"How do you know where we're going?" I asked. Without a

smartphone, we had no GPS, and the car certainly didn't have a navigation system. All it had was a radio with giant knobs and an orange dial to indicate what station we'd landed on.

"I memorized a map," Anthony said. He drove with one hand on the wheel, his left resting on his thigh. He'd left his window cracked as we'd driven through the Bay, perhaps to keep himself awake with the cool air, but now had closed it. His hair was still brushed back from his face like the wind had run its fingers through it.

"Always prepared," I said after an eye-watering yawn. "How long are we driving?"

"Until we get there."

I rolled my eyes at his vague answer and stuffed my sweater pillow into position to lean my head against the window. The low rumble of the car and the bouncy suspension as we rose and fell over the highway's various lumps was enough to lull me to sleep. "Anthony?"

"Yeah?"

"Are we someplace safe now?"

A pause filled the car while he weighed his answer. "I'd say so, yeah."

"Good. Then tell me the whole story. You said you would when we were someplace safer."

He softly chuckled as I yawned again. "You really want to hear it?"

"Of course I do. It'll keep us both awake. Start from the beginning and don't leave anything out."

He sighed. "Okay. Here goes."

I kept my eyes on the taillights ahead of us, glowing red like sets of eyes in the dark. Despite my various aches and pains, when Anthony's warm voice poured over me like I'd slipped into a bath, I felt myself relax.

"I met Portia when I was seven. Well, I guess more accurately, I met her brother, Jake, when I was seven, and she was the annoying little sister who wanted to follow us like a shadow. But she was cute." He paused to laugh quietly and fondly before his voice turned darker.

"My dad split when I was a baby, and my mom drank away her problems. Their dad is a piece of shit who hit their mom. None of us really had anyone looking out for us at home, so we looked out for each other—and Uncle Lou, of course. He always kept an eye out. When he'd come around for dinner at my mom's, he'd always ask if Jake and Portia were joining, so, of course, I'd run down the street and go get them. Their mom was doing her best to keep herself alive, so she took any chance to have the kids off her hands. So we ended up spending a lot of time together." The fondness had cautiously crept back into his voice. He sounded almost reluctant to let it, as if he'd knowingly let it lure him to a cliff—with certain pain at the bottom.

"When we were in high school, Jake fell in with a really bad crowd. Basically, a street gang. One night, there was this fight, and both Jake and this kid from another gang got shot. They both died."

"Oh, my God." I noted how bluntly he'd said it, as if it would only feel like striking himself with a club, instead of a knife, if done right. "I'm so sorry, Anthony."

He gave his head one shake and thickly swallowed. "It was a long time ago."

"That doesn't mean it doesn't still hurt." I softly placed my hand on his leg.

He looked down at it and blinked a few times. I felt his eyes flick to my face before he returned them to the road and kept speaking. "After Jake died, the gang came after Portia—the other kid's older brother, specifically. He was their leader—the head asshole. I mean, he was an adult harassing a teenage girl.

The guy was scum. He said she was going to pay for what Jake took from him. It got really bad. Portia was afraid to leave the house, to go to school. She got death threats. It went on for almost a year. I told Uncle Lou about it because I was so worried, and because I'd promised her brother I'd look out for her. Lou cared about Portia too, obviously. They were both over for dinner one night, and she was skinny as a rail by then. All cheekbones and dark circles from all the stress. She wasn't sleeping or eating anymore. Uncle Lou pulled me aside and asked me in the most serious tone I'd ever heard him use if I wanted him to *take care of it.*" He paused and flashed his gaze to me again.

I was wide-awake, riveted, and pretty sure I knew where this story was going.

"I didn't know too much about his business at the time," he went on, "but I knew he didn't have a normal job. He'd come and go a lot; he wore expensive clothes and nice watches. He drove that big, old Cadillac around like a king. One time, when I was ten, my mom was between jobs and our electricity got shut off. Uncle Lou got it turned back on, and then came over with this thick envelope. I hid around the living-room corner and watched their whole conversation as he tried to get my mom to take it. She kept refusing, saying it was wrong and she didn't want it, and they got in an argument. He left it on the kitchen table when he went. My mom went to her bedroom and shut the door. I could still hear her crying when I went into the kitchen and opened it."

"What was in it?" I asked when he paused, doing my best to slip my voice gently into the stream without disrupting his narrative.

"Twenty thousand dollars. I spent half the night lining the bills up in stacks on the kitchen table and counting them. I kept losing track and having to start over. It was more money than I'd ever seen in my life. I knew Uncle Lou loved us, but people didn't just *give* that kind of money to each other. Unless . . . they had lots of it. That's when I realized he could make things happen; he could *fix* things, like no one I'd ever known." He heaved a heavy breath. "So fast-forward to when he asks me about Portia. I was eighteen, about to go off to college, and I didn't want to leave Portia—because I knew she wouldn't be safe. So I said yes, not really knowing what *taking care of it* would entail."

His words were as loaded as I expected them to be. "I thought you said Lou wasn't a hit man."

"He wasn't. But he knew a couple. You can find anyone to do pretty much anything for the right price." He stroked his hand over his jaw; he was reliving that conversation where he'd said yes and perhaps still feeling the weight of his decision. "So he tells me he'll take care of it. But then my mom gets wind of things, and swears she'll never speak to either of us again if he goes through with it. She'd always known what line of work he was in and had tried to keep me away from it; she never knew about that night I counted all the cash. They went back and forth for a while, but then Lou says I'm an adult now, and leaves the decision up to me. Since he and Portia were the most family I'd ever had, I said yes, again. And he took care of it."

My eyes were wide as saucers as I blinked. I swallowed hard. "And then what happened?"

"I went off to college at Penn."

"You went to Penn?"

He turned to look at me. "Yes. Uncle Lou paid for it. Should I be offended by how surprised you sound?"

"I—No! Sorry. I didn't mean it like that." My cheeks burned.

A small smile twitched his lips. "Sorry, not all of us can have PhDs from Berkeley, Dr. Collins."

My flush only burned deeper. "How do you know that?"

"There's this thing called Google."

"Ah. Yes, well, in my defense, I Googled *you,* and there was nothing there, so I couldn't possibly know anything about your education—which, how does one even accomplish that? You have no digital footprint—even in shady places."

He flashed me another coy grin. "*You* looked in shady places for me? I thought you were a professor, not a hacker."

"That is not the point. I want to know how you managed to erase yourself from the Web."

"I know people."

I sat up and turned toward him, engaged. "See, *that* is a piece of this story I'm truly interested in. How do we get from the kid from Queens, with a rough homelife, to a Penn undergrad majoring in . . ." I trailed off, thinking of everything I knew about him. I took my best guess, *"Business?"*

"Econ, technically."

"Econ?! I didn't exactly have you pegged for a numbers nerd."

"I told you, I'm the suit."

"Yes, there are obviously many layers here, but I want to know how *you* ended up in this line of work. How did you go from straitlaced econ major to a not-bad-guy financial consultant slash fixer? Do they offer that as a minor at Penn?"

"Who said I was straitlaced? And no, *Pen,* they don't."

"I see what you did there."

"I take opportunities where I see them."

"But really. What happened next?"

"I was getting there, but then you took us on an alma mater detour."

"Sorry. Continue, please."

I sat back against my seat and prepared to keep listening.

"So, after it all happened and I went off to school, I kept an eye on Portia from a distance. I'd go home on weekends to visit; she'd take a train out to see me. She was doing better, but she still wanted out of her life. She wanted to be free. When I was in my junior year, she finished high school and moved to California and never looked back. She reinvented herself."

"*I'll* say. There was nothing about this when I searched her online, and there is *a ton* of stuff about her online. And as I am saying this out loud, I am realizing the same reason I saw none of this online is the same reason there is nothing about you online."

"Now you're keeping up," he said with a grin.

"Damn. What's the going rate for a thorough internet scrub?"

"Not cheap. You saw the suitcase in the trunk. But we make exceptions for friends and family."

"Love a good discount. So, where are we now? Portia is in California, and you're still at Penn, with your pocket protector and calculator, and you're wooing dates with enthralling discussions of your favorite Excel formulae."

"That is an egregious stereotype."

"Tell me *one* part of that sentence that is not accurate."

"I didn't date."

"Another surprise."

"Why is that a surprise?"

"Are you really going to make me tell you how attractive you are, again? The *ego* on you, I swear."

He blushed, and I smiled.

"We are never going to get to the end of this story, if you don't stop derailing it."

"Sorry." I made a motion like I was locking my lips and throwing away the key.

"So, yes, I'm finishing school, and Portia is in California. I'd considered moving to the West Coast after I graduated, but

Uncle Lou was still in New York; and to be honest, I was kind of hoping to fix things with my mom." His voice fell off. Aside from when he'd told me his best friend had died, this statement carried the most weight—like a rain cloud the color of a bruise waiting to split open.

"And did you?"

He sucked his teeth with a defeated flick of his head. "Still trying. And I didn't make it any easier for myself when Uncle Lou offered me a job working with him and I said yes."

"Okay, *now* we're getting somewhere."

He shot me a glare, and I pressed my lips together again. "I moved back to New York and interned at a brokerage firm after college, and the finance world was not all I'd hoped for. The hours were brutal, and the competition was cutthroat. Everyone was five seconds away from a heart attack or an aneurysm—I literally saw someone have an aneurysm one day. I could feel my soul leaving my body after a year."

"Fair. I've seen *The Wolf of Wall Street*."

"Yeah, well, I'm not one of those guys."

"No. Your career path sounds much more . . . *tame*?" My voice pitched upward because I could not find the right word, and the one I landed on sounded as equally sarcastic as it did serious.

Based on his smirk, I could see he interpreted it as the former. "It was tame, compared to all this." He gestured out the windshield at the dark night. "Like I told you before, I was the suit side of things for Uncle Lou."

"And what exactly does a *suit* for a fixer do?"

He shrugged one shoulder. "Whatever Uncle Lou needed. I worked in an office. I was making calls and doing research and balancing books. The job was like half PI, half accountant. Uncle Lou would say, 'I need this information on this person'; then I'd go find it. No questions asked. Or he'd tell me to transfer a pile of money into some account, and I'd do it. And, of course, I was keeping his income on the legal side of financial affairs by overseeing several business ventures in his name. People are willing to fork out a lot to make their problems go away; he had to put all that money somewhere. Uncle Lou brought me on as temporary at first, a trial period and basically to save me from the corporate scene, but I liked it too much to quit. It was the most interesting work I'd ever done, and I didn't want to give it up."

"So you didn't."

"I didn't. It's been thirteen years now."

"That's quite the trial period. And in that time, I have to imagine you've seen some things, present situation excluded. I mean, you seem to have a lot of street smarts for a numbers nerd with an Ivy League degree who works in an office."

He partly frowned. "Yeah, well, like I told you: rough childhood. Most of my smarts came from before this job, and Uncle Lou kept me away from the on-the-ground stuff, but I have picked up a thing or two, I guess."

"Like how to throw someone over a wall?" I said with a sly grin.

He softly chuckled with a shake of his head. "A surprisingly useful skill."

"So, why did Lou move to California?" I asked, remembering I had watched him move in next door to Libby five years ago.

"Well, my mom still wasn't talking to either of us, and he said he needed a change of pace as he got closer to retirement. Honestly, I think he had some heat on his tail. You can only do his job in one place for so long before *you're* the one who needs a fix. But he gave me this whole speech about California being a *land of new opportunity,* saying there was a whole different set of problems out here that needed fixing—what with the entertainment and tech industries. Turned out he was right."

I marveled at how one man's decision to uproot and move cross-country had put everything in motion to land me in a classic Camaro cruising down the midnight highway with his nephew.

"Why didn't you come with him?"

He half shrugged again. "Because I'm a city rat. It's too sunny here, and you all are too nice. Everyone smiles and wants to stop and chat—neighbors bake each other *pies,* for God's sake." He shot me a little grin. "Not to mention your appalling public transportation system."

"Did you try my sister's pie?"

"Yes. It was delicious," he said bitterly.

"Of course it was. Okay, so now we're up to speed: Lou is in California, and you're still in New York. What is Portia up to?"

"Making the worst decision of her life," he said. "When she first told me she met someone, I was happy. I thought, 'Good, finally some stability for her.' She invited me out to drinks to meet Connor when they were visiting New York once. He was there on business, and she'd tagged along. She had stars in her eyes that night. I'd never seen her so lovesick, and I'd known every boyfriend she'd ever had. Don't get me wrong—it was a fantasy at first. Private planes, penthouses, limitless shopping sprees. He gave her the world on a platter. But he was possessive, and demanding, and extremely jealous. He kept her on a leash. Locked in a cage. She was an object to him. It got to the point that she couldn't breathe without his permission. He had control over all her finances, her travel, what she ate, where she went, who she talked to." His voice had grown strained. His knuckles were white where they gripped the steering wheel.

"She hid it all, of course. All the social media posts, the gala appearances, the magazine interviews. No one knew, but she couldn't lie to me. I've known her since she was four years old. I could see straight through the real-life princess she'd molded herself into and back to that terrified teenager afraid for her own life."

I tried to picture what Anthony saw when he looked at Portia and I thought back to that day she visited campus and the sad cloud that seemed to hang over her.

"I noticed it too," I said.

He looked over at me in curiosity.

"That day I had coffee with her on campus, she was nothing but nice and friendly, but I couldn't shake this feeling it was an act. A performance."

His head bobbed in a sad, slow nod. "You were right. It was."

"So, what happened? What set all this off?"

The air inside the car grew tense, crackling with electricity. I could feel his rage simmering from deep inside him. "A few days before she disappeared, she showed up on my doorstep. She and Connor were in New York for a short visit. Him for business; her to attend a charity event. It happened to coincide with EnViSage backing out of that deal with StarCloud."

The words set off a lightbulb in my mind. "Wait, that actually has something to do with all this? The deal with Star-Cloud?"

He didn't scold me for another interruption, perhaps finally accepting I was a very dynamic listener. "Yes."

"I *knew* it! A multibillion-dollar deal going bust and the CEO's wife going missing within days is too shady not to be connected. What happened?"

The air thickened with tension again. His voice strained. "Well, that night she showed up at my door, she was a mess. Trembling, crying. She had a cut lip and a black eye, and the first thing she said to me was her husband was going to kill her."

"Oh, my God."

His hand tightened on the wheel again. "It wasn't the first time he'd hit her, but it was the first time I'd ever seen her that terrified. I brought her inside my apartment. She said after their fight, she ran from their hotel room—before her body-guard could follow—and came straight to me. She was . . . It was really bad, Penny. I wanted to go kill him myself. Once I got her to calm down, she explained what had happened. Turns out, that deal with StarCloud fell through for good rea-son. EnViSage is essentially broke. Connor has been stealing money from his own company for years, and Portia found out about it. When that high-profile merger suddenly didn't hap-pen, the FBI took notice. Apparently, Connor has been on their radar for a while, and this was enough for them to offi-cially come knocking."

I opened my mouth to speak, and he cut me off.

"And before you ask, *no,* I will not tell you what Portia specifically knows about her husband. She hasn't even told *me* all of it; and the fewer people who know, the better, given Con-nor is willing to kill to keep it quiet."

I snapped my mouth shut and swallowed hard, because that was the exact question I was going to ask.

"Let's just call it *large-scale fraud,*" he said. "So news of the failed deal comes out, and the FBI takes notice. They hear that the Slates are in New York for a few days. Unfortunately—or probably intentionally, the more I think about it—they come knocking when Portia is alone in their hotel room. She swears she didn't tell the agent anything, and only talked to him long enough to find out what he wanted. I said *unfortunately* be-cause Connor showed up while the agent was still there, and, of course, to him, it looks like his wife is ratting him out to the Feds. The agent leaves, Connor goes berserk and beats the shit out of Portia, and she comes running to me."

My heart was pounding and aching at the same time. I was hardly breathing.

"She fell apart right in front of me. I couldn't stand it. I begged her to leave him, to file for divorce, to just fucking run—and she wanted to, but she said it would be impossible. He'd never let her go. And now that he thought she'd talked to the Feds, she was sure he was going to kill her."

The words hung inside the car with a chill. I shivered and spoke softly.

"So you made her disappear."

"That was the plan, yes."

"What went wrong?"

He sighed another breath, which was deep enough to make him wince. "All of it. Portia wanted to stay in the city for the charity event, and we needed time to prepare anyway. I told her to give us three days and we'd have it figured out by the time she got back to California. Lou was not happy. Certainly, not about the rush—he was methodical to a fault and took time to plan everything—and definitely not about a job involving Connor Slate. He warned me it was a huge risk, and that pulling together a convincing disappearance in three days was near impossible. But I didn't care. I had to get her out.

"We built a whole new identity for Portia—that's what was in the safe and why I needed the key: her new passport and ID. Uncle Lou had it all ready to go. The plan was to stage a kidnapping. She goes missing, and we make sure Connor—who would be the prime suspect—has an alibi, so they all think she's really gone, even him. Maybe it would be seen as retaliation for the StarCloud deal, we didn't know. We weren't really thinking things through, because we were moving so fast. It was my fault it got so sloppy, but Lou cared about Portia enough to go along with it. We planted the shoe in the woods by their house to make it look like there'd been a struggle. We had her picked up and moved to a safe house, where Lou was going to meet her with her new identity, and then we'd put her on a plane, and she'd be gone. Forever." His voice wavered at the end, and I wondered if a permanent goodbye between them was supposed to be part of this disappearing act. "Connor was always going to look for her when she disappeared, even if he believed she'd been kidnapped. But she was supposed to be gone. Untraceable by even him."

"So, what happened?"

"The night after she gets to the safe house, I get a call Lou never showed up with her IDs. An hour later, there's a knock on my door in Manhattan. That motherfucker who had you tied up in the basement is standing on my doorstep and tells me my uncle is dead and I'm next—if Connor doesn't have Portia back by the next day."

My whole body tensed at the mention of the tweed man, and I suddenly didn't feel very bad for stabbing him. "How did they know?"

"I don't know, but I would guess Portia's bodyguard. He knew the plan. We had to have him in on it, or it would have been impossible, given he never left Portia's side. She swore we could trust him, and I believed her. But it turned out his loyalties remained with Connor after all. I mean, he didn't protect her from her own husband abusing her, so, clearly, he had priorities."

I thought back to the man I'd seen on campus that day with Portia, and in all the photos online. He was so stoic and faithful. Given what Anthony had told me about her life, I'd imagine Portia had trust issues, and if she trusted her bodyguard, she must have had reason to.

"Maybe he regretted never protecting her at home, so he was loyal now, and they killed him because he wouldn't talk," I offered.

"Maybe. Or maybe he talked, and they killed him for even considering helping her escape."

I shivered again, unsure which theory was true, and not really wanting to think about the body in the closet anymore. "Why weren't you there?" I asked, and almost immediately regretted it by the way his shoulders slumped.

"I should have been for something this important. But we moved too fast. Uncle Lou knew all the intricacies of making things happen on the ground and was better at it anyway, so he put it in motion before I could get there. I was still in the city tying up all the logistics of it. I thought we'd been careful enough. I should have listened to him. It was too risky from the start, but we were desperate." He shook his head and briefly gazed out the side window. His disappointment and his guilt were thick enough to taste.

He went quiet, and I let the silence linger so I could organize all the new information and let it sink in. I'd been right about a few things, but mostly wrong. Anthony was not a bad guy. Sure, perhaps he was tangentially connected to some uncouth activities, but at least this situation with Portia was a rescue mission and not the murder conspiracy I'd believed it to be. I studied his profile against the window's midnight backdrop. A divider with bushy oleander plants separated us from any oncoming traffic, so the only light came from the moon and the dim glow of the car's dash. It bathed his skin in a deep golden hue. I'd been right about how enigmatic he was. I'd learned so much in the past few hours and felt like I'd still only scratched the surface. Part of me still couldn't believe I'd ever crossed paths with him.

"How does the estate sale fit into all this?" I asked. "Seems like a strange event to throw into the mix."

He scoffed like the frustration was fresh. "Yes, it was. It's Uncle Lou's Realtor's fault. I was listed on everything as next of kin, so I was getting a million phone calls when he died. His Realtor called about the house, suggested an estate sale so we could get it on the market ASAP, and I said yes without even thinking about it. Next thing I know, she's asking if I'm available that Saturday to run it—and, by the way, it's already been advertised. It was a moving train. I couldn't stop it. So I fly out, and I'm dealing with the mortuary, funeral services; keeping the murder out of the news, because I didn't need that added heat; Googling how to run an estate sale; trying to pick up where Lou left off to get Portia the hell out of Dodge; and a goddamned *body* shows up on my back porch."

I blew out a breath, trying to lighten the mood. His anxiety over what must have been hell to deal with hung on him like a tangy cologne. "That's quite the to-do list. Is Detective Warner on Lou's case too? How did you convince him to keep it under wraps?"

"He is on the case, but he's not the one who kept it under wraps. Uncle Lou had connections in the press, and I called in a favor."

I had a sudden moment of realization. "Wait. That night in your kitchen when you told me someone didn't want news about Portia's bodyguard getting out, you were talking about yourself, weren't you? *You* kept it out of the news."

He nodded. "Yes. Until Portia is someplace safe, I don't want word getting out that someone is picking off people in her inner circle. It will be too messy. People just know Lou died, not how. And thankfully, her bodyguard doesn't have a family that is going to come around asking questions anyway."

A pang of sadness hit me at thought I'd been right about nobody mourning the bodyguard. "What was his name?"

"Tyler."

I wasn't sure if that was a first or last name, or perhaps he was mon5nymous, like a celebrity, but I paused in a moment of silence for Tyler.

"So, does Warner know all this? That both deaths are tied to Portia?"

"I'm sure he has suspicions by now, but I certainly didn't tell him. After I pulled strings to keep Uncle Lou's murder quiet, and then Tyler showed up in my closet, Warner was ready to arrest me. Mr. Mitchell, the lawyer you met at the station, used every trick in the book short of bribery to get him to let me off."

I thought back to the day of the estate sale and how quickly the crime scene tape had come down. "I wondered how you managed to clean that up so quickly that day. Little did I know. And sorry if I added to the stress. I had no idea what was going on."

He glanced sideways at me, and his frown tugged up on one side. "Yeah, I was already losing it, and then this feisty professor shows up and starts yelling at me about candlesticks."

"Yelling at you?" I said with a gasp, completely scandalized. "For the tenth time, I was only trying to prevent a rip-off in progress."

"Well, you got a lot more than you *bargained* for."

"Good one."

A yawn suddenly hit me like a rogue wave. I shielded it with my hand and felt my eyes swim with moisture. "Was it the same case with the funeral? It was already in motion, so you had to see it through, even though you were in a rush to help Portia?"

"Yes and no. It was partly to keep up appearances. I didn't want Connor to think he'd rattled me—and I knew all of Uncle Lou's clients would want to pay their respects. But also"—he shrugged his bulky shoulders—"I wanted to. For Lou. So I planned it."

I reached over and squeezed his arm in sympathy. "What are you going to do with the house now? Or, well, I mean, after all this is sorted out."

He tilted his head and looked at me from under his lashes with a grin. "I admire your optimism that this is going to get sorted out."

"Uh, it *better* get sorted out. Otherwise, you can turn around and take me home right now, because I still have to make tenure before summer is over."

His laugh was tight and laced with uncertainty. "And what exactly does making tenure involve?" He shot my earlier question about his job back at me.

"Chaining myself to my desk to crank out research papers, serving on committees, teaching courses, earning awards, getting grant funding, presenting at conferences, and mostly sucking up to the old white men who run my department and university until they decide I have jumped through enough hoops to be unfireable."

"You have to do all that this summer?"

"No. I've been doing all that for the past five years. I still have to finish some of it, but if I don't submit my case—basically, a portfolio documenting all that—by the end of this summer, my clock is up and I'm no longer eligible."

"And then what would happen?"

I turned sideways and gave him a serious look, not liking what he was implying. "Let's hope it doesn't come to that, and thank you for voicing my biggest fear, but I would lose my job and have a hard time finding another one."

"I see. So it is very important not to mess this up."

"Correct."

He thoughtfully stroked his chin, like he was realizing the full weight of my situation. "Have you always wanted to be a professor?"

"Pretty much. Both my parents are professors. Though sometimes I wonder if I'm really cut out for it."

"What makes you say that?"

I shifted, feeling the familiar wave of insecurity wash over me. "Well, for starters, I'm constantly fighting an uphill battle in a male-dominated field. Many of my peers are particularly skilled at questioning my qualifications and overlooking my work. It's mostly just exhausting, but when it happens enough, you start to wonder."

"Fuck them," he said sharply.

I jumped in surprise and laughed as heat splashed my cheeks.

"Sorry," he said with a soft grin. "But seriously, fuck them. As far as I can tell, you're brilliant."

I was thankful for the cover of darkness shielding my deep blush. "Well, that's kind of you to say, but you don't have much to go off of."

"Sure, I do. You got us out of the Slates' house, didn't you? And you put the pieces together about Portia on your own. And on top of being smart, I think you're pretty brave. I can't imagine being a professor prepares you for being kidnapped and chased, and you've handled tonight like a pro."

I snorted. "That's generous. I was mostly just reacting to the situation."

"Are you capable of taking a compliment? Or did those insecure cavemen you work with train it out of you? Stop downplaying what a badass you are."

"I—" I snapped my mouth shut when his words landed like a little epiphany.

Did I downplay my abilities? My competence? When I paused to consider, I felt the reflex to deflect praise coiled under my tongue like a spring. Had that always been there? I frowned and mentally spit it out.

I looked over at him and caught his eye. Even in the dim light, I felt like he could see right through me. He gave me a nod, like he knew his words had penetrated. Perhaps he was right. I'd thought the scariest thing I had to face down was my tenure committee, but I'd escaped a kidnapper tonight.

I chewed away the shy smile bending my lips. "I am not a badass."

"I beg to differ. The move with the chair in the basement was one of the most badass things I've ever seen. Give yourself some credit."

My traitorous lips betrayed me and fully bent upward. "Okay, fine. I guess that was a little badass."

"Mmm-hmm. And if you can survive all this, then I have no doubt you can survive whatever a bunch of stuffy old professors are making you do to make tenure." He said it with enough conviction to boost my confidence and flutter my heart.

"Thank you."

"You're welcome. Glad to see you're already making progress on the compliment front."

I sat back against my seat and smiled.

We cruised along in a comfortable silence for several moments. When he spoke again, his voice came out warm and soft. "To answer your earlier question, I don't know about the house. I did plan on selling it, but then . . ." Even in the dark, I noticed the shy flush in his cheeks. His eyes said *but then you showed up.* It sent my belly loose with tiny flapping wings.

"But then some feisty professor's nephew opened your closet, and a body fell out, and now you're on the lam with said professor, who everyone thinks is your girlfriend, heading to some undisclosed location to finish the very dangerous job of rescuing your childhood friend, who is married to a megalomaniac billionaire, who wants to kill both of you?"

He cast me a look like he wanted to laugh, but knew he shouldn't. "That about sums it up."

"Hmm. Well, I, for one, am rooting for you. You seem like a solid guy. And I'd rather you didn't die."

He snorted. "Thanks. I'll do my best."

I yawned again and repositioned my sweater pillow, taking comfort in his words even if we were joking around. "Tell me your favorite childhood memories. What were Portia and her brother like as kids? What were *you* like?"

A warm, slightly surprised sound popped from his mouth. Almost like he didn't believe I was interested in knowing. "Sure. I've got a few stories."

I listened to the soft hum of his voice, a velvety blanket over the car's purr, and eventually gave up trying to keep my eyes open.

CHAPTER 11

"Penny."

I woke to the sound of Anthony's voice softly murmuring beside my ear. For a second, I imagined I was lying next to him in a cocoon of warmth, but quickly remembered I was smashed up against a car window, with a pilly, old-man sweater as a pillow.

I sat up and rubbed my eyes. The neon glow of a VACANCY sign smeared the pitch-black night with pink outside the windshield. "Where are we?" I asked. My voice croaked out thick and dry. I reached around for my bottle of water.

"Nevada," Anthony said as he unbuckled. "I need to rest. I'm not safe to drive anymore."

"I can dr—IVE," I said through a roar of a yawn. Tears leaked from my eyes.

"You don't even know where we're going, and you've been asleep for two hours."

I stretched my arms and felt my back pop. "Exactly, I'm fresh as a daisy. *And*—I know this might come as a shock to you—you *could* tell me where we're going."

He opened his door without acknowledging my umpteenth request for the information. "Stay here. I'll be right back."

"I'll come with you," I said, wanting to stretch my legs and get some fresh air.

"No."

"Why not?"

He leaned back in the door, with his hand on the roof. "*Because*. Don't you remember Sadie back in Woodside? If you go in there with bruises on your face, they're going to think I put them there. If I go in there beat up, they'll think I got in a bar fight. We don't need anyone calling the cops and reporting we're here. Connor's resources are limitless, remember?"

I peered out the windshield at the row of yellowed doors lined in the crumbling green building like a set of rotten teeth. They had plaques with numbers beside them and actual doorknobs with keyholes. An air-conditioning unit protruded from each room's window like a boxy tumor. Enough of them were wheezing to suggest they might have to flick on the NO on the VACANCY sign soon.

"You really think they care about who's hitting who at this place?" I asked.

"I would hope so," Anthony said. "I'll be right back." He shut his door and left me in the parking lot.

I sat in the silence as I watched him stalk off toward the front office. The motel had maybe twenty rooms total. Two by ten stacked on top of each other, with an iron-railed staircase leading up to the second floor. It looked like the type of place people rented by the hour, used for shady crimes, or, as in our case, stopped for the night out of desperation.

Anthony had only said we were in Nevada. He didn't name a city, and judging by my sweep out the rear window, revealing a diner and a gas station flanked by darkness across the street, I would guess this little oasis wasn't even on a map.

The mini-mart sign, blazing in white and blue above the gas station, caught my eye as I yawned again. I assumed there'd be a functioning shower in the motel, but it didn't look like the type of place where I could call the front desk and request a toothbrush. Anthony was still in the office, and I decided to try my luck with the mini-mart's toiletries selection while I waited.

Before I crossed the street, I popped the trunk and borrowed a few bills from the suitcase. The desert night air hung paper dry and still hot from the day. I felt it warm and heavy in my lungs with every breath. The parking lot was half full, and I noticed a single pickup truck over at the gas station. Otherwise, there were no signs of life.

Across the street, the gas station's fluorescent lights sizzled overhead and turned me a sickly shade of blue. The mini-mart's door *bing-bonged* when I opened it, and the smell of bleach and refrigerated cardboard immediately greeted me. The employee behind the register, a twentysomething kid with a hoodie and patchy goatee, didn't even look up from his phone when I entered. His lack of interest suited me fine while I shopped.

The door *bing-bonged* again as I found the aisle containing the store's meager selection of travel-sized products. The man who'd been pumping gas outside entered, looking as gaunt and tired as I felt. He wore a baseball hat and a denim jacket and headed straight for the refrigerator while I scanned the shelves.

"Yes!" I quietly cheered at the sight of toothbrushes dangling from a hook, alongside little boxes of toothpaste. I grabbed some toothpaste, toothbrushes for Anthony and me, along with a miniature stick of deodorant for each of us, and a bottle of Tylenol, because my head was still throbbing, and I wasn't about to pop one of those mystery trunk pills. New underwear was too much to ask for, but I did find a first aid kit that wasn't thirty years old, a little bottle of superglue to try a trick I'd seen on TV, lip balm, a tube of vanilla-citrus-scented body lotion, and some cheap concealer, which would probably make my skin break out, but would at least help cover bruises.

For good measure, I also grabbed a pack of powdered doughnuts, some Red Vines, two bags of Doritos, and a trucker hat with *The Silver State* scrawled on it.

The cashier looked bored by our transaction and, thankfully, didn't ask questions about my strange outfit, though I felt him eye it with curiosity. He placed my price-gouged middle-of-nowhere purchases into a plastic bag and bid me a good night right as the man pumping gas stepped to the register behind me.

"You from out of town?" he asked in a grumbly voice.

I flashed a look over my shoulder at his absurd question. Why else would I have been buying travel products and junk food in the middle of the night at a gas station? I gave him a tight smile and nodded, wondering if he was a local making a midnight run for the beer in his hand. He was large, with dusty boots and what looked like dried blood caking the knuckles on his right hand. He snapped open the beer and took a swig before he'd even paid for it.

"Just passing through," I said neutrally as I turned to leave. And then for good measure, I added, "My boyfriend is getting us a room across the street. He's a cop." My face hardly flushed at the lies, but I'd already been kidnapped once today. Bending the truth to deter interest from this stranger felt reasonable, if not necessary.

He gave me a thin-lipped grin and set his beer on the counter. "Have a good night."

Back across the street, I found Anthony pacing the parking lot and tugging on his hair.

"What's wrong?" I asked, sure the person at the front desk was a Connor Slate spy and had reported us and we'd have mere minutes to get back on the road.

He immediately stopped pacing when he saw me and closed the gap between us in three enormous steps. "Where were you?" He reached for my shoulders with both hands and shook them. He was too distracted to wince.

The panic in his eyes threw me for a loop. "I—I was across

the street," I stuttered. I dug my hand into the bag and pulled out a toothbrush. "I wanted to brush my teeth."

He blinked at the blue plastic stick in my hand, like it took him a moment to realize what he was seeing. "A toothbrush?"

"Yeah. I got you one too. Along with some other stuff." I dropped my brush back inside and held the bag open for him to see.

He studied the snacks and toiletries and closed his eyes to let out a big breath. "I thought something happened to you. I came out and you were gone." When he dropped his hands from my shoulders, I immediately regretted their absence.

"Sorry. I was only gone for a second. I didn't mean to worry you."

"It's okay. Sorry I yelled at you."

I softly smiled at him, feeling equally bad for upsetting him and warmed by the fact he cared enough to worry. "It's okay. Tell me I get to take a shower in the next five minutes, and I'll forgive you."

He looked over his shoulder at the motel in all its desperate roadside glory and dug in his pocket. When he pulled out his hand, a single key looped onto a key chain, with a faded 4 on it, hung from his finger. "They only have one nonsmoking room available." He almost sounded like he was apologizing. His cheeks turned pink, all the way to the tips of his ears.

I tilted my head in confusion, and then remembered. "Ah, right. Nevada. Home of public indoor smoking."

"Yeah. I told them we'd take it for the night. There's only one bed—but it's a king, so . . ."

I suddenly understood why he was blushing so hard. I looked down at our feet and pushed my hair, which had grown limp and oily, behind my ear. "Got it. Well, I'm pretty tired and could probably sleep anywhere, so it's fine."

"Right. Me too." He nodded and pivoted for the car. "We need to take everything inside."

"Everything?" I asked as he opened the trunk. I wasn't sure how I felt about sleeping next to a bag of guns. The tall, brooding man slinging the bag over his shoulder, sure, if I had to, but a bag of weapons made me uneasy.

"Yes. Safer to have it with us. We'll only be here a couple hours anyway. I just need to rest."

I realized then I had no idea what time it was. Probably close to 2:00 or 3:00 a.m. if we were all the way in Nevada, and Anthony said I'd slept for two hours.

"I can get them," I told Anthony when he reached for one of the suitcases. I pushed his hand out of the way and heaved the money and the clothes out of the trunk. He let me, likely because the duffel bag looked like it weighed half a ton, and he was already struggling to carry it with his injuries.

Luckily, our room was on the first floor, about ten feet from where we'd parked. When he unlocked the door, a puff of musty but cool air burst out to greet us. The room had one king bed, as advertised, and not much else. A TV sat on a dresser, and two lamps flanked the bed on matching wooden nightstands. The bed's duvet, with gaudy orange and burgundy stripes, looked fit for Lou's suitcase. At least several cushy-looking extra pillows were piled at the headboard.

"I want to take a shower," I said, suddenly bone tired at the thought of actual sleep.

"Me too. You go first."

I dumped over the bag from the mini-mart onto the foot of the bed and grabbed the lotion, the floral-scented deodorant, a toothbrush, and the toothpaste. "Enjoy the spoils."

The small bathroom had scratchy towels and a selection of generic shampoo, bodywash, and a milky conditioner, which all smelled exactly the same. But the water was hot, and I didn't really mind it stinging the cuts at my wrists and ankles if it meant washing off the day. Once my skin was scalded pink and fresh, I dried off and slathered myself with the lotion from the mini-mart. I could already feel the dry air sucking the moisture from my skin. The tiny luxury felt indulgent and lovely.

I put the banana shirt and my underwear back on, but nothing else, seeing as it fell to my thighs and made for a nightgown anyway. When I rejoined Anthony in the room, he'd turned on the TV to a sitcom rerun and propped himself on the bed. His eyes were drooping closed until he heard the sound of my voice.

"All yours," I said.

He snapped awake and eyed me in my makeshift pajamas, with my hair wrapped in a towel. He muttered something that sounded like *Right. Sure,* and climbed off the bed. His gaze took a brief tour of my legs before he looked away and stumbled toward the bathroom.

"Do you need help?" I called after him. "With your shirt?"

"No. I got it," he muttered, and closed the door.

He was in there for an age. Long enough that steam leaked from under the door in wispy white clouds and I wondered if he'd lain down in the tub and had fallen asleep. Perhaps a shower with broken ribs was slow going.

After I treated the largest of my abrasions and cuts with ointment and Band-Aids from the new first aid kit, I noted an ice bucket beside the TV and got an idea. "I'll be right back!" I called. I removed the towel from my hair and stepped into my pink shoes before slipping back outside. On the way into our room, I'd seen a vending machine and an ice maker, near the office. I filled the bag inside the little bucket with ice and carried it back.

Anthony had emerged from the shower when I returned. I tried to pretend I'd gained an immunity to seeing him in his underwear, but the flutter in my belly said I had not. As did the funny loop my blood took through my veins. He was pulling on a new shirt from the suitcase, this one a solid teal color and still ugly. "Where'd you go?" he asked.

"Ice." I held up the bucket. "For your ribs. I also have something for that too." I pointed at the now-exposed gash on his forehead. He'd removed the ripped-dress bandage to shower, and the wound was angry, red, and still wet-looking. "Sit." I commanded and pointed at the bed.

Perhaps he was simply too tired to protest because he did what I said.

"Leave it open," I said when he started to button his shirt. "For the ice." I held up the bag when he gave me a curious look. I crawled onto the bed and knelt on his right side. He propped himself up against the pillows again, with his legs out in front of him. The muscular limbs were miles long and his boxer briefs very short. He set a pillow in his lap, and I ignored the significance of it. "This is going to be cold," I warned, and gently placed the ice on his abdomen.

He immediately sucked in a breath and tensed.

I grimaced. "How is it?"

"Cold. But nice. Thank you." His breath was minty and fresh. He'd washed himself with the identical shower products that I had, yet he somehow smelled better. Little water droplets clung to his collarbone, where he'd missed with the towel. It all did a number on my senses.

I stuffed another pillow under the ice to help hold it in place and reached for my other remedy. "Okay, I saw this on a TV show, so don't sue me if it doesn't actually work, but since you won't go for medical help and you need stitches, we're improvising."

He dubiously watched me pull the cap off the little plastic bottle. "Superglue?"

"Yes. Supposedly, it's the same as what they use in the ER."

"I seriously doubt that."

"Well, it's what we've got. Now hold still." I leaned closer to him and aimed the bottle's nozzle at the cut above his eyebrow. I was on my knees, and my bare thigh sat very near his.

"Is this ever going to come off?" He looked up at my hands hovering over his face, nearly going cross-eyed. I felt his warm breath on my skin.

"I don't know, but a permanent glue patch is better than an infection."

"Is it? You can clear up an infection with the right drugs. I'm not sure what can be done for glue."

"Well, either way, this ugly mug of yours will have more character now. Either from a scar or a glue patch."

"I think I'll take the former." He winced when I pinched his skin together to close the wound. "Ouch."

"Sorry. Almost done."

He grew quiet while I glued his face back together. His lashes tickled my palm when I got close enough. I felt his eyes studying me and had to concentrate to keep my hands steady.

"There," I said, once I finished. "Now it needs to dry so you don't glue yourself to the pillow." I softly blew on it and felt him twitch. His right hand rested on the pillow in his lap and moved several inches closer to me. "How's the ice?" I asked between breaths.

"Helping."

"Good." I kept blowing. I waved my hand to fan a small breeze.

"You smell like a Popsicle," he said.

"A Popsicle?"

"Mmm-hmm. One of those orange ones with vanilla ice cream in the middle. I love those."

"That would be thanks to the mini-mart's finest available skincare."

"It smells good."

The air took on a new charge between us. One that may have always been there, but never at an intensity that felt like standing on a very high cliff and wanting to leap, simply for the thrill of the rush.

"Penny," he said as I recapped the glue bottle. The lights were low. His eyes soft. My heart trilled somewhere high in my chest.

"What, Anthony?"

He blinked his long lashes. "I want to say I'm sorry. For all of this. I never meant for you to get involved."

I held his gaze and realized telling him it was okay would be lying because nothing was okay. So instead I did what I most wanted to do in that moment and kissed him.

If he wasn't expecting it, he didn't show it. He kissed back almost immediately. So quickly, in fact, I pulled back in surprise and began apologizing in a fluster.

"I'm sorry—I shouldn't have—I didn't mean—Was that okay?" My words came out disjointed and messy, and I was *mortified,* but he looked at me like it was the most ridiculous question he'd ever heard.

"Are you kidding me?" he said, and shoved his hand into my damp hair, palming the back of my head and pulling my mouth back to his.

Our second kiss landed with purpose, and I sank into it. It was hungry and soft and fiercely hot all at once. He bit at my bottom lip and then sucked it between his. I rose on my knees and leaned into him with my hands on his shoulders. His right hand swooped down to my hip. The fabric of the banana shirt slipped beneath his grip as he pulled me closer. I heard the ice crunch between us before I felt the cold, but the feel of his tongue sweeping mine melted it away.

I got greedy and kissed him deeper. He reciprocated, drawing me in like he was drinking me. I nibbled at his lip and slid my hand lower on his chest. It summoned a moan from deep in his throat, which turned into a wince.

At the sound, I pried my hands off and paused. "Sorry!"

His lips were swollen and wet; his cheeks flushed. But he was clearly in pain. "It's okay." He reached out for me, but I held back.

"Anthony, I think we should stop."

"But I don't want to stop. Do you want to stop?"

"No!" I shook my head. My heart was still pounding. "Not at all. I just wonder if maybe we should come back to this when your ribs aren't broken." I indulgently traced my finger over the contours of his chest. The hairs tickled. I bit my lip.

"Please don't do that."

"What?" I asked, suddenly embarrassed for taking liberties.

"Bite your lip like that." He reached up and used his thumb to release it from my teeth, where I'd bitten it again. "It's unbelievably sexy, and I will end up breaking all my bones tonight if you don't stop."

The flush that scorched my cheeks was hotter than a desert summer day. I bashfully looked down and tried to straighten my hair for distraction.

"You're doing it again."

"Sorry. I don't even notice it."

"I do," he said, and reached for my chin. He brushed his thumb over my bottom lip in the smoothest, slowest stroke, and I thought I might burst into flames.

I groaned in frustration and flopped my arms on my lap. "Well, now what am I supposed to do? You can't say things like that and expect me to go to sleep," I whined.

He softly laughed and adjusted the ice bag. "It's probably a good idea that we stop, given my state. You just have to hold back like I've been doing."

"You've been holding back?"

"Penny, I've wanted to kiss you since the candlesticks."

I was going to die. He was going to kill me. This half-naked man, lying up in bed next to me, with the world's most kissable lips and melt-me eyes, muttering romantic nothings, would be the end of me. Forget the bag of guns and the whack jobs chasing after us. Anthony Pierce was going to murder me with lust.

"You are impossible," I said. "Can we kiss for, like, five more minutes, and then go to sleep?"

He laughed and clutched at his side. "I don't think that would be a good idea."

"Three?"

"Penny."

"Okay, two. Final offer."

"Fine. Deal."

I lay down with a smile. He carefully rolled over on his side and scooted down on the pillows to face me.

"Hi," he said. His minty breath fluttered against my face.

"Hi."

"Two minutes," he warned with a stern look, like he was telling himself as much as me.

I bit my lip and excitedly nodded.

It might have been the best two minutes of my life. His hands, his mouth. The heat of his body as he pulled me close to tangle his legs with mine. It was two minutes so good it erased my awareness we were in a scuzzy motel on the run from kidnappers. I felt completely at peace when we fell asleep together in ugly shirts and our underwear.

I woke when a beam of light cut across my face with a blast of heat. It pulled me from the warm, dreamy fog of sleeping next to Anthony. At one point in the night, I'd woken and felt his hand on my hip and his chest against my back. The slow cadence of his breath had lulled me back into a bottomless sleep, where I'd never felt so safe. Now he wasn't beside me, and I wondered if it had all been a dream.

I sat up, exhaustion still clawing at me, and shielded the light with my hand. "Anthony?" I said as I blinked the sleep from my eyes. I saw his silhouette at the window, peeking out a slit in the curtains and holding a gun down by his hip. I gasped and pulled the sheet tight to my chest. I was suddenly wide-awake. "What's wrong?"

At the sound of my alarm, he turned and let go of the curtain. He was fully dressed and looked like he'd been awake for a while. He set the gun on the nightstand and came to sit next to me. "Nothing. But we should get going soon."

I nervously chewed my lip and felt his eyes studying my face. I could feel that my hair was a tousled mess from sleeping on it wet. I remembered what he'd said about biting my lip and released it from my teeth. "If it's nothing, then why are you looking out the window with a gun in your hand?"

"I'm only being cautious." His voice was serious, his eyes hard. The soft, pliable man I'd fallen asleep kissing seemed to be gone.

I tucked my knees up to my chest and squeezed them, remembering why we were in this motel room and feeling foolish for thinking last night was anything other than a stolen opportunity created by the circumstances. "Okay." I sounded defeated and sad, and I felt an ache in my chest that whatever heat had blossomed between us had died. My vulnerability got the best of me. "Was last night real?" I asked in a quiet voice. I squeezed my knees again.

He slightly leaned back and considered me with a tilt of his head. A layer of scruff a shade darker than yesterday coated his jaw, and I wondered if he normally shaved every day and I'd simply never seen him having skipped one. I rather liked the unkempt look. "It felt pretty real to me." His eyes flashed with a glint of the flame from the night before.

"Really? I mean, you weren't just high on expired trunk pills and kissing me because we were stuck here?"

A smile curved half his mouth, and he reached for my hand. "Penny. Since the candlesticks, remember?" He laced his fingers between mine, and a swell of winged creatures swarmed my empty belly.

"Are you sure?"

He reached for my face, his left arm more mobile now, and pulled my lips to his. The kiss was soft and polite, but held a deep hunger that made me want to tackle him. The rough scratch of his chin sent my blood looping dizzily.

"Does that answer your question?" he said in a low growl when he pulled back.

"Uh-huh." I'd lost the capacity for more sophisticated words.

He kissed my hand that he was still holding and stood from the bed. "Get dressed. We can grab something at the diner before we leave."

"How much farther are we going?"

"Not much. We'll be there later today."

I reeled in surprise, somehow having convinced myself this journey was never-ending. "Really?"

"Yes. I actually need to make a phone call." He fished the burner phone out of his pocket.

He'd reminded me I needed to make a phone call too, and as much as I wanted to stick around and eavesdrop, I desperately needed to pee, and I had to prepare for what to say to my sister.

By the time I brushed my teeth, washed my face, found another hideous shirt, and blotted the grape-colored bruise on my temple with some probably toxic mini-mart makeup, I was ready to call Libby. Anthony was carting luggage back to the car while I sat on the bed. He'd left the phone at the bed's foot like he knew I was going to ask to use it. It was 8:00 a.m. My sister and her kids would normally be done with breakfast by now, although I couldn't say how normal anything was, given the situation.

Libby's phone number was one of the few I had memorized. She answered on the third ring.

"Hello?"

"Hey, Lib."

"Penny! Where the hell are you? *What is happening?*" she shouted with the exact intensity I expected. I leaned away from the phone.

"I'm okay, Libby. I wanted to call and tell you that. I'm with Anthony."

"*Anthony?!* Where did he take you? Did you know he told me *not* to call the cops?"

"Yes, and you didn't, right?"

"*Of course I did!*" she screeched. "I don't care what the hot guy next door says. If my sister goes missing, I'm calling the police!"

I smacked my hand to my forehead. "Libby! He told you not to for a reason!"

"Give me *one good reason* why I shouldn't have, Pen. *One!*"

"I—" I started and stopped, not sure how to answer. Of course Anthony wasn't the bad guy she thought he was, but I wasn't sure how much of the truth I could explain.

Libby took advantage of my silence. "Warner knows you're gone and *he* had something to do with it."

"You went straight to Warner?"

"Of course! Who else would I call?"

I groaned, thinking of what Anthony said about Warner wanting to arrest him. My sister had only stoked the fire, and I needed to clear things up. "Lib, I need his number so I can call him and tell him I'm not missing."

"But you *are* missing! I certainly don't know where you are. Where are you even calling from?"

"*Libby,* please just give me Warner's number."

The sound of her fading grumble said she'd pulled her phone away. I reached for the pen and notepad sitting on the nightstand, ready to write it down.

"Here it is," she said, and recited it. I quickly wrote it down.

"Thank you. Anthony told me you called Mom. Is she there with you?"

"*Yes,* she's here. And I swear, if you don't come back home and save me from her, I'm going to kill you myself."

A laugh accidentally popped from my lips. I could picture her yanking on her hair and pacing around her kitchen in leggings and socks.

"Are you *laughing* right now?"

"Of course not. Try to calm down, Lib. I'll be home soon. And don't kill Mom."

"Penny! This is not the kind of adventure I meant when I said you needed more adventure! Where are you? Can you at least tell me that? We are worried sick."

Guilt flooded through me. I didn't know how much I could say. Telling her where I was might make her come look for me—which would have been a challenge anyway, since I didn't even know.

I picked at a thread on the duvet. "Right now, I'm in a motel room, but we're about to get back on the road."

"*On the road?* What, are you guys like road tripping?"

"Something like that."

"To where?"

I laughed again. Darkly this time. "I wish I could tell you."

She grew silent in one of her judgmental pauses that spoke volumes.

"Don't worry, Lib. Things will be fine," I said, trying to believe it myself.

She sighed. "I want you to be safe, Pen. And to come home."

"I am safe."

"Are you?"

"Yes. Anthony is with me."

He walked back in the door again right as I said it and lifted his head at the sound of his name. His eyes warmed.

"Do you trust him?" Libby asked.

I watched him hoist the duffel bag over his shoulder. He'd found a T-shirt in the suitcase, and it clung to him in all the right places. He gave me a small grin and headed back out the door. If I was going to call Warner, I needed to do it out of Anthony's earshot.

"Yes," I told Libby. "I have to go."

"Okay, but, Penny—"

I jammed my finger into the button to end the call before she could finish. Then I immediately punched Warner's number into the keypad.

This early on a Wednesday morning, I imagined him sitting at his desk in the middle of the police station.

"Detective Warner," he answered.

"Hi, Detective Warner. It's Penny. Collins."

A pause passed and his voice took on a concerned edge. "Hi, Penny. What can I help you with?"

I stood from the bed to peek out the door and make sure Anthony was still busy with the car. My words came out in a rush. "Listen, I know my sister told you I'm missing, but I'm not. I mean, I *was* kidnapped, but I escaped—and Anthony had nothing to do with it. Well, other than when he came to save me."

Warner paused. I could hear his shock over the phone. "Penny, where are you?"

"Someplace safe, don't worry. For now, at least."

He let out a flustered breath. I imagined his dark brow folded in concern. "I don't understand. Why are you telling me this?"

"Because I wanted to call and clear up any confusion over what my sister might have told you. Anthony had nothing to do with my disappearance *or* with his uncle's murder *or* Portia Slate's bodyguard showing up in his closet."

I feared I had divulged too much, but the latter part of my sentence got his attention.

"How do you know about either of those things?"

The truth just kept coming, and I hoped I wasn't thwarting any of Anthony's plans by sharing it, but I needed Warner to know. "Because the man who kidnapped me is the same man who killed them both. He told me before I got away."

A stunned silence passed.

I peeked out the door again and saw Anthony close the trunk. I wrapped my hand over the receiver to shield my voice. "Look, Daryl, I know this all sounds unbelievable, but I swear I'm telling you the truth. Anthony is innocent. If you go to Connor Slate's house, you'll find Lou Griotti's old green Cadillac somewhere on the property—and my phone! They took that and Anthony's phone when he came to rescue me, and they moved Anthony's car. We had to flee on foot when they started shooting at us. We're still running from them. *They* are behind all of this. Connor and his henchmen."

"Penny, what are you—"

"I'm telling you, *that's* who you want for your murders. Please don't tell my sister any of this. I have to go! Bye!" I barely got the last words out before Anthony appeared in the doorway.

"How's your sister?" he asked.

I fought to control my breath and heart rate. I swiped my hair out of my face. "Not happy, but she'll live. Ready?"

He gave me a curious look before he nodded. "Yes."

We drove across the street to the diner, which seemed unnecessary, but Anthony insisted on having the car within sight and as close as possible. He filled up the tank at the gas station before we went for breakfast. We sat at a booth. I ordered a short stack of pancakes and bacon. He got a ham steak and eggs. We shared an entire pot of coffee. I'd replaced my Silver State hat and threw on the aviators from Lou's suitcase. Anthony wore a baseball cap that shielded the gash on his forehead—that was perfectly sutured with the superglue, thank you very much—and had his hair flipping out over his ears. Paired with the T-shirt and vintage jeans, he looked ready for a weekend stroll. It felt a little like we were on a date.

Minus the part with the strange man at the counter staring at us.

I took my last bite of bacon and wiped my fingers on my papery napkin. I hadn't brought up the man because I was hungry, and I didn't want Anthony to make us leave before I had breakfast. I spoke softly. "I don't mean to worry you, and don't look, but the guy at the counter has been watching us since we got here."

Anthony's eyes widened. His head turned toward the counter.

"I said *don't* look!" I hissed.

The man sat sideways on a stool as he ate, leaning his elbow on the counter, with his body open to the dining room. Aside from him, it was us, another couple a booth down, a family with kids behind Anthony, and a handful of singletons at the counter. The place was a roadside diner stereotype: red vinyl seats, checkered floor, greasy menus, absolutely delicious food.

"He was in the mini-mart last night," I whispered in case it was relevant. "He asked if we were from out of town."

Anthony's eyes widened again. "You talked to him? What did you say?"

"I said we were passing through. And you were a cop."

This time, he rolled his eyes.

"What? He's got *truck stop serial killer* written all over him. I was not about to let him think I was alone."

"Well, if you'd stayed in the car like I told you to . . ."

I dismissed him with a wave of my fork and then stabbed my last bite of pancake. "I'm sure it's only a coincidence. He's not *watching* us. He's probably just curious about our weird clothes."

"I look normal today," he counterargued.

The undeniable fact squeezed my full belly with nerves.

Anthony drummed his fingers on the table. He pulled out his wallet to drop down cash to cover the bill, plus a generous tip. "I'm going to go to the bathroom. Stay here and check if he watches me go."

"What? Don't leave me here alone!"

"It's just a test. I'll be right back." He shoved out of the booth, and when he stood to straighten his shirt, I caught a glimpse of the gun tucked into his waistband. The bathrooms were on the far end of the diner, back by the entrance and in the direction I'd been facing the whole time. I watched him go with a knot in my throat. As he passed, the man at the counter pivoted to sit straight on, and then turned his head to watch him walk the length of the room.

Great. If I had any doubt he'd been watching us, it was gone now, and then only further erased when he *got up and followed him* into the bathroom.

"Shit," I hissed. I tried and instantly failed to convince myself it was all a coincidence. We were being watched, if not followed. And now the man with dusty boots and bloody knuckles had gone into the bathroom with Anthony.

"Shit. Shit. Shit."

The little boy at the next booth heard me and curiously tilted his head. He had a milk mustache and syrup-coated sausage fisted in his sticky hand. My heart suddenly ached for Max and a day at home with my family.

But no. I was in a roadside diner in the middle of nowhere with no one to call for help, and my fake boyfriend—who wasn't really fake anymore—had been stalked into an enclosed space with a menacing stranger.

In a snap decision, I reached for the steak knife they'd given him for his ham and tucked it up my sleeve. The icy blade pressed along my wrist, and I gripped the wooden handle. My heart beat in my throat and my eyes glued to the corner where the bathrooms were. If he wasn't out in ten seconds, I was going to go check on him.

Ten.

The little boy at the next booth took another bite of his sausage link.

Nine.

His mother noticed how sticky his hands were and intervened with a napkin.

Eight.

The waitress behind the counter let out a bark of a laugh at something a man sitting there said.

Seven.

A trio of new customers entered the front doors.

Six.

Someone in the kitchen *dinged* the bell for order up.

Five.

I poked the knife's tip into my arm and couldn't stand waiting anymore.

I slid out of the booth and walked with my head down to the bathrooms. No one really looked up, but they had no reason to. They were none the wiser I had a steak knife up my sleeve and was potentially walking headfirst into danger. My heart was absolutely pounding. I'd begun to sweat. The blue button-down I'd tied at my waist clung to me like polyester plastic wrap.

In the small hall outside the bathrooms, I paused for a breath. Both the women's and men's doors remained shut, hanging still on their hinges. I strained to hear anything to tip me off there was more than normal bathroom activity going on behind the men's grubby door, but the nearby kitchen was too loud: the cooks chatting, a radio bleating tinny music, the slap and hiss of food being prepared.

I waited the final four seconds of my countdown and turned the knife blade-out in my hand. I held my other hand out to push open the door, shaking all over at what I might find on the other side, when I heard a gunshot.

I froze. My blood turned to ice. My body refused to move. I stood there like a stone statue as people out in the dining room screamed and I feared the absolute worst. The entire universe narrowed to a single point. The moment lasted an eternity.

And then the door swung open, and Anthony came barreling out. He grabbed my outstretched hand like I'd been reaching for him and pivoted me in the other direction in one swift move. Before I could take a breath, he was dragging me toward the exit at a full run.

The diner had erupted in chaos. The cooks were shouting; the waitress was screaming; the customers were ducking in their booths.

"Did you shoot him?!" I heard myself scream.

"Only in the leg. We've gotta go!" Anthony said, and yanked me back into the hot morning sun.

"Oh, my God!"

Thanks to his preparedness, the car was parked right outside the door.

"Get in!" he commanded, and let go of my hand.

I sprinted for the passenger side, still trembling and my ears ringing, when sight of a black pickup truck caught my eye.

"Penny! What the hell are you doing?!" Anthony shouted when I ran off in that direction.

Without answering, I dashed to the truck and plunged the

steak knife still in my hand deep into the front tire. It exhaled an angry hiss, and the truck sagged. I left it embedded there and ran back to our car.

"Now he can't follow us!" I wailed, and wrenched open my door.

"Why do you have a knife?!"

"Because I was coming to save you!" I threw myself onto the front seat.

"How do you know that's his car?" Anthony said as he cranked the ignition. People were starting to pour out of the diner.

"I saw him getting gas last night. Now go!" I slammed my door and smacked the dash.

He hit the gas, throwing us in reverse at first, and then left a plume of smoke behind us as we peeled out onto the road. I twisted in my seat to look out the back window. A cook had run out into the parking lot and was waving a rag at us. Half the customers were probably on their phones dialing 911 already. Anthony put the muscle car's full muscle to use and sped us away from the scene with a thunderous roar.

When I caught my breath, I looked over at him to see a bright red ring around his neck.

"Oh, my God. Are you okay?" I reached for him, and he flinched.

"I'm fine. He got an arm around me for a second."

The furious shade of scarlet coloring his skin and the dappling of bruises on his collarbone suggested it was more than a second.

"Who *was* that guy?"

"Someone working for Connor."

I looked out the back window again and didn't see anyone chasing us. Not yet at least. "How did he find us?"

"I told you: limitless resources."

I sighed and squeezed my fists with worry. "Well, that bodes well. Where are we heading now?"

He stared out the windshield, eyes focused and both hands gripping the wheel as we tore down the road at near ninety miles an hour. The blip of a town was already in the dust behind us. His words came out with a grit that put a dazzling shiver in my blood.

"To put an end to this."

CHAPTER 12

We drove for four more hours. The scenery didn't vary much: endlessly straight roads bending with the horizon, flat plains with scrubby little bushes, rolling hills, the occasional mountain range popping up and disappearing. Anthony's eyes darted to the rearview mirror like a Ping-Pong match between it and the windshield. Every once in a while, a car would hug our bumper, and my heart would vault up into my throat. Anthony's knuckles would turn white on the steering wheel, and then the car would whiz around us to pass on the two-lane highway.

If we were still being followed, no one had caught up yet.

Shortly after the sun had crested the sky's midpoint and begun its slow descent into another blazing summer afternoon, we pulled off into a town bigger than our previous stop, but still small enough to count as the middle of nowhere.

"Dare I ask where we are?" I said. I shifted and felt my blood recirculate after becoming one with the vibrations of the road for so long.

"Elvin, Nevada," Anthony answered.

I looked out the window at the passing scenery. Old trains, squared-off brick buildings, a small casino. It had all the markings of an old foothill mining town. "Is this our final destination or another pit stop?"

"Semi-final. We're not staying here, but this is where Portia is."

The announcement made me tingle all over. *Finally.* "And what's the plan, once we get to her?"

He shot me a glance, which I did not like the weight or silence of.

"You *do* have a plan, right?"

He stroked his jaw and did not answer.

"Anthony! We came all this way, and you don't have a plan for what's next?!"

"I'm working on it! I told you, it's complicated."

I grumbled and sat back in my seat, wondering if I'd ever see my apartment again. "I'm never going to make tenure."

He reached over and squeezed my hand. "Yes, you will. I promise. I'm going to make this right."

We rolled down a central street, which landed somewhere between *quaint* and *dismal.* Half the storefronts were abandoned, and the other half looked stuck several decades in the past. "Why this place?" I asked.

"Could you find it on a map?" he said.

I watched another block pass, this one entirely occupied by a rectangular park shaded in leafy green trees. An old man sat on a bench; a middle-aged woman walked a dog. Even from inside the car, I felt the town's insularity. No one came to live here because they wanted to; anyone here had been here all along.

"Probably not."

"Exactly. Plus, there's an airport." He pointed off to the north where I saw a landing strip and row of tiny propeller planes. The little municipal airport lacked soaring air traffic control towers, the staple of international hubs, but it could get the job done for a private jet.

"I'm guessing the Slate family jet is off the table for an evacuation?" I said, remembering what he'd said about putting Portia on a plane to disappear.

"Unfortunately."

"So, what are we going to do, then? Dig our way out in one of these old mine shafts?"

"Let's hope not."

He pulled onto a street with cracked pavement and side-walks bumpy from trees doing their best to provide shade from the relentless sun. The modest houses sat far apart and had patchy lawns and sun-bleached cars in the driveways. We drove to the dead end of the street and turned into the carport of a brick house, with plain white shutters and a rosebush out front. A generic silver sedan, with a Nevada plate, sat parked in front of us.

"We're here," Anthony said, as if it wasn't obvious. A nervous energy suddenly hung over him. He seemed to be in a hurry.

I climbed out of the car and followed him to the house's side door, which entered from the carport. He knocked twice, and we waited.

I was buzzing with tension too, feeling like I stood on the precipice of something huge. All this time, all this way. What we'd come for waited on the other side of the door.

"Who the fuck is it?" a deep, imposing voice said.

If I'd expected Portia to throw open the door and greet us with a welcoming smile, I quickly adjusted. Of course she wasn't here alone. I imagined whoever was on the other side holding a gun, similar to the one still tucked into Anthony's waistband, maybe an even bigger one.

"It's me," Anthony said.

"Me who?"

"Gio, come on. It's Anthony. Open up."

"Nope. Not a chance until I'm sure."

"You can be sure, I promise."

"Nice try, pal. Tell me something only Anthony Pierce would know."

Anthony sighed. "Fine. Your name is Sergio William Bryant. Your mom is Dominican; your dad is from Texas. You served ten years in the Marines. You talk a lot of shit, but you're allergic to cats and cry at Disney movies."

A pause passed before the sound of several locks being unlocked clattered against the door: chains, latches, and finally a dead bolt. The door swung open, and one of the largest men I'd ever seen filled it like a tree trunk holding a gun. His full lips split into a grin.

"About time you showed up."

Anthony grinned back and stepped inside. I followed into the small entryway, and before any of us could say another word, a blond woman shoved forward and threw herself at Anthony.

"Tony!" she cried, and latched on to his middle.

My friends call me Tony. His words from that night in his kitchen came back to me as I watched them embrace. It was completely familial. I felt my eyes mist over as Portia wiped at her own eyes and leaned back to look at him.

"Ouch! Careful," he said with a grimace. "My ribs are broken."

"Your ribs are broken? *Oh, my God,* and your face! What happened?" She clucked at him like a little mother hen, pinching him and gasping every time she noticed a new injury. "Did Connor do this to you?"

"No. I actually haven't had the pleasure of running into him during all this, but I'm fine."

"You're not *fine.* You need—"

"Portia, I'm fine." He took her hands in his to stop their fluttering exploration of his wounds. He gave her a soft smile.

She tsked again and wiped another tear. "I'm so glad to see you." She went in for another hug, but stopped halfway. "Oh, sorry. I won't do that again."

"It's okay." He turned toward me with a hand out. "This is Penny. She—"

Portia gasped again and launched herself at me. I wondered if she was a naturally affectionate person or perhaps simply craving physical contact after having been locked up so long. "Tony's girlfriend! I'm *so* happy to meet you." She squeezed me with surprising strength.

"Oh, I'm not his—" I cut myself off, instead of correcting the mistake that set this whole journey in motion. I wasn't so sure it was a mistake anymore, and the affection flowing from Portia, her pure joy at meeting who she thought was her friend's significant other, felt like a ray of sunshine. "Yeah," I said. "I'm Penny."

She gave me a final squeeze and let go to wipe her eyes again. "We've been watching the news, and I saw you together, and—wait." She tilted her head, looking closely at me, as if for the first time. "I know you."

I nodded, still trying to gather my bearings that Portia Slate was standing right in front of me. Not only because the whole world was looking for her, but also because she was Portia Slate, wife of famed billionaire and socialite darling. "Yes. We met at the university where I teach last year. You came when—"

"When we donated the computer lab. Yes! I remember. How did you meet Tony?" Her face folded into confusion as she glanced over at him.

He did one of his signature hair swipes and quietly laughed. "That's a bit of a story."

"Well, I would *love* to hear it. I am starved for company. No offense, Gio." She threw a smile at the man who'd crossed over to the living-room windows to peek out into the street. He still held his gun at his hip.

"None taken. I can only lose so many poker hands. I'll take a fresh sparring partner. Don't trust this girl; she's a hustler."

She playfully poked her tongue out at him.

Gio let the curtain fall and stalked back over to us. The floor shook with each step. I noted the tattoos curling the dark skin on his arms, which were thicker than my legs. "Were you followed?"

Anthony rubbed a hand on the back of his neck. It was starting to bruise from the diner bathroom incident. "We ran into some trouble at our last stop, but haven't seen anything for a few hundred miles now."

Gio nodded. "Good. But we gotta move soon, Tony." He nodded over at Portia. "Pretty, famous girl in this town is going to stick out like a sore damn thumb if we stay much longer. People are starting to notice."

Portia twisted around to face Anthony and pressed her hands together in an apologetic pose. Guilt was written all over her face. "I'm staying hidden, I promise. It's been so long, and I needed some fresh air the other day. It was only a short walk. No one saw me, I swear."

Anthony's jaw twitched. "You went outside?"

"For, like, five minutes."

"Portia!"

"I know! I'm sorry. I'm going stir-crazy in here. I was only supposed to be here for a day, and it's been *twelve.* I don't have my phone; Gio lets me use his, but only to check the news. We've watched all the movies and played all the board games. The daytime TV is turning my brain into mush. I—"

"Okay!" Anthony said, holding up his hands. "I get it. It's time to move."

Portia exhaled an enormous breath, relieved. I noticed then she wasn't wearing what she'd gone missing in: leggings and a fleece. Obviously, the blue running shoes had been a decoy. She wore jeans and a silky blouse, with a pair of slip-ons. One of those carelessly casual celebrity outfits that probably cost a thousand dollars. It struck me that if she'd planned to disappear for good, she probably had supplies lined up to take with her.

I was still wearing a men's polyester shirt, likely older than me, and the same underwear I'd had on since the funeral.

"Um, Portia," I said shyly, unable to believe I had the nerve to even ask. "Do you have any extra clothes I could change into?"

She turned to me and took in my appearance. A little gasp snuck between her lips as pity folded her brow. "Of course. Come with me." She grabbed my arm and pulled me toward the hall, excited like friends going to play makeover at a slumber party. I willingly followed and wondered if anyone would ever believe that Portia Slate let me borrow her clothes.

Down the short hall, we passed a bathroom and another bedroom while she led me to the main bedroom. The house lacked any kind of personality. It wasn't decorated beyond the necessities, and I wondered how many times it had been used as a hideout and for whom.

"Gio gave me this room because he thought I'd be more comfortable," she said, and led me into a room about the size of my bedroom in my apartment. A queen-sized bed, with a fluffy white comforter, took up most of it. A small dresser had a few books stacked on top of it, and a nightstand held a lamp. Two suitcases sat propped in the corner. A door opposite the closet opened to a bathroom. "We had clothes sent here to get my new life set up, once I was gone, but I unpacked when it seemed like it was going to be a while. What do you need?" She opened the closet to show it full of clothes.

"Um. Everything," I said with a deep flush.

"Got it." She nodded and went to the dresser. "So, how exactly did you meet Tony? I know he wasn't seeing anyone in New York; he never sees anyone. And he's only been in California for a few days."

I sat on the bed and kicked off my shoes. I began to untie the shirt knotted at my waist. "Well, turns out my sister lives next door to his uncle. I happened to be there the day of the estate sale. My sister and her kids and I were there when, um . . . your bodyguard was found."

She solemnly stared at the floor and blinked a few times. Her head tilted in question. "Are those my shoes?"

"Oh," I said with a small laugh. "Yeah. I borrowed them when we were escaping your house."

She did a cartoonish double take. "What?"

I didn't know why I was embarrassed to tell her, but I found myself blushing ten shades of scarlet. "After that photo of me and Anthony was on the news, I guess your husband thought I was his girlfriend and had me kidnapped as leverage to get information on you."

"Oh, my God." She slowly sank down on the bed beside me, her mouth hanging open in shock. "Tony didn't tell me that. I thought you were just with him."

"Like, along for the ride?"

She nodded, still looking shocked.

"No." I quietly laughed and tucked my hair back. "I just happened to be there that day. When that photo ended up on the news, my life spiraled out of control. The truth is, I'm not his girlfriend. It was all a misunderstanding. But the wrong people misunderstood, and now here we are."

She gaped at me, still managing to look beautiful with her mouth opening and closing like a fish. "Penny, I am so incredibly sorry. Did they hurt you? Are you okay?" She gave me a once-over, like she'd done to Anthony when we'd arrived, checking for injuries. She clucked her tongue at the bruise on my temple, which was clearly showing through my shoddy mini-mart makeup job. I'd avoided looking at the bruise on my arm from the chair, but I imagined it was not pretty.

"I'm a little banged up, but I'll be okay."

"This is all my fault," she said, and held her face in her hands. "It was such a bad idea. I can't believe how much it has fallen apart."

I snorted. "You sound like Anthony."

She popped up out of her hands. "What do you mean?"

"He thinks it's his fault. He said it was his idea."

Her face flattened into a frown. "He would say that. I guess it was both of us, really. I wanted a way out, and he thought he could give me one. But he's always been like that—trying to save everyone."

I thought about what he'd told me about stepping in after her brother died and how he'd implied fixing problems was part of his nature. "He told me about your brother. I'm so sorry, Portia."

She flashed her eyes with a sad smile. "Yeah. No one really knows the truth about Jake. Anthony made sure of that so I didn't have to talk about it publicly. I think part of the reason he did that was so *he* wouldn't have to talk about it either. It's the worst thing that's ever happened to both of us."

"I'm sorry," I said again, and wished I could offer something more comforting. Her pain swelled into the room like a balloon. I felt it in every inch of the space.

She sadly shook her head. "Ever since my brother died, I don't think he's ever really let himself care about anyone, except me, Lou, and his mom, but that was already hardwired so it doesn't count. He doesn't want to get hurt again, so he uses his job as an excuse not to get close to anyone."

"Well, I mean, for good reason." I held up my wrists to show off my zip tie bruises.

She gingerly touched one, with a soft cluck of her tongue. "That unbelievable asshole. *God,* I can't believe I married him." The bitterness in her voice replaced the pain from a moment before. "At least Tony was there to save you, right?"

"Yeah, but he walked straight into a trap. *I* had to do some of the saving because of it."

A quiet laugh, which sounded warm and familiar, bubbled from her mouth. "For someone who pretends to be closed off from the world, he leads with his heart an awful lot."

My face warmed again. "What do you mean?"

"I mean, it was only a trap because it worked, right? He came looking for you, so he obviously cares. And if you're still with him now, I'd imagine he gave you some speech about not letting you out of his sight—until you are safe."

My burning cheeks and tiny smile gave me away. "How do you know that?"

"Oh, because he does the same thing to me. Except he doesn't kiss me. That would be gross."

I jerked sideways, like I'd been caught doing something illegal. Embarrassment washed over me anew. "What? How did you . . . ? We didn't—"

Portia only laughed. "Oh, I *knew* it! That shy look on his face when he introduced you. He's so obvious. You both are."

I fought not to bury my face in my hands. I wanted to crawl under the bed and hide. Apparently, the chemistry between us was obvious to complete strangers, as well as lifelong friends. "I guess you could say that's what got us into this mess in the first place."

She sighed again. "What a mess, indeed. Come on. Get changed and we can have lunch." She handed me some clean underwear and a pair of socks. She left the closet open, which I took as an invitation to shop, and stepped out the door.

We wore the same size, so I could have chosen anything, but I opted for something close to my style: leggings and a T-shirt. All of it was better than a ripped dress or an old men's shirt from a literal trunk sale. The bruise inside my left arm from the chair shone a spectacular and horrifying shade of purple. I didn't want to look at it, so I found a gray hoodie. I slipped her shoes back on, now with socks, and made my way back from the room.

I found them in the kitchen, where Portia and Gio were busy prepping lunch. The small, square room was hardly big enough for two cooks, especially with one of them the size of Gio. They maneuvered around each other like cogs in a machine, clearly having practice utilizing the space. Anthony and I took two of the four chairs at the round dining table and watched.

"I made this *barbacoa* last night. You picked a good day to show up for leftovers," Gio said. He pulled a pot from under the counter and started it on the stove. Portia retrieved a plastic storage container from the fridge and handed it to him behind her back.

"Gio was a cook in the Marines," Anthony told me.

"Really?" I asked in surprise.

"Yes, ma'am," Gio said. "I know what you're thinking: a guy like me was probably rappelling cliffs and rescuing hostages."

"That, or fighting sharks barehanded," I said.

He laughed. "I had my fair share of field ops, but I was also running a kitchen and keeping dozens of men fed every day."

The pot began to sizzle on the stove when he dumped in the *barbacoa*. The tempting smell of spices and sweet sauce was already making my mouth water.

"And now you're what, a safe house landlord and personal chef?" I asked.

"I prefer private security agent," he said with a friendly smile. "And what do you do?"

"I'm a professor. How did you meet Anthony?"

He looked over his shoulder as he stirred the pot. He nodded at Anthony, prompting him to tell the story.

"Uncle Lou," Anthony said simply.

A heaviness settled over the room.

"I was really sorry I couldn't be at the funeral," Gio said.

"Me too, Tony," Portia added, and came over to squeeze his shoulder.

The air sat thick with sadness I could feel while still being on the outside of it. I was not bound in sorrow the same way the three of them were, but I ached with empathy.

"Uncle Lou would have understood," Anthony said. Then he shook his head with a breath, resetting. "Speaking of Lou, we need a plan for next steps."

"Well, given how much time has passed, and the fact Connor is aware of said plan, the original plan is shot to hell," Gio said.

"Maybe not entirely," Anthony said. "You still have your new IDs, Portia?"

"Yes. They arrived yesterday morning." She slipped out of the room and back down the hall.

"This is what was in the safe that you needed so badly?" I asked Anthony.

He nodded. "Primarily, yes. I shipped them here so she'd have them when things got complicated. I didn't want to have them on me in case we got intercepted."

Portia came back with a Swedish passport and a small square ID card. They looked as real as any official documents, and as real as the fake ones I'd seen in Lou's trunk. "So, what's the plan?" she asked.

"Well, a private flight is obviously out," Anthony bitterly said. "Connor has grounded anyone who'd be willing to fly you." He picked up the passport and flipped it over. "We could always go by car. Canada is an option, or somewhere in South America. We'd have to get a new set of these though, which will take a while. Otherwise, I have no idea how we're going to get you to Sweden, unless Gio knows someone with a boat."

"I know a couple, actually," Gio said, wearing a pair of bright red oven mitts and carrying his pot of *barbacoa* over to the table. "But unless you want to hide in a shipping crate across the Atlantic and risk someone being there waiting for you on the other side, it's not a great option. Soup's on."

"But it's not a *nonoption*," Anthony said, and reached for the tortillas Portia had set on the table.

Portia sat next to him and across from me and grabbed her own tortillas. "I know sacrificing my standard of living is all part of this deal, but a shipping crate might be where I draw the line."

"Even if it means saving your life?" Anthony asked.

She leveled him with a stare. "Tony."

"This is delicious," I said after my first bite. "Gio, you have a gift."

He turned to me with a pleased smile. "Thank you, Penny."

I chewed and thought for a moment about a possible suggestion. The situation was just another puzzle. All we had to do was assess the situation and make a plan. "What about a commercial flight?"

They collectively looked at me, and I felt like I'd been called on in class.

"What do you mean?" Anthony said.

I swallowed a succulent bite—Gio truly was talented. "I mean, why do we have to find a private pilot willing to fly when Portia has a new ID ready to go? Can't you hop on a commercial flight in disguise?"

The silence that settled over the table made me wonder if they found the suggestion foolish and were too polite to tell me, or if they really hadn't thought of it before.

"That"—Anthony said with a thoughtful tilt of his head—"is actually an interesting idea. The only reason we were going to go private originally was because it was safer. The new IDs were to set up her life, once she landed, not necessarily to *get to* her new life. But we might as well use them if we have them. A passenger on a commercial flight is going to be harder to find than booking a private one. Penny, you're brilliant." He put a hand on my arm and squeezed.

I proudly smiled and gave them the benefit of the doubt that Portia only flew private, so a commercial flight really hadn't occurred to them. "Where's the closest international airport?"

"Vegas," Gio said. "It's like a four-hour drive from here."

"Perfect."

"There's only one problem with that," Portia interjected. "Connor is never going to stop chasing *you* if I disappear." She directed her statement at Anthony, but it went without saying that I was swept up in the concern too.

Anthony cast me a look like the problem may have not been much of a problem if it were only him running forever, but because I was along for the ride, everything was different.

"Can I ask a question?" I said as I had a thought. They looked on encouragingly. "Forgive me if this is too intrusive, but, Portia, why didn't you talk to the FBI when they first came to you?"

Her jaw immediately clenched and she glanced sideways at Anthony.

I held up my hands. "Don't worry. He didn't tell me any details. I only know the FBI is interested in your husband, and they approached you about it."

Portia's face flushed. She visibly shrank as her shoulders hunched inward. She tucked her hair back, and her voice grew softer. "Well, for starters, Connor would kill me if I talked to the Feds, and second, I'm not exactly sure what I can say to them without implicating myself, given I knew what he was, um . . . doing."

The confident, polished socialite I saw online and in the news vanished right in front of me. She was the sad woman from campus, the frightened teenager Anthony had described. Simply broken.

Anthony reached out and squeezed her arm. "That's why we opted for disappearing. Seemed like the best option."

I gave Portia a gentle, sympathetic smile. "I don't blame you. I probably would have done the same. I make my living dealing with men who think they run the world. None of them are as powerful as your husband, of course, but I know what it's like to navigate egos. And I've seen plenty of men let their ego get the best of them. They don't realize this enormous, swollen opinion they hold of themselves eventually becomes a vulnerability. It's kind of ironic, really."

Anthony cast me a curious look, as if he knew my thoughts were spiraling toward a solution. "What are you suggesting, Penny?"

"I'm saying, Connor doesn't expect her to talk to the Feds, because he knows she's afraid—and he knows she hasn't talked at this point, because he would have been arrested by now." I turned my gaze to Portia and looked at her head-on, feeling a solution take shape. "He thinks he's scared you into not talking, so talk. Catch him off guard."

She paled like I'd suggested she jump into a tank of sharks. "Won't that get me in trouble too, because of what I know?"

"Not necessarily, if you do it right."

A heavy silence fell over the table. Anthony leaned back in his chair, and Gio pursed his lips with a sharp exhale through his nose. Based on their body language, I could tell they understood what I was suggesting. Portia still looked lost.

"What does that mean?" she asked with a wide blink of her eyes.

Anthony sat forward again and stroked his jaw. "She's talking about federal witness protection, Portia. You testify against your husband, give them what they want, and they'll provide you with protection." Tension splintered his voice. He scrubbed his face with a hand and sighed. I sensed he knew it was a good solution, but not one he wanted.

Gio tapped his thick fingers on the table. "The professor makes a good point, Tony."

"Yeah, I know she does," he snapped.

Portia turned to him with a hopeful look in her eyes. "Would that work, Tony?"

Anthony flinched. "What? You can't be serious, Portia. They might just arrest you too."

She swallowed hard, steeling herself. "With what I know about Connor, I think it would work, but I need to think about it."

"Think about it?" Anthony cried. "What is there to think about? You'd be signing your life away forever."

"That's what we were going to do anyway," she snapped back.

"But this will be different."

"How?"

"Because *I* won't know where you are!" he burst.

Their exchange had picked up the biting cadence of squabbling siblings. The silent pause crackled like the air between lightning strikes, and it fully settled over me that Anthony's reluctance came from the fact federal protection would mean he'd never see her again. If he had succeeded in making her disappear, he would at least have known where she was, but doing it on the record would mean Portia Slate would cease to exist completely. I almost regretted my suggestion, for the pained look on his face.

He took a heavy breath. "Portia, federal protection means you'd *really* be gone if it worked. Basically, it would be what we were going to do, but all above ground. I'm talking new life, new identity. Away from everyone . . . *including me.*" His last words came out thick and strained.

A heavy silence returned to the table. Anthony stared at his plate. Gio finished another taco. I pushed food around with my fork. Portia raked her gaze over all three of us, one at a time. I couldn't help feeling like I'd crashed a party with my suggestion.

Portia eventually pushed back from the table and stood. "I think I need a few minutes."

"Portia, wait—" Anthony tried, but she was already gone.

CHAPTER 13

Portia never returned to lunch. The rest of us finished eating in an awkward silence, until Gio declared it was time to clean up. I helped and then went to find Anthony when I couldn't locate him inside any of the house's limited square footage.

At the back of the house, a short chain-link fence outlined a modest backyard that edged up to a sweeping expanse of nothing. Beyond the patchy lawn and single shady tree was an open field of dirt and the same scrubby bushes we'd passed along the highway. It rolled out like a brown-and-green carpet, all the way to hills too far off to know if they might count as mountains.

Anthony sat in a plastic chair beneath the patio overhang; he was staring out into the abyss. I noted a few playthings in the yard, a tricycle fit for a toddler and a toy tractor, and wondered what situation would involve needing to stow a child at a safe house.

"Hey," I said by way of greeting, and sat in the chair next to him. A small glass table with an empty ashtray and a potted cactus sat between us.

"Hey," he said, sounding desolate. The air around him throbbed with pain.

"I'm sorry if federal protection was the wrong thing to suggest. I was only trying to help. I thought—"

"No, it was the right thing to suggest. I just don't want her to do it."

My heart twisted at the sorrow in his voice. He'd already lost his uncle, and now here he was facing down never seeing his lifelong friend again. One by one, the people he cared about were disappearing. I reached over the spiky, little cactus and placed my hand on his arm. "How are you doing with all this?"

He looked down at my hand, and where I thought he might shrug it off and quip about being fine, I was taken by pleasant surprise when he didn't. The hard edge in his eyes melted away to a soft vulnerability. "Not great," he said simply. "I feel like I failed."

I aimed for a casual shrug. "I wouldn't say you *failed,* necessarily. Things just didn't go the way they were planned, but you're likely still getting to the same ending, more or less."

"Yeah, and the *less* part is I'm going to lose Portia too, if she goes through with this. Both her and Uncle Lou gone in one fell swoop." He waved his hand like he was scooping up the air and throwing it aside.

I wasn't sure there were words I could say to soothe that certain ache, but I tried anyway. "Anthony, if it weren't for you, Portia might be a very different kind of *gone* at the hands of her husband already. The kind no one comes back from. So you're saving her after all. It just doesn't look the way you thought it would be."

My argument seemed to resonate with him. He gave me a reluctant nod. "I guess you're right. But I can't say the same for Uncle Lou. It's my fault he's gone."

That was, admittedly, a trickier topic to navigate. "Lou was an adult who made his own decisions. You didn't coerce him into anything, Anthony. And like you told me: He cared about Portia too. Do you think he would want this to end any other way than with her safe?"

He looked sideways at me, and the tiniest smile tugged at the corner of his mouth. "You're good at this."

"At what?"

"Pep talks."

"Is that what this is?"

"Seems like it."

"Huh. I was aiming more for comforting words for someone in need, but I guess that's essentially the same thing."

"Well, I appreciate it, whatever the intention."

We both fell quiet and gazed out at the brittle yard. The landscape was rather beautiful in a parched, barren way.

"Tell me about your uncle," I said. "What was he like? What's your favorite memory of him?"

Anthony cast me a befuddled look. "Is this part of the pep talk?"

I shrugged. "Sure. I just have a hunch you haven't gotten to talk to anyone about him in all this, and I'm here to listen. We've got nothing but time and desert views." I spread my hands at the beige canvas before us.

"All right. Uncle Lou was . . ." Anthony trailed off, pausing like he wasn't sure what to say. A sheen suddenly glossed his eyes, and I thought for a moment I'd made a mistake in asking. But then his lips twisted up into a sly smile and he took on the guise of someone in on a very good secret. "Clever. He was very, very clever. And loyal, obviously. And had an odd, dark sense of humor, but I guess that comes with the territory." He looked down at his lap and quietly laughed. The sound made my heart sing. "For example, he asked me to pick up his car once, and I kept hearing something rattling around in the trunk. I pulled over to check and it was a fake skeleton with a Happy Halloween sign tied around its neck. I nearly had a heart attack."

I gasped and threw a hand over my mouth to cover my smile. "He did *not* do that to you."

"Oh, but he did," he said, still laughing. "He told me I was too serious a lot. 'Lighten up, kid. Life's not that bad.'" He put on a husky voice with a thick New York accent.

"I agree with your uncle on this sentiment. When was the last time you took a vacation?"

He went quiet long enough to make me tsk in dismay.

"If you have to think about your answer this hard, it's been way too long."

"Does last night in that motel count?"

"Definitely not. I'm talking, toes in the sand, cocktail in a coconut, under a palm tree, turned off your phone, and probably got sunburned because you fell asleep—that type of vacation."

He shot me a grin. "Is that your ideal vacation?"

"Minus the sunburn, yes."

"Sounds nice."

"It would be. Especially if I had someone there to rub sunscreen on my back to prevent the sunburn." The words slipped out, and I realized it sounded like I was inviting him.

A vision of him lying beside me in a pair of board shorts, chest glistening with salt water or sweat or both, it didn't matter, hit me like a truck. How we got from fond family memories to beachside fantasies, I wasn't sure, but I had to blink several times and shake my head to find my way back.

Based on the look on his face, he may have been envisioning the same thing.

"Tell me more about Lou," I said for distraction, before I needed to be hosed down from getting carried away imagining a full tropical fantasy.

He sat back with a soft smile and then launched into another story.

I listened to him talk for over an hour. The anecdotes ranged from funny to frightening, from sometimes sad to heartwarming. The light in his eyes grew brighter with each one. It was the most animated I'd ever seen him, and the warmth in my chest expanded at a startling rate. Clearly, he was very fond of his uncle, and I was growing fonder of him by the minute.

Right as he finished a story about an A-list actress, whose reputation they'd salvaged after an unfortunate incident with an assistant involving a thrown latte, I heard the rattling of aluminum cans coming from around the side of the house. I turned to see Gio approaching with a trash bag slung over his shoulder. He'd put on sunglasses and a camo-colored hat.

"Hey, Professor. Do you know how to shoot a gun?"

"No," I said, and noticed he had one holstered at his hip.

"Do you want to learn?"

"Not particularly."

He split a grin and dropped the trash bag on the ground. "Come on, I'll show you. It might come in handy." He bent over to dig in the trash bag and pulled out several empty beer cans.

"I appreciate the offer, but I generally strive to avoid situations with firearms."

"Sure. We all do. But you never know. It's best to be prepared. Stay here." He trotted off toward the fence, which was a good thirty yards away. I watched, knowing where this was going, as he carefully balanced five beer cans on top of it, and I thought about how I couldn't hit a single one of them with a cannon, let alone a handgun.

Gio came trotting back; there was a smile on his face. "Basic target practice." He pulled the gun from his hip. "Now, your stance is more important than you think. This isn't like the movies where you can do stuff one-handed and hanging out of a car."

"I guess I missed the part where I agreed to this lesson," I said flatly.

My sour mood did not deter him. He waved me over. "Come here. I'll show you proper technique."

I cast Anthony a look, and he responded with an encouraging shrug. "Badass, remember?"

I shyly blushed and stood from my chair. "If we must."

"We must," Gio said. "Now . . . feet like this, arms like this." He demonstrated and aimed the gun at the cans when I walked over. "You want to be locked, but relaxed enough to absorb the kickback." He pulled the trigger, and one of the cans leapt off the fence and split into a crumple of jagged aluminum.

I flinched at the deafening sound and listened to it flood out into the empty field in search of something to echo off.

"Just like that," Gio said. "Your turn." He held the gun in one hand and pivoted to me with his other arm open in a welcoming gesture.

"You're the same as Anthony, assuming I can simply *do* things like you can. I work at a desk all day; I don't climb walls and shoot things."

"Never underestimate yourself. Come on." He swung his arm around me and put the gun in my hand. Then he kicked my feet farther apart with his toe. "Little bend in the knees, shoulders square, hands like this. You got it! Now take a breath and—"

I mentally muttered the word *badass* as I pulled the trigger and automatically closed my eyes. I didn't hear the *plink* of a beer can being obliterated—only the *bang* of the gun and its vibrations rattling every bone and nerve in my body.

"Not bad!" Gio encouraged. "You might have better luck if you keep your eyes open though. Try it again."

I shook the sting from my arms and aimed again. The second shot skipped off the dirt past the fence.

"Better," Gio said. "Try lowering your arms a little." He reached over and gently bent my elbows and used his hand to aim the gun half a tick down. He was remarkably calm and confident, considering we were handling a deadly weapon. My heart was hammering. "Don't forget to breathe."

I took a breath and mentally ran through his list. Feet like this, arms like this, eyes open, breathe.

The third shot hit a can—not the one I was aiming for, but still—and I gasped in surprise.

"There you go!" Gio said, and clapped.

"Nice shot, Penny!" Anthony called from behind me.

I turned my head to see a small grin playing at his lips. It did feel like an accomplishment, though not one I was terribly proud of. I weakly smiled back at him.

We kept shooting, until Gio had to reload the gun several times, and a small graveyard of beer cans littered the fence line. I didn't feel cool and powerful, a sexy gunslinger. I was trembling the whole time and hated every second of it. But I did feel more confident. If things ever went sideways and I needed to shoot something, I would at least know how to.

"Not bad," Anthony said to me once the gun was safely out of my hands. His eyes softly crinkled at the corners. The day had moved into early evening. The soaring sky was a dusty shade of blue above us. Shadows ran long.

"Thank you, though I hope I never need to be even remotely adequate at that skill."

"Too bad, Professor, because you're already there," Gio said as he gathered the trash bag. His eyes snagged on something at the corner of the house, and we all turned to see Portia, who had emerged from inside.

Anthony immediately stiffened at my side. Even from a distance, I could see the decisive look on her face. Something had shifted over the past few hours.

She casually approached with her hands in her pockets and scuffed her shoe at the dirt. "I've made a decision."

"Portia, no—" Anthony started, but she stopped him with a raised hand.

"I want to, Tony. It's the only way out. For all of us."

"But what if it doesn't work? What if they arrest you too?"

She nodded and swallowed, steeling herself. "That's a risk, yes, but I'm willing to take it. Because what's the alternative? We figure out how to get me to Sweden and I look over my shoulder for the rest of my life? And you do too?" Her voice strained with fear. She took a calming breath and came closer. "Look, this plan was always a moonshot. Getting away from Connor on our terms was a one-in-a-million chance. We tried, okay? But it's time to stop. I don't want to keep making it worse. I mean, look at you, all bruised and broken." She turned to gesture at me. "And poor Penny was kidnapped. And Gio has been stuck in this house for days, playing Texas Hold'em for Monopoly money with me!" Gio shrugged, like it was no bother. She turned back to Anthony with a pleading look. "Please, Tony. It's time to put an end to this."

He looked at her with a sheen glossing his eyes. His throat bobbed with a thick swallow. I felt like I was intruding on a private moment. "But, Portia, I promised Jake I'd watch out for you."

"I know you did, Tony. And you have. My whole life. For once, let me protect *you*."

Anthony held his face in his hands with a sigh. I thought he was going to flat-out refuse, and we'd be stuck as fugitives forever, but he didn't. Not yet at least. "How would this even work? Do you have someone at the FBI to contact?"

My heart lifted. For the first time since getting knocked out in Lou's back office, going home felt like a real possibility and not a distant hope.

Portia nodded. "Yes. The agent who came to the hotel that night in New York. Agent Ives. He gave me a card, and I kept it before Connor showed up and . . ." Her voice trailed off.

I noticed Anthony's fist clench. Neither of them wanted to relive it.

"Okay," he said. "So—hypothetically, if we're even going to do this—we call Ives and tell him you're ready to talk. We'd need to meet him somewhere so he can take you into protective custody, and we can't do it here. I don't want this place on anyone's radar."

"Well, I can't go back home," Portia said. "Everyone is looking for me there."

"Everyone is looking for you *everywhere,* Portia," Anthony said. "We need someplace off the grid."

We all silently stared at one another, as if one of us might have a list of obscure but convenient locations for clandestine meetups. I was honestly a little surprised Anthony didn't.

"What about the opposite?" Gio suggested. "Kind of a hiding-in-plain-sight situation."

I thought back to what Gio had said about Portia getting recognized in the small town where she'd been hiding out. Perhaps a place with too many faces to keep track of was the way to go. "You know, that's not a bad idea. A crowd could be helpful here. Good suggestion, Gio."

"Thank you, Professor. And also, I assume we want this to happen quick, and this Fed is going to have to fly in if he's in New York. If we're in the middle of nowhere, how's he going to get to us easily? And more important, how's he going to get Portia *out* easily, assuming it all goes well?"

"Another solid point," I said.

We all looked at Anthony, since he was the most likely to dissent.

"What do you think, Tony?" Portia eventually asked.

Anthony studied the desert view before looking at Portia. A silent conversation passed between them, and then he turned his gaze over to me. We had our own tête-à-tête, which managed to encompass everything from arguing over candlesticks to hiding in a closet, from escaping a basement to kissing in a roadside motel, from fleeing an attacker to standing here, staring at each other with our future—in many senses—hanging in the balance.

He looked back to Portia. "Are you sure you want to do this? It can't be undone, and it might not even work the way we're hoping. You could end up in prison."

She reached out and squeezed his hand. Her eyes had glossed with moisture, and she nodded. "Nothing could be worse than the prison of being with Connor. Let me set us all free, whatever it takes."

Anthony held her gaze for a long moment before letting out a big breath. "Okay."

Portia sagged with an exhale, and I felt it in my bones.

Gio clapped his hands together with a grin.

"Why are you smiling?" Anthony asked.

"Isn't it obvious? There's only one place nearby that fits all our criteria." He looked at us expectantly.

I knew the answer, but didn't want to steal his thunder.

"It all ends in Vegas, baby."

We discussed the rest of the plan while we had dinner. Anthony knew a guy—of course he did—who could get us a suite at the Venetian for free. Apparently, Lou had cleaned up a particularly messy weekend in Vegas on this guy's behalf, so in return, he had a standing reservation at one of the glittering towers on the Strip. We counted the win because it saved us from leaving a paper trail with our names or any form of payment. Anthony also called Mr. Mitchell, the lawyer who'd been there the day of the estate sale. If things went south with Portia's confession and they wanted to arrest her, we needed someone on standby to help.

Portia had kept the card from Agent Ives. She called him and told him she was ready to talk and she'd meet him tomorrow in that suite at the Venetian. He confirmed he'd be there by 5:00 p.m.

It felt remarkably simple, but federal agents apparently made quick accommodations when a witness was ready to talk.

Later that night, Portia and I split her bed and Anthony took the couch. It was the only option, seeing there was no way Anthony and Gio could share a bed unless they spooned all night, and the couch wasn't exactly big enough for two people either.

I lay on my side, facing away from her, and thought about what was going to happen tomorrow. I didn't have much part to play, other than passenger. Anthony wanted to stick around long enough to make sure Portia was safe and, hopefully, not under arrest, and then we were headed home. Gio was tagging along to Las Vegas as an extra escort. Even so, the thought of it had my nerves jumping.

"Penny," Portia whispered in the dark. "Are you awake?"

"Yes," I said quietly. Apparently, I wasn't the only one unable to sleep.

"I want to say thank you. For helping us come up with a plan. If you hadn't said what you said, I don't think I would have had the courage to stand up to my husband."

I rolled over onto my back to face the ceiling. I didn't think I'd said that much, but my words apparently resonated. "You're welcome."

"You're right. I've spent so long afraid of him that he won't see this coming." She paused for a long moment. "And I don't want you to think I'm a bad person. For not turning him in sooner. It's just . . . I couldn't."

I blinked in the dark, unsure what to say. The situation was surely complicated, and seeing she feared for her life, I wasn't about to blame her for keeping her mouth shut for her own safety. But still, a niggling curiosity, like an itch in need of scratching, squirmed inside my brain. Connor Slate was a kingpin of my industry, and here I was whispering secrets in the dark with his wife.

Temptation got the best of me. I sat up and turned on the bedside lamp.

"How long have you known?"

She rolled over to face me. "Years," she said with an exhale, which sounded miles deep. And then a dam broke loose. "*I never did anything illegal, unless you count knowingly spending money that had been embezzled. But I couldn't even find out if that was a crime, because Connor would know I asked someone for legal advice. Everyone is in his pocket. He's been siphoning from his own company for years. You know how I found out? After one of those foundation events I was forced to attend, like the one where you and I met. I'd hosted a group of twenty for a private luncheon in the city, and the foundation's credit card got declined when I went to pay.*"

I could see the haunted look in her eyes. Surely, someone in her tax bracket would find a declined credit card distressing, but her face said the embarrassing inconvenience was only the tip of a very large iceberg. "Obviously, I was mortified and didn't want to make a scene, so I used a personal card to pay for lunch. Knowing Connor would get an alert, since he monitors all my personal spending, I texted him a heads-up the corporate card got declined. He never responded. That night when I brought it up, he told me he must have forgotten to pay that bill and said not to worry about it." She blinked a few times and held my gaze with a gritty stare. "Connor doesn't forget anything, Penny. And we have accountants, who handle our money anyway. I knew something was off, and after some very careful digging, and because I honestly didn't want to be embarrassed by having the card declined again, I discovered the foundation account used to pay that card's bill was empty. All the money had been moved and redistributed into our personal accounts. And it wasn't just the foundation—other corporate accounts I have access to had been skimmed."

When she stopped talking, I noticed I'd stopped breathing. "What did you do?" I whispered.

"Nothing," she said with a single shake of her head. "I couldn't confront him about it because he would deny it and then punish me for even questioning him." Her words were matter of fact, but I heard the tremor in them. The fear she worked so hard to mask and the sting of memory from times she'd crossed her husband's lines. "So I pretended I didn't know. The guilt ate me up inside, but I had to keep up appearances. I couldn't stop spending money like normal because he would wonder why. But I wasn't the only one who noticed something was off. The FBI started coming around, and when they cornered me that night in New York after that deal went bust, I was terrified, but part of me thought, '*Finally* a way out.' I honestly think I might have confessed everything if Connor hadn't come home. What a difference five more minutes would have made." She paused and took a deep breath. "And now here we are instead."

Here we are, indeed, I thought. My curiosity over the *what* and *how* was satisfied. I partly wished I'd never asked. Anthony had told me Connor was committing large-scale fraud and left it at that. Portia hadn't gone into too much more detail, but I knew a secret about one of the most powerful—and apparently dangerous—men in the world. A secret he was willing to kill over.

"How do you think he found out you were trying to leave?" I asked.

She sighed a weary breath. "I think he figured it out through Tyler, my bodyguard. When we told him the plan, he swore to me he'd help me finally find a way out. He'd always done as much as he could to protect me from Connor, but knew it was never enough. I think Connor got to him about the plan, and he refused to talk, so they killed him. Tony isn't convinced, but I know he'd never betray me like that. I trusted him."

I mulled her words and thought back to the conversation Anthony and I had had in the car. Portia and I were on the same page about Tyler's loyalty, but I wondered if we'd ever know the truth.

I pulled the sheet up tighter around me. "I'm sorry he's gone."

"Thanks. Me too," she said solemnly. She paused, and I listened to the sounds of the quiet house. Gio snored from the next room over. I imagined Anthony out on the couch, sleeping with a gun.

"I'm really sorry you got dragged into this, Penny," Portia broke the silence. "But I'm glad—" She stopped short and took a breath. It sounded like she was trying to ward off tears. "I'm really glad Tony met you." The sheets rustled as she moved. "He's been trying to save me my whole life. I know this isn't what we were planning, and I'm going to miss him terribly if this all goes well, but this is the only way to save us all."

The sudden emotion in her voice caught me. "Are you scared?"

She blinked, and I saw the whites of her eyes shining. The look of determination on her face said she'd thought through all the consequences of her decision. "Yes and no. I mean, I'd rather not end up in prison, but assuming things go well, and I don't end up there, I'm not scared. I've reinvented myself out of necessity before; I can do it again." Her mouth twitched up at one corner. "I'm sad I wouldn't get to see Tony anymore though. But I'm glad he has you now. Well, that's awfully presumptuous of me; you've only just met. But still. I'm glad." She shyly blushed and smoothed her hair.

I found it oddly satisfying to have her blessing. It was true I'd only just met Anthony, but it was also true Portia was one of the most important people—one of the only people—in his life. And like the rest of them, she was about to disappear, one way or another. Knowing she was happy for him before she went made me smile.

"I'm glad too."

She wiped her eyes with an inelegant sniffle, which made her seem impossibly human. "If this works, just don't let him come looking for me, okay? That will ruin everything."

I quietly laughed. "I'll do my best, but no promises. And I'm really sorry, Portia. That it has come to this." I couldn't imagine being in a situation so dire that going to prison or completely disappearing was plan A.

She softly shook her head, rustling her hair against her pillow. "I can't change the decisions that got me here. All I can do is move forward. I want my freedom back, if I can have it. You know what freedom feels like to me?"

"What?"

"A sunny day at the beach. The wind in my hair, sand under my toes. Nothing but the water in front of me, endless. And no one watching me. When I can have a sunny day at the beach again, free and all to myself, I'll know I'm okay."

I softly smiled to myself and wondered if we'd ever cross paths on a beach someday. "That sounds nice."

"It will be." She adjusted her pillow with a sigh. "And I want you to know that no matter what happens tomorrow, everything will be all right. Good night, Penny."

"Good night, Portia." I clicked off the light and plunged us back into darkness. The soft sound of her voice carried both a resolve and an optimism that helped me close my eyes and fall asleep.

CHAPTER 14

We woke early the next morning. Gio cooked breakfast while the rest of us packed up. I wondered if Gio would return to the house or if there was a between-clients safe house cleaning crew who came through and turned it over for the next guests. Since I was already comfortable with him, especially after our shooting lesson, and because I assumed Anthony and Portia would want to spend any time together that they had left, I offered to ride with Gio for the trip.

Anthony held me back in the driveway before we climbed into the cars. "Penny, I just want to say thank you for yesterday. For asking me about Uncle Lou." He looked at me, and his eyes dazzled a deep honey brown in the morning light. "That was very kind of you."

I gave him a gentle return smile. "Sure."

He swiped a hand through his hair. We'd ventured into feelings territory, and it had us both nervous. "So I can't promise a tropical vacation quite yet, but when this all works out, can I maybe take you on a date?"

I couldn't fight the flush that ignited in my cheeks. I took a step closer to him. "I admire your optimism that this is all going to work out."

He quietly laughed at my callback to our night on the road.

"Uh, it *better* work out, because I know a professor who has to make tenure by the end of summer."

"Too bad taking down a megalomaniac billionaire and setting his wife free won't count toward my case."

"You should talk to your committee about that."

"They'd be pretty hard to sway."

His playful smile faltered at the corners. He wrapped an arm around my back and his voice grew serious. "Penny, I'm really sorry about dragging you into all of this."

I exhaled a long, tired breath. "I mean, it's collectively the most terrifying thing that's ever happened to me, but if I hadn't tried to buy those candlesticks, I never would have met you, so it's not all bad news."

He impishly grimaced and brought his face closer to mine. "Just mostly bad news."

"Meh. The good might outweigh the bad." I hungrily outlined his lips with my eyes.

"You are giving me entirely too much credit."

"Have you *seen* yourself in a hideous grandpa shirt from a trunk suitcase?"

"Stop. You'll inflate my ego."

"I don't think it can get any bigger," I countered.

"There's always room."

"Are you going to kiss me anytime soon?"

"Is that what you're waiting for?" he asked, his interest obvious.

"That, or for you to run out of quips."

"I've got endless quips. Countless quips. Limitless quips—"

I pushed up on my toes and kissed him. He tightened his arm around my back, and I felt his smile against my lips. It was the first time we'd kissed standing up, and having to reach for it somehow made it all the sexier. He leaned into it hungrily, and I welcomed him. His tongue swept over mine, and I reached up to fist my hand in his hair. It was silky and thick, and tugging on it coaxed a little moan out of him. The sound made me want to climb him like a tree.

I held back, only because his ribs were still broken.

We kissed under the soaring Nevada sky, with the thrilling excitement of it still being one of our first, but also with an uncertain desperation, realizing it might have been one of our last.

"See you in Vegas," he said when he eventually pulled back and planted one last kiss on my temple. He climbed into the Camaro. Portia tucked into the passenger seat, and I joined Gio in the silver sedan of no remarkable make or appearance.

"This car is generic on purpose, isn't it," I said to Gio as we pulled away from the house.

"Yes, ma'am. One of the most common cars on the road, actually. Harder to spot. Not exactly as exciting as *that,* but it gets the job done." He pointed out the windshield as Anthony turned the corner in front of us.

The morning sun winked off the Camaro's glossy sheen. With Anthony in the driver's seat, wearing a pair of sunglasses, and Portia's blond hair blowing out the window, they looked like a couple of movie stars. I wondered if we'd looked that sexy fleeing across the state in the middle of the night. I somehow doubted it.

"Did you know Portia before this?" I asked.

"No, but I care about her now. Being in close quarters with someone for several days can change things."

"I'll say."

He detected the smile in my voice and glanced over at me. "Didn't exactly expect to meet Tony in all this, did you?"

"No, definitely not. I wasn't planning on meeting *anyone* anytime soon. I'm focusing on my career right now."

He sighed a dreamy sound. "Gotta love life's curveballs."

I softly smiled and felt the sun splash my face through the

window. We rolled out of the tiny town and onto the highway, where traffic was nonexistent. Compared to the rush and noise of a city, the rural emptiness held a certain shock factor—shocking in that I enjoyed it. I silently wondered what it would be like to live someplace so remote. So removed from the world's radar.

"Where's home for you, Gio?"

"Wherever it needs to be."

I turned to him in surprise. "Really?"

He nodded. "I go where the jobs take me, but I guess if I had to choose a home base, it would be where my folks are in Texas. That's where I grew up."

"Interesting." I had a vision of him as a little boy wearing a cowboy hat. "Do you have any siblings?"

"Yes, ma'am. I've got an older brother, who thinks he knows everything."

I snorted a laugh. "I have one of those, except a sister."

"Ah, I knew I sensed a kindred youngest-child spirit. My brother is a neurosurgeon, so I guess he's got a leg to stand on. He's pretty smart."

"Hmm. Do you think he can stitch me back together when my sister tries to kill me after all this?"

He chuckled a warm, jolly sound. "What does your sister do?"

"Besides try to set me up with every man under the sun? She's a stay-at-home mom."

"Ooh, a know-it-all *and* a meddler! The best kind. Does she know about Tony? Or is she going to be heartbroken when you tell her that her matchmaking skills are no longer needed?"

I shot him a glare that was halfhearted and mostly smile. "Actually, she was the one who introduced us. At the time, she didn't know about all *this*"—I gestured at the car and our general surroundings—"and I'm sure she would have had an opinion, but too late for that."

"That's right. You're in it now, baby sis. No turning back!"
He thumped his hand on the steering wheel for emphasis.

I laughed. "How long have you known Anthony?"

"Long enough to know he cares about you. *A lot.* I've never
seen him on the ground for a job. Granted, this isn't a normal
job, but the fact you're here with him says a lot."

A wave of insecurity hit me. Through all the hiding and escaping and running, I wondered if what had sprouted between
me and Anthony grew from the situation and not something
more organic. I felt oddly comfortable sharing my vulnerability
with the hulk of a man beside me, who I'd only known for a
day. "Portia said the same thing. You don't think it's a matter
of circumstance?"

"No," Gio said, shaking his head. "You're here because of a
choice. He made the choice to come save you. People don't
risk themselves for people they don't care about."

As his words landed, I realized I wasn't only trying to get
back home, but I was also helping Anthony. *Because I cared
about him.*

"You're remarkably intuitive, Gio."

"Thank you. Now, find us a good radio station. We've got a
long way to go."

We pulled into Vegas midafternoon.

Las Vegas in the daylight always felt naked to me. As if
someone had turned on all the lights inside a club, and I could
see the imperfections and blemishes: the dirty sidewalks, the
faded signs, the used-up people still awake from the night before. As a place designed around the debaucheries of nighttime, the sunshine did it no favors.

Also, it was hot as hell.

The Venetian sat at the north end of the Strip, almost like an
endcap to the main drag. A few more resorts scattered beyond

it, but most of the foot traffic of boozed-up revelers walking the Strip any given night ended their journey at the ode to Italian opulence.

We skipped the valet and navigated the maze of a parking garage. When we parked among a field of other cars, we climbed out into the musky, exhaust-tinged desert air. Portia had let me borrow an outfit a little classier than athleisure: jeans and a silk blouse. I still wore the pink running shoes. She, on the other hand, was dressed down in leggings, a hoodie, a low ponytail, and oversized sunglasses. Along with Anthony and Gio in their streetwear, we looked like any pair of couples checking into their hotel for a stay in Vegas.

Given the whole point of this trip was to meet a federal agent, Anthony felt it best to leave the bag of guns in the car. No one in Vegas was going to question a suitcase of cash, but a bag of guns was another thing altogether. We carried the green suitcase full of clothes, and Portia's two roller bags so we didn't look completely out of place showing up for a supposed stay.

A parking garage elevator delivered us to a glossy marble walkway a world away from the concrete tomb we'd left. The acrid smell of smoke already curled in from the casino floor the second we stepped inside. We found our way to the registration desk inside a towering room with marble pillars and a dizzying checkered floor. I gazed up at the gold accents and domed ceiling, feeling like I could have been in an Italian palace. It was positively buzzing with activity. Guests zipped around, dragging luggage or swinging shopping bags. Women clicked by in sharp heels and carried tiny handbags. Men hung off each other, loudly laughing and enjoying the revelry. I saw a few clusters of people in business attire, with lanyards dangling from their necks; they were in town for a convention. All walks of Las Vegas life were on full display.

Gio, Portia, and I hung back while Anthony approached the

registration desk. He briefly had to wait in line, so Gio and I formed a protective yet casual-looking wall in front of Portia to shield her from onlookers. But as far as I could tell, no one was looking at us. Anthony got to the front of the line, and I imagined him speaking some code word to the clerk. When she snapped into action and produced keycards almost instantly and with no paperwork, I assumed I hadn't been far off.

"Seriously?" I muttered. "Just like that?"

"Just like that," Gio muttered back. I hadn't realized he'd heard me.

"All set," Anthony said when he rejoined us. "Luxury king suite, twentieth floor."

"*Damn,* Lou had style," Gio said. "What else will dropping his name in this town get us?"

Anthony pocketed the keys with a grin and led us to another bank of elevators.

I seriously wondered what the answer to Gio's question was. "Did Lou have any connections with, I don't know, Michelin-starred restaurants or anything?" I asked, trying to sound casual.

Anthony shot me a knowing look over his shoulder. "There's hardly an industry his business didn't touch."

"Good to know."

Visions of the kinds of favors at Anthony's fingertips unfurled before me as our elevator arrived. We stepped in, and before the door slid shut, a young couple slipped through to join us. From the rigid shift in his posture, I thought Anthony was going to tell them to get out—and, arguably, the car *was* pretty full with Gio inside it—but he didn't. Instead Portia shrank back into the corner, and Anthony and Gio strategically stood in front of her. All four of us stopped breathing.

Luckily, the pair was too drunk in love to pay any attention. They hung off each other, gooey-eyed and giggling, probably legitimately drunk, and departed on the fifteenth floor, none the wiser they'd been in the presence of the missing woman all over the news.

I released a breath when no one else climbed in after they left.

"Guess you were right about hiding in plain sight," Anthony said as he jabbed the button to close the doors. A noticeable tension released inside the small space as we continued our journey.

"I told you Vegas was perfect," Gio said. "Everyone here is too focused on their own pleasure to see beyond their nose. Just a bunch of hedonists."

When we arrived on our floor, the tension from the elevator returned. Every step toward the room felt like a step closer to danger. Although the whole point of this mission was to remove the danger. Still, heading to a covert meetup in a Vegas hotel room, accompanied by a suitcase of cash—even if the cash wasn't part of the deal—made for one hell of a jittery journey.

The lavish suite had walls in shades of ivory and cream, and its furniture was purple and gray. A sunken living room boasted a view of the Strip. The marble bathtub was big enough to swim in. I almost regretted we were only using it as a base camp and not staying for a weekend.

"So, what's the plan from here?" Gio asked from where he'd generously spread himself on the sofa. His arms layered over the back of it like logs.

"We wait," Anthony said. "And we prepare. Agent Ives is meeting us here in two hours."

Portia had busied herself at the minibar. Bottles of top-shelf liquor clinked as she lifted and set them back down. She settled on vodka and began uncorking the cap.

"Portia, I'm not sure that's the best idea right now," Anthony said in a gentle tone.

She yanked off the cap and reached for a glass. Her hands

visibly shook. "Tony, I'm about to turn my husband over to the FBI so he doesn't kill me, and in hopes they don't arrest me with him. I think I am allowed to have a drink," she snapped. She poured half a glass and sipped it. "Can someone get me some ice?"

Gio popped up at the bite in her voice. "I'm on it."

He stalked back over to the door as Anthony came around to Portia. He put his hands on her shoulders and coaxed her into taking a deep breath. I heard him muttering to her and didn't want to intrude. I took the opportunity to find the phone to call my sister. It sat in a cradle on a nightstand beside the enormous bed.

I sank onto the crisp linens and felt the mattress embrace me. After splitting a bed with Portia last night, and the motel bed the night before, it called to me like a Siren. It took all my strength not to fall back against the pillows. I wondered if anyone would mind if I took a nap for the two hours before the FBI showed up.

Libby answered on the second ring, probably tipped off by the strange area code. "Hello?"

"Hey, Lib. It's me again."

"Penny! *Now* where are you?"

I flinched and realized she was probably going to yell at me every time I called, until I came home. Luckily, that event was on the horizon.

"Getting ready to come home."

"Why aren't you home already?"

I gazed over at Anthony and Portia still chatting by the minibar. The backdrop of the Strip in daylight loomed behind them. It felt garishly bright from the other end of the long room.

"Because we have to take care of something."

"*We?* Are you still with Anthony?"

"Of course I am. And we'll be home tomorrow." The plan

was to see Portia off, assuming things went well, and they took her into protective custody; use the room for the night; then we'd leave first thing in the morning for the long drive home.

Libby sighed. Her voice took on a pained and weary plea. "Penny, please just put an end to whatever is going on. I need to know you are safe."

I ached at the sound of her distress. "That's what we are doing, Lib. I'll see you tomorrow." I hung up before my guilt got the best of me and made me cry.

"Who's thirsty?" Gio asked when he barged back in the door with a bucket of ice. He made his way to the minibar to deposit it.

The suggestion didn't sound half bad. The last three days had been hell, and I had no part to play in what was about to happen anyway. Gio and I were going to head down to the casino while the room was occupied and then meet up with Anthony, once Portia was securely gone. Having a drink with her now seemed like a proper way to send her off.

"I'll take one," I said, and pushed up off the bed.

"I like your style, Professor," Gio said, and scooped some ice in a glass. "Tony?" he asked, and pointed the little silver shovel at him.

"No thanks," Anthony said.

Portia clucked. "Tony, come on. Best-case scenario here, we're never going to see each other again. The least you can do is have a drink with me." Her voice already sounded looser. I noticed her glass was nearly empty. She handed it to Gio to re-fill.

"Portia—" Anthony started, his voice pained like he was going to scold her, but she cut him off with a raised hand.

"Don't tell me not to say that. It's true: If this works, none of you will ever see me again after tonight." She looked around at each of us in turn, and I felt my throat thicken with an acute sadness over the reality of it all. I'd only known her for around twenty-four hours, minus our professional encounter a year ago, but it felt like longer, and I cared about her and wanted her to be safe. She gave me a soft smile; I felt she knew what I was thinking. Her eyes washed over with a shiny sheen. She swallowed hard. "You've all been through so much for me. You've scarified so much, and there's no possible way I could ever thank you. But please know that my decision to turn in Connor is as much to set myself free as it is to set you all free. You don't deserve to be caught up in any of this, and I'm sorry you are, and this is what needs to be done. So, please, before I go, do me one more favor and let me have one final drink with my friends."

I couldn't hold back the tear that spilled over my lid. I dashed it away with a quick hand as Gio sniffled. Anthony was flushed and rapidly blinking, obviously fighting to keep his eyes dry.

Gio elbowed him and whispered loud enough for everyone to hear, "Dude, you're going to look like a huge jerk if you say no right now."

Portia and I laughed wet, soggy sounds. She leaned her head over on my shoulder and clinked her glass to the one Gio had handed me.

Anthony finally caved, smiling reluctantly. "Fine. Pour me one."

Portia cheered and looped her arm through his.

We stood in a little huddle, a hodgepodge of humans brought together through a bizarre chain of circumstances, and some-how already loyally bound. We clinked glasses.

"To freedom," Gio said.

"To sunny days at the beach," Portia added.

"To friendship," Anthony said.

They all turned to me, and the outsider status I'd felt back in the safe house's kitchen when they were mourning Lou vanished. I was theirs now. And they were mine.

"To new beginnings," I said, and then we all drank.

We killed the remaining two hours before Agent Ives was set to show up eating room service and laughing, behaving like we really were in town for a fun weekend. Portia declared she didn't want her final moments as herself to be a solemn occasion, so we lived it up. And she sobered up. She cut herself off after her second drink to be prepared to talk to Agent Ives. I was the only one who kept sipping, and mainly because I was nervous.

I couldn't shake the sense of a ticking clock counting down to some imminent detonation.

At ten to five, Gio and I said our goodbyes to Portia. The occasion left both of us puffy-eyed and looking like we'd suffered an allergy attack. Anthony kissed my temple and promised to come find us in the casino when everything was said and done.

I kissed him on the mouth and told him what he was doing was selfless and brave. I left him flushed and shyly grinning.

Gio and I made our way down into the casino. Time didn't exist on the floor—literally; there were no clocks—but I could tell the evening crowd had started to descend. The skirts were shorter, the laughter louder, the cocktails flowing. It was pregame happy hour for whatever the night would hold. Dinner, a show—a night losing and winning money, only to break even before bed. The room was intentionally disorienting: a glittering, flashing maze of lights and sounds designed to snare attention and not let go. I kept my eye on the elevator bank, not wanting to lose sight of our way back to Anthony, as we walked past a dimly lit, roped-off room full of poker tables.

"High rollers," Gio muttered. "Speaking of . . ." He glanced over his shoulder before he turned toward me and flashed a wad of cash from inside his jacket.

I playfully gasped, still a little woozy from the farewell drinks. "You *didn't*. Is that from the suitcase?"

He gave me a sly, guilty grin. "Figured we could have a little fun while we wait."

"Well, I am not much of a gambler, but I am not opposed to a slot machine."

"*Pfft.* Might as well light this money on fire if you're going to do that. Let's play a real game. Come on." He led us to the cashier and exchanged several hundred dollars for chips. "For the esteemed professor," he said with a small bow, and placed a stack in my hand.

"Thank you, kind sir."

"My pleasure. Now, who on this floor are we going to take to school tonight?"

We both gazed out at the options. I didn't have the heart to tell him I'd gambled only once before, and would not be taking anyone to school, unless he meant giving them a lecture on probability sampling.

"Ah! Craps, my favorite," Gio said, and nodded toward an oblong table near the room's center.

I followed on his heels, making sure I could still see the elevators. "Craps? When you said a *real game,* I thought you meant one that involved actual skill and not just random chance."

"Craps does involve skill. You've got to guess right. That's a skill."

"Perhaps, if you're skilled at lucky guesses."

"I'm skilled at all sorts of things." He gave me a devilish grin and approached a table. Other gamblers easily cleared space for us to join. I positioned myself to keep an eye on the elevators. "Stop looking, Professor. He's not even here yet."

I flinched in embarrassment. "How did you know I was looking?"

"Because you haven't taken your eyes off that corner since

we got down here. Relax. And he's not going to show up with FBI written on his forehead, so you don't even know who you're looking for." He casually threw down some chips on the table. "This is going to take a while, so you might as well throw in."

I knew he was right, but the thought of waiting and hoping it all went off without a hitch had me feeling helpless. I didn't know how long it took to give a statement to the FBI, but I imagined it wasn't instant.

I sighed and dropped a few chips on the table.

"Now we're talking," Gio cheered me on right as a cocktail waitress materialized at my elbow.

"Something to drink?" she asked in a honey-sweet voice. She had cleavage up to her chin and eye shadow the color of a peacock. She balanced a tray on one hand littered in empty glasses bobbing with melted ice and lipsticked straws. A tip jar stuffed with singles sat between two expired lime wedges.

"Um, vodka soda, please," I said. "With a splash of lime."

"Sure, hon. And for you?" She turned her adoring gaze onto Gio.

"G and T if you please."

"Of course, sugar. Be right back." She winked at him and squeezed his arm.

"I think you have a fan," I said when she sauntered off.

He shrugged. "They treat everyone like that to keep them on the floor. Nothing like free booze and flirting to get people to spend cash."

"Sounds like you speak from experience."

"I've been around the block. Now let me show you how this is done." When it came his turn to throw the dice, they looked like something out of a child's toy set in his hand. The waitress eventually returned with our drinks, and despite the circumstances, I found myself having fun after a while. It may have been the booze. Or Gio's belly laugh. Or the fact he was actually *really good* at craps, despite logic suggesting that wasn't possible, and his enthusiasm was contagious.

I'd lost track of how much time had passed, but was feeling a little tipsy by the time Gio had a small mountain of chips in front of him. I turned away from the table for a breather.

"He has to be here by now, right?" I muttered, recalling why we were even in a casino in the first place.

"What?" Gio muttered over his shoulder, still facing the table.

"Ives. We've been down here for twenty minutes? A half hour?"

"Long enough for me to double my winnings so Tony won't notice the cash missing from his suitcase," he said, and playfully stuck his tongue out sideways.

I sucked the end of my drink through the straw until it made a sputtering sound. The waitress with the peacock eyes was likely to appear any second to offer to refill it, but I didn't need another. Not until we were in the clear.

"I want to go check on them," I said.

"Definitely not. We can't go up there until it's done. Tony is going to come find us after."

Discomfort hung over me like an itchy blanket. I was suddenly antsy.

"Professor, relax. Throw in another bid."

"Sorry. I'm not very good at standing by and waiting. I just want to know what's happening."

"We are destroying the house at craps, that's what's happening. *Ooh!*" he shouted to a round of cheers from the small crowd at our table. I glanced backward to see another little mountain of chips being pushed his way.

When I turned back to face the elevators, a face in the crowd caught my eye, and I thought I might be hallucinating.

"What?" I murmured in shock.

I blinked several times, thinking maybe my vision had be-trayed me, but no. It was still him.

"Gio!" I whispered, and clawed at his bulky arm. He was busy high-fiving the man next to him. *"Gio!"* I called more des-perately, and yanked on him.

"What?" He turned to me, and the look of confused ex-citement melted from his face at the look on mine. "What's wrong?"

I knew I'd had alcohol, and I knew I was in a hot room crowded with smoke and noise and flashing lights, but I knew I wasn't imagining things.

"Is that Connor Slate walking toward the elevators?"

Gio instantly tensed and whipped his head around, all signs of frivolity gone. He followed my pointing finger, and his mouth fell open. "Ho-ly shit."

Connor stalked the edge of the room with the threat of a shark swimming in dark water. He wore an open jacket over jeans and a collared shirt and looked both like he didn't care about being seen and like he would flatten anyone who got in his way. Notably, he was alone.

"What the fuck is he doing here?" Gio whispered under his breath as Connor made his way to the elevator bank.

I scrambled for an answer, still struggling to believe what I was seeing and understand it. The chances of Connor Slate randomly booking a room at the same hotel we were at on a Thursday night were slim to none—and no one even knew we were here. Anthony had called in a favor for the room, but whoever was on the other end of it had no idea why. I didn't tell anyone. Gio didn't tell anyone. Of course Portia and An-thony didn't. That only left—

"Shit," Gio said at the same second I figured it out. He looked down at me with a tempered rage in his eyes. "That FBI agent is dirty. He told Connor we're here."

My horror seemed to dissolve the alcohol in my system, instantly sobering me. I slapped a hand over my mouth. "Limitless resources," I muttered.

"What?" Gio asked, having completely turned his back on the craps game.

The pieces unscrambled and snapped sharply in place. I suddenly saw it all. I gripped Gio's arms in a desperate panic. "Gio, Connor must have bought him. He was afraid Portia was going to talk, so he bought off the agent she was going to talk to. That night in New York, he saw them together, Anthony told me. Connor knew Ives was a threat, so he put him in his pocket. He cut off Portia's resource before she even tried to use it."

Gio had gone rigid in shock. I could see thoughts tumbling in his eyes as he tried to work it all out.

But I was two steps ahead of him. "Gio, this meeting was a setup. Connor must be here to . . . finish this. They have no idea he's coming. They are sitting ducks up in that room. We have to warn them before he kills them both."

I spun away from the table, abandoning the chips and all sense of self-preservation. My only thoughts were of Anthony and Portia not knowing they'd walked into a trap.

"Penny, wait!" Gio called after me. He caught up in a few steps and, to my relief, didn't grab my arm and try to stop me. I knew I liked him for a reason. He was definitely a *run toward the danger in an emergency* type of person. And we were running. Heads briefly turned to see what the fuss was, but everyone went back to their games once we passed.

I was out of breath and fighting the booze bubbling in my veins when we reached the elevators.

"Where'd he go?" Gio asked as he scanned the area.

I'd lost sight of him too, but the bank of elevators was in full use, and he had to be in one of them. "Up! He went up!" I said, and smashed my finger into the call button. I paced in a circle, sweating and swearing. The swarm of guests getting ready to go out for the night was working against us. Everyone had somewhere to be, and the elevators were jammed. The lights above each closed door indicated which floor the elevator was on, and none on either side of the bank were even close.

"Stairs?" I turned to Gio with a desperate hope.

"That's twenty floors, Penny. We'll never make it."

It wasn't a real suggestion; I would have died by floor five, no doubt, but I still had to say it. "Call Anthony," I said with a gasp. "The burner phone; you have that number, right?"

"Yes." Gio nodded and reached for his phone as I jammed the elevator call button again.

I tuned out his attempt and paced again. "Come on, come on, *come on!*" I growled at the wall of still-closed doors. I willed one of them to open while at the same time, I willed Anthony to somehow hear my desperate warning. *He's coming. Get out.* I thought it as hard as I could in case there was a remote possibility he could sense it.

"He's not answering," Gio reported with a shake of his head.

"Damn it."

Visions of the worst-case scenario swam in my mind. Connor showing up with a gun, catching them off guard. Anthony dead. Portia gone. Agent Ives never even having materialized at all.

"Hurry up!" I shouted at the wall. I'd lost my cool completely. Furious tears blurred my eyes. A fiery rage pushed heat into my face and made me want to scream.

Finally, *mercifully,* an elevator *dinged* behind us.

We both spun around and threw ourselves at it. A loud, fragrant crowd of women in glittery dresses with TEAM BRIDE sashes stepped out in a clatter of heels. I shoved my way through them, parting a sea of Chanel Number 5.

"Hey, watch it!" one of them snapped at me when I nearly stepped on her foot.

"Sorry!" I flung myself into the empty lift and pressed the button for the twentieth floor, over and over.

Gio stepped in behind me and turned to face the open doors. He spread his arms out to prevent anyone else from entering. "Sorry, this is an emergency, folks." He said it calmly and rationally and looked like he could snap over his knee anyone who protested, so, thankfully, none of the annoyed guests dared argue.

The doors slid shut, and I prayed no one between us and floor twenty was waiting for a ride to go up.

"Call him again," I commanded. My hands were slicked with sweat. I shook all over.

"I don't have a signal in here," Gio said, and jammed his phone back in his pocket.

I watched the floors light up as we rose into the sky, all the while my heart beating faster and harder. "What are we going to do when we get there?" I asked.

"Assess the situation and then come up with a plan of action." He sounded like he was reciting tactical orders.

"Right. Of course," I said, fully intending to follow his lead, but then we arrived on our floor with a *ding,* and all sense abandoned me.

I shoved my way around him and ran into the hall. "Anthony!" I cried. Panic had taken over again. I had to get to him. I had to save him.

"Penny! Get back here!" Gio hollered behind me. I heard his thunderous steps crashing down the hall as I ran.

Our room wasn't far from the elevators. I had to turn left and then left again; then it was a straight shot down a hall with an emergency exit at the end.

I was halfway down the hall when I heard a door slam, followed by a gunshot.

"*No!*" I screamed, and froze in my tracks.

Gio caught up and passed me. He shoved by and headed toward our door with a gun, which he'd apparently had the whole time, drawn at his hip. He paused to listen and held a finger to his lips as I caught up on trembling legs. My heart was in my throat and my eyes swimming with tears again.

There was nothing but silence on the other side.

Gio got out his keycard and reached for the handle right as the door flew open.

Anthony came tumbling out into the hall, gasping and swearing. He crashed into Gio and tripped before Gio caught him and set him on his feet.

"Anthony!" I cried, and lunged for him.

He was struggling to breathe. Maybe he'd been punched in the gut? But I didn't see any gaping gunshot wounds.

"Are you okay?! What happened?" I gripped his arms and saw he had a gun in his hand.

"He took Portia!" he gasped on a pained breath. "Connor. Is. *Here*. The FBI agent is—" He cut off with another gasp and doubled over, pointing behind him back into the room. "Setup."

I quickly pieced together his broken sentence and looked through the open door. Someone in a suit writhed on the floor, gripping his right leg. The agent had shown up after all.

I hunched over to meet Anthony's eyes. He was still gasping and holding his side in pain. "Did you shoot someone in the leg again?"

He nodded, his eyes alight with understanding. "And he . . ." he trailed off with a wince. "Ribs."

It all made sense. "And he hit you in the ribs, and now you can't breathe?"

"Yes," he forced out with another wince. "And Portia. *Gone.*"

I glanced over my shoulder to look for them and make sure

we weren't drawing attention. Hopefully, no one else heard the gunshot. No doors flew open, so I assumed we were in the clear.

"Where'd he take her?" Gio asked. "We just came from the elevators, and there was no one else there."

Anthony stood and fought for a full breath. He squeezed his eyes shut in pain, but pushed through it. "They just left, so if they weren't at the elevators, then . . ." He looked over at the emergency exit. "They took the stairs."

The implication hadn't fully settled over me before he was twisting out of my grip and shoving his gun into his waistband. He met Gio's gaze for a silent conversation.

"Go, man," Gio said. "I'll take care of this asshole." He nodded at the man still on the floor losing blood.

"Thank you," Anthony said, and started for the stairwell.

"Wait, are you *serious?!*" I blurted, hurrying to keep up. "Anthony, we're twenty floors up, and you can hardly walk!"

"We'll lose them otherwise!" he called over his shoulder.

Of course it would end with a staircase. *Of course* it would. Because climbing walls and running through the woods wasn't enough. And I, of course, wasn't going to let him go alone. Not after all we'd been through, and not when he looked minutes from collapsing.

I grumbled and followed after him.

"What are you doing?" he said, picking up his pace to a trot now. "Stay here with Gio."

"Are you kidding me? You don't get to play Rambo without supervision in your condition."

"Penny, go back!"

"Shut up, Anthony! I'm coming with you!"

He cast a scowl over his shoulder when he reached the door to the stairwell and pushed it open.

"Professor!" I heard Gio shout from behind me.

I turned to see him partway down the hall. He held up his gun, indicating he was going to toss it to me; and then to my horror, he tossed it to me. "Just in case!"

I caught it with a zing of terror. I considered dropping it and running away. Just booking it to the elevators and finding a flight home or maybe to someplace warm, tropical, and very far away—but as soon as I had the thought, I knew I wouldn't do it. No. I'd grown too attached to this ragtag group, and putting an end to this mess was the only way to get my life back.

So, convincing myself I possessed even an ounce of the courage they all had, I shoved the gun into my waistband and followed my no-longer-fake boyfriend as he chased a madman into the stairwell.

CHAPTER 15

Twenty flights of stairs was a truly monstrous task. Going down was at least better than going up, and Anthony had been right. We weren't the only ones in the stairwell. There was another set of footsteps clamoring down below us, punctuated by intermittent sounds of protest.

I had to imagine Connor was dragging Portia, and the sounds of her struggling only made me want to run faster.

But wanting to run and being able to run were two different things. My legs were trembling and my lungs heaving. I kept one hand on the railing as we spiraled down at a dizzying angle. I quickly fell behind. When I stopped to catch my breath somewhere around the tenth floor, I heard a pitiful yelp, which made me lean over the railing.

At the bottom of the narrow chamber, I saw Portia sprawled on her hands and knees, looking like she'd tripped or perhaps been shoved. Connor came into view and squatted beside her. He spoke in a low tone, but given the shape of the stairwell, his voice carried like he was standing right beside me.

"You think you can run from me? After everything I've given you? And not only run, but *turn me in*?" He grabbed her ponytail and yanked her head back.

"Connor, please," she begged. Tears mangled her voice.

"Please *what,* darling?" he hissed. My skin crawled at the sound. The menace in his voice was sharp as a sword.

"Please. I won't tell anyone anything! I swear," she sobbed.

"Well, it's a little late for that, don't you think? How am I ever supposed to trust you again?" He stroked her hair and said it with a facetiously loving coo, which turned my stomach. "Turns out I can't trust anyone to do anything right. That's why I'm here on my own—to clean up this *mess* you've made."

He released her with a shove, and then stood from his crouch and kicked her in the stomach.

"Stop!"

I didn't even realize the word had come from my mouth until Connor whipped his head up to look at me. Anthony appeared over the railing five floors below me to do the same.

I gulped when they both saw me, and I hardly jumped out of the way in time when Connor pulled a gun and shot at me.

The ringing shattered off the walls of the echo chamber. I'd never heard anything so loud before, and I feared I'd never hear anything else again, but a second gunshot assured me I had not lost the sense completely.

"Connor, stop!" I heard Anthony shout in a muffle from below. It sounded as if I had cotton in my ears. The eardrum-splitting ache was unreal.

A door slammed far below. I peered over the railing to see Portia gone, and Connor twisted around to look at a bloody gash on his calf.

Anthony had grazed him with a bullet.

Connor fired off another shot at us before he disappeared from view too.

My ears were still ringing, equaling the worst stereo feedback in history, when I heard the door slam again. Anthony's hurried steps followed the sound, and we were off once more. He was still out in front of me, several floors below. I tried to catch up, but between shaking in fear and how fast he was moving, I lost him.

The final ten flights passed in a blur, perhaps because of the adrenaline cranking through my system, or perhaps the pure terror at the idea someone was going to die.

When I arrived at the bottom of the well, I found a small pool of blood from Connor's injury and noticed a line of droplets leading to the door.

Perfect. They were leaving a trail. As I followed it, I wondered if Anthony had grazed his leg on purpose for this exact reason.

"Street smarts," I muttered to myself. I opened the door, not sure where it would lead me, and found myself facing another hallway. This one was long and concrete, and ending in a heavy set of double doors.

The blood told me that's where they went, so I followed.

It took me outside, and I suddenly found myself gazing up at the famed Las Vegas Strip. The lights were just now beginning to come to life. They dazzled, as if taking the baton from the sun sinking in the dusty sky. Billboards flashed and hotel towers glittered. An enormous volcano erupted flames into the sky. Another night in Sin City geared up for the midweek crowd.

Except the blood did not lead toward the showstopping glamour. It turned to the right, away from the lights and into a quieter end of town. I followed it along the dirty sidewalk, gummed up with spilled drinks and cigarette butts, fully aware I was outside in public with a gun in my pants, chasing after two men with guns and a woman running for her life. I didn't know what I would do if I caught up to them, but I couldn't lose track of them now.

Maybe Portia was running to a bus, or a hospital, or a police station. Maybe she was simply running because she didn't know what else to do. When the trail led me down a street to a construction site, I decided she was either very smart or very desperate, since the place was dark, abandoned, and dangerous. The perfect place to hide. Or to be killed without anyone knowing.

The blood trail got harder to see, the closer I got to the dark skeleton of a building. I reflexively reached for my phone to use the flashlight, but remembered I'd been without it since Tuesday night.

I went inside despite the dark.

The small, in-progress building was boxy, and so far, there was only concrete with exposed rebar sticking out like spindly ribs. The exterior walls were yet to be closed off, but the air inside still hung thick with the earthy smell of sawdust and cement. Piles of lumber and steel rods were stacked against walls. A few sheets of plastic hung as partitions. The night air moved freely through its gaps and open spaces.

I strained my ears for signs of Anthony, Portia, and Connor, but with not much to echo off in the unfinished space, sound seeped out into the surrounding streets.

My heart pounded in my ears, but my legs had finally stopped shaking. I took slow, steady breaths in an effort to keep calm as I ventured deeper into the dark, all the while aware of the gun in my waistband. I was definitely playing the worst game of hide-and-seek ever. When I spun around, heart in my throat, at the sound of something behind me, which turned out to be a sheet of plastic fluttering in the breeze, I realized it was entirely possible Connor would find me in this maze before I found him.

I swallowed in fear at what that might mean.

I started taking lighter footsteps to stop my feet from scraping the bald floor as I continued following the blood drops. Somewhere in the building's deep belly, I lost track of the trail.

Another stain had cropped up, which looked nearly the same in the dark, perhaps grease from a power tool. Going right would take me deeper into the building, and going left would take me closer to its edge, back toward the streetlight.

I opted for left, in hope I could find the blood trail again.

After the length of an unfinished room, I came to an abrupt stop when I heard voices. They came from in front of me, toward the light. I took three quick steps in that direction and paused again.

"Please, Connor," I heard Portia beg.

He'd caught up to her, and I froze with fear.

But a relieved breath snuck out of me that at least she was still alive. I wouldn't fully exhale until I heard Anthony too. I hoped he was hiding around a corner at a strategic angle to step in and save the day.

I crept closer as silently as I could and came to a partial wall I could peek around. I held my breath as I stole a look in the direction of Portia's voice and had to stifle a gasp. Connor had her at gunpoint, which was not unexpected, but to my equal-parts relief and horror, Anthony was standing right next to her.

He was still alive too, but not for long if Connor fired the gun aimed at him.

Anthony and Portia both stood with their hands up. Anthony's gun was on the ground in front of them. Connor had his back to me, and Portia never took her eyes off him, but Anthony flicked his gaze in my direction. When he saw me, I noticed his jaw tighten at the same time relief blinked across his face.

It dawned on me with a sick sense of irony that *I* was the one hiding around the corner at a strategic angle and primed to step in and save the day.

Of course I was.

I turned away and pressed my back into the cold concrete

wall. The gun in my waistband pulsed like a living thing, reminding me of its presence. I closed my eyes and took a tight breath, unable to believe it had come to this. I should have been at home in my sweatpants working on a research paper. I shouldn't have been anywhere near a gunpoint standoff in the middle of Vegas, wondering if I had the courage to intervene.

But I was.

"It doesn't have to end this way, Connor," I heard Anthony say.

The sound of his voice sent a soothing warmth spilling into my blood; at the same time I noticed the fear in it.

"Oh, but it does," Connor said. "I clearly can't trust my wife, and you've gone and made a mess of everything with your little plan to make her disappear. Did you *really* think that was going to work? You know I have eyes everywhere. I knew as soon as her bodyguard tried to pretend she wasn't up to something. He should have known better than to try to lie to me."

I heard Portia gasp, and I imagined the look on Anthony's face at confirmation she'd been right. Tyler had stayed loyal to her and refused to talk. My heart ached for him.

"Do you know how easy it was to get Agent Ives in my pocket?" Connor went on. "I only have to wave a little money at someone and they do whatever I say. Except you, Portia. You're the only one who's never done what I say. At first, I liked it. There was a thrill in someone saying no to me. But now you've grown tiresome. And problematic." His voice took on an even more sinister edge. He sounded nothing like the man I'd seen in TED Talks and prime-time interviews.

Every hair on my body was standing on end and my nerves on high alert. I dared to peek back around the corner.

"Connor, I said I'm sorry," Portia begged. Tears streaked her face. She was hideously frightened yet still beautiful. "I know I messed up."

He laughed a cruel, dark sound. *"Messed up?* Baby, what

you did is so far beyond *messed up*. Mistakes can be fixed, but there's no coming back from betrayal. As far as I'm concerned, you've sealed your own fate. You've got no one to blame but yourself." He shook his head in disgust. "I should have left you in the trash where I found you. You're both trash. And so was that piece of shit uncle of yours." He swung the gun back to Anthony, and I flinched on his behalf.

The hurt on his face was almost too much. He tried to hide it, but I saw right through the façade. I thought back to our conversation at the safe house and how his eyes had lit up when he told me stories about Lou. He loved his uncle. And he loved Portia. None of them deserved to die at the hands of this monster, who thought he ruled the world.

Something snapped loose inside me and I made a decision.

I swallowed the fiery, terrified lump that had shoved up into my throat and tried to maintain consciousness as I reached for my gun. If I wasn't mistaken, it was the same one from my shooting lesson. I flipped off the safety, like Gio had shown me, and nodded at Anthony so he knew what I was going to do.

He couldn't nod back without giving me away, but I saw the acknowledgment on his face. I couldn't miss the absolute terror there too.

Before I could talk myself out of it, I sucked in the most frightened breath of my life and ran through Gio's list at warp speed, forgetting half the details and skipping the other half, because this was nothing like the backyard and beer cans. I braced my shoulder against the wall, silently muttered *badass* once more, aimed for Connor, and pulled the trigger.

My eyes snapped shut. The shot jolted through my body. I stumbled back and tripped. My wrists throbbed in pain when I caught myself. An ache shot up my spine. I scrambled back behind the wall just as another gunshot split the air.

The silence that followed thundered with ringing and my pounding heart. Terror screamed through me as I waited for what would come next.

Who had the second shot hit? What was happening on the other side of the wall?

I couldn't bring myself to turn around and look.

I was still on the ground, numb, with tears streaming down my face, when Anthony suddenly appeared. He was on his knees in front of me before I blinked twice.

"Penny! Penny, you're okay. Look at me. You're fine. We're all fine." He kissed my temple and squeezed me in his arms, tighter than I had ever been squeezed before. I could hardly breathe from his grip and my own tears.

"Is he—" I choked on the words I didn't want to say. "Is he . . . dead?"

Anthony cupped my face in his hands and wiped my tears with his thumbs. "Yes, but you didn't kill him. You missed."

"I m-missed?" I gasped as he hugged me again. Relief shook his body in waves.

"Yes. But you distracted him, and that's all we needed."

I wiped my eyes and looked over his shoulder to see Portia standing over her husband's body with Anthony's smoking gun in her hand, looking like the freest woman alive.

If I'd been asked a week ago what being a fixer entailed, burying a body would have been high on the list. I'd learned there was much more to the job, but it felt fitting our journey was culminating with such a token activity.

"You know, the busted ribs are a sorry excuse for not helping," Gio said from where he stood waist deep in the hole he'd been digging. Sweat poured off his brow and stained his shirt. The desert night was thick with heat and pitch-black other than our headlights.

We'd driven deep into the empty wilderness outside Las Vegas, where the blistering sun baked the dry earth all day and wind swept away tire tracks. We were nowhere near a road, out where the unforgiving land was all too ready to swallow secrets.

After the scene in the construction site, I went back to the hotel to find Gio while Portia and Anthony stayed behind to wrap Connor's body in one of the conveniently available plastic sheets hanging from the ceiling.

I'd found Gio alone, and when I'd asked what happened to Agent Ives, I feared the worst when he said he'd *taken care of it*. But then at the look on my face, he told me to relax, and he only meant he'd sent him to a hospital in a cab and warned him that if he didn't want Internal Affairs to find out about tonight, he'd never speak of it again.

In the time it took us to procure a shovel and transport Connor's body to the Camaro's trunk, night had completely fallen. We packed up and left, figuring it was best to flee Vegas before anyone caught on to what had happened.

Somewhere between the Strip and California, we pulled off the road into the dirt and drove by moonlight far enough to worry we were lost. We parked the cars facing each other so the headlights intersected on a patch of dirt that would be Connor Slate's final resting place and began to dig.

"Hey, I did my part transporting the body," Anthony said. He leaned on the Camaro's hood between the headlights with his arm slung over my shoulders.

Gio stopped digging and stood up straight to wipe his brow. "Fair. But you could at least take a short shift."

"Sorry, G. Doctor's orders," he said with a shrug and motioned to me.

I gently elbowed him—on his right side, of course. "I'm not that kind of doctor."

"True, but you still told me to take it easy, so."

"Convenient interpretation, but okay." In truth, I was happier, the less he was involved. He wouldn't let me take any part in helping dispose of Connor's body. I was basically a kidnap victim again, along for the ride. I would have preferred if he wasn't involved either, but someone had to fix the latest problem.

"I'll finish it," Portia said. She stood at the edge of the hole, dust gently stirring around her feet in the headlights, and reached for the shovel. "It should be me."

Gio looked up at her with a tilt of his head, possibly prepared to protest, and then held out a hand to help her into the hole. Gio climbed out with a grunt and wiped his hands on his shirt. "Got any water?"

"Backseat," Anthony and I said at the same time.

Given the trunk was occupied with a dead billionaire's body, all our travel necessities had been relocated to the Camaro's backseat.

"You sure this is going to work?" I asked for the tenth time.

Anthony nodded for the tenth time. "Yes. With Portia still *missing*, people will think Connor had something to do with it and skipped town to avoid arrest. He's a billionaire; everyone will assume he's got the resources to disappear. No one is going to look for him here."

Despite my nerves over the whole situation, it was a fair argument. Portia couldn't exactly come out of hiding, because then she'd have to explain where she'd been, which would inevitably lead to questions about what had happened to her husband. Seeing that she'd killed him, it was best she stay hidden. The original plan to make her disappear was back on, only now, she wasn't running for her life.

"And if they ever do come looking for him," Gio said after draining half a water bottle and then pouring the rest on his head, "they're never going to find him." He held his arms out to gesture at the empty expanse around us. We were miles from anything. I knew for certain I'd never be able to find this location again if I tried.

"And you were right, Penny," Portia said from the hole. "My husband's ego was his downfall after all. He showed up here alone, thinking he could handle things by himself." She blew a loose strand of hair out of her face and half smiled. "Little did he know what he was up against."

I smiled wanly back and felt Anthony tighten his arm around me. Their reassurance smoothed over me like a balm in the dry desert air. "I have to tell you something," I said to Anthony. It seemed like as good a time as any to confess.

He leaned sideways to look at me with a grin. "What, you've been an undercover FBI agent this whole time and are going to arrest us all when we get home?"

I laughed. "No. But it does have to do with the police and going home."

He raised his brows in question.

"So remember how you said you convinced my sister not to call the police when I was kidnapped? Well, you weren't as convincing as you thought. When I called her from the motel room the other morning, she told me she'd called Warner that day. As soon as she told me, I called him to explain I wasn't missing, because I didn't want him to think you had anything to do with it. I ended up telling him about being kidnapped though, and that the tweed man confessed to killing your uncle and Portia's bodyguard. I told him to go look for the Cadillac and our phones at the Slates' house as evidence. I'm sorry if that complicates anything, but telling him the truth felt like the right thing to do." I scrunched up my nose in apology, worried he might be about to scold me.

But he didn't. He let out a long breath and tilted his head in consideration. "That . . . actually might help matters."

"Really?" I asked hopefully.

"Yes. Because if word gets out Connor Slate's personal employee was involved in two murders and a kidnapping, Connor disappearing will make all the more sense. With all these crimes piling up around him, people will *really* think he skipped town."

"Huh. I hadn't thought of it that way, but I guess you're right."

"Yeah. Things have a funny way of working out sometimes."

I leaned my head against his shoulder and let out a long breath. Sure, we'd have some explaining and maybe a little more fixing to do when we got home, but the loose ends seemed to have tied themselves up for the most part.

"Do you think she's going to be okay?" I lowered my voice and nodded toward Portia. Only the top of her head poked out from the hole where she was bent over digging. A shovelful of dirt came flying out every few seconds.

"Yes, I think she will be okay. She's going to have to get on a plane for real now, but since none of Connor's people will be looking for her with him gone, she'll easily be able to disappear."

I watched her continue to dig and thought about how she'd saved herself in the end. The journey had been long and winding, and she could have shot her husband at any time in the past, but doing it under the current circumstances left her off anyone's radar as being responsible for the crime. I wondered fleetingly if killing her husband had been her long game the whole time.

"Good." I pulled in a deep breath of the warm desert air and let it settle in my lungs. "And what about you?" I asked, nudging him. "Are you going to be okay?"

He turned to look at me. The moonlight bleached him out like a black-and-white portrait. My glue job was still holding up on his brow. He blinked his long lashes and gave me a soft smile. "That depends. Are you still on for that date when we get home?"

A mirroring smile bent my mouth upward. "I think that can be arranged. But does that mean you're sticking around? Not selling the house?" The nerves that suddenly hollowed out my belly made me realize how much I cared about his answer.

He pursed his lips, considering. "It's probably going to be a tough sell, what with the body in the closet and all."

"This is true."

"And, I mean, I don't really *need* to sell it for financial purposes."

"Oh?" I said, completely aware he was swimming in money, given the suitcase in the backseat and what I'd seen in Lou's bankbook.

"Yeah. I've got a rich uncle, haven't you heard? He died and left me everything." He pointed over his shoulder with his thumb and gave me a cheeky grin.

"Well, that was generous of him."

"Sure was. Only thing is, I think he left me his business too, and I'm not exactly sure what I'm going to do with his clients." The jovial tone dropped from his voice.

"Oh yeah. That."

He may have had my heart cartwheeling, but there was the fact his job entailed illegal activity. I tried to picture him with a desk job—a real one—and all I could see was him showing up in all black to rescue himself from the banality. He would hate it, but I wasn't sure I could stomach knowing he was up to things like what we were doing right now—if there was any future for us.

I reached for his hand and laced my fingers through his. "Maybe the econ degree can come back into play. You can move to the suburbs and become an accountant. Take up golf."

He huffed a laugh. "Perhaps. At least I don't have to make any major career decisions tonight." He kissed my hand and squeezed it.

The sound of the shovel landing with a hard *plink* on the dirt pulled us out of our conversation. Portia had tossed it up out of the hole and was climbing out, streaked with sweat and dirt. Of course she was still beautiful, even rising like a murderous zombie from the grave.

"It's deep enough," she declared as Gio walked over to help her out. "Put him in."

Anthony took his cue to retrieve the body from the trunk. He and Gio wrestled the plastic sheet out of the Camaro and carried it over to the hole. Anthony winced in pain with each step, but carrying a body ten yards was at least easier than digging a grave.

They dumped him in with no ceremony, and when Gio reached for the shovel to begin the process of burying him, Portia held out her hands.

"Wait!" Her voice cracked in the dark night. I couldn't make out the emotion, but it sounded like a mix of complex feelings. "One last thing," she said. She reached for the rings on her left hand and pulled them off. My stomach bottomed out that she was going to drop the five-carat monstrosity into the grave, but she replaced it on her finger. Then with a breath so big, I felt it in my soul, she only dumped the wedding band.

"Goodbye, Connor." She nodded at Gio, signaling him to replace all the dirt, and turned back for the car.

Anthony and I watched as Gio filled the hole. The process was much quicker than making the hole, but it still took a while. When he finished and patted the dirt flat with the shovel, Anthony slung his arm over my shoulders and kissed my temple.

It was the end of one journey and the start of another. I

couldn't say what would have happened if I hadn't tried to buy the candlesticks, or what was going to happen now. But I knew the person beside me had sharply divided my life in two. I'd always have a before and after Anthony Pierce. And under that sweeping midnight sky with endless possibility rippling around us, I knew I wanted to find out what came next.

"Let's go home," he said to me with a tired breath.

I smiled at him, knowing he could see it in the dark. "It's about time."

CHAPTER 16

Of course we couldn't go straight home.

We had to put Portia on a plane, and since none of us ever wanted to set foot in Las Vegas again, we detoured through Los Angeles. We said our goodbyes, and she used her new identity to fly off to Europe. Gio refunded the cash he'd nabbed from the suitcase as a parting gift, and then departed to his own undisclosed location, but heavily hinted he'd be sticking around Southern California for a while.

Before our long drive home, Anthony and I got a hotel room for the night—a nice one—and spent a lot more than two minutes doing a lot more than kissing. Very carefully, of course, seeing his ribs were still broken.

We left the city in a dreamy haze and cruised up the state. He even let me drive for some of the journey, since he was the one who had no idea where we were going this time.

When we pulled into his driveway in the early evening, it was right in time for the golden-hour sun to melt the sky and leave everything dripping in soft light. He cut off the car's rumble, and a peaceful finality settled in the air.

We made it. We were home.

I glanced over at my sister's house and noted two cars in the driveway—the minivan, and my mother's. A third sat at the curb.

Anthony saw me looking and squeezed his hand on the back of his neck, suddenly shy. "Penny, would it be all right if I walk you home?"

I blinked at him in surprise. For the last hundred miles or so, versions of this moment had cycled through my mind. How were we going to say goodbye? A kiss? A hug? Perhaps escape upstairs to his bedroom before anyone next door even noticed we were home?

I'd admittedly lingered on the last scenario for an indulgent amount of time.

But in all my iterations of this moment, I hadn't thought he'd offer to walk me home.

"I—um . . ." I mumbled in mostly surprise. I was flattered and fluttering and also seriously wondering about his mental state. "You know my mom's over there, right? And my sister called the cops on you."

He quietly laughed as a charming flush curled into his cheeks. "Yes, I know. That's why I want to do it. I want to apologize and set things straight. You're the best thing that's happened to me in a long, long time, Penny, and I don't want to mess this up."

I blinked at him again and wondered at how he'd gone from curt stranger to mistaken boyfriend, from suspected criminal to rescuer, from traveling companion to rescuee, from lover to man who wanted to come in and meet my mom—all within the span of less than a week.

"I, um. Okay," I said. My face offered up a matching flush.

"Okay," he said with a smile.

We climbed out of the car, looking less like fugitives than we had in days. We'd swung by a mall in L.A. for some clothes from this decade. I was back in jeans and a tee, and he in the same, but all black, of course. He slipped his hand in mine as we walked down his driveway and crossed over to Libby's property.

"You're going to walk in holding my hand? You really are a glutton for punishment," I teased him.

"If I'm not mistaken, *this* was your sister's original intention in introducing us." He held up our clasped hands to signify what he meant. "So she's really only got herself to blame here."

I snorted. "Try telling her that."

I realized as we climbed Libby's front steps he was right. Despite my protests that day, my sister's plan had come to fruition. The plan she'd been scheming at, for most of my adult life. Little did she know the guy who'd finally stick was the one she'd never have picked if she'd known the full truth.

Funny how things worked out sometimes.

I took a bracing breath as I reached for the front door. It flew open before I could grab the handle, and where I expected to see my sister's furious face, I saw her empty entryway. Until I looked down.

"Aunt Penny!" Max wailed, and threw himself at me. He adhered himself to my legs and squeezed like he was trying to pop me. He tilted his head up to give me a goofy grin. "I missed you."

My heart was fit to burst. I let go of Anthony's hand to reach down and hoist him up into a hug. "Oh, my Maxy. I missed you too!" I buried my face in his soft neck, which smelled like little boy, and deeply inhaled. His scent made my mind flash back to moments over the past few days when I'd thought I'd never see my family again. My throat suddenly ached with hot tears.

"*Mom!* Aunt Penny is back!" he screamed right in my ear. I flinched as he wiggled, wanting to be set down, but I held my grip. First, because I didn't want to let him go; and second, because I selfishly wanted him as a shield from his mother. I stepped inside, with Anthony on my heels.

Max cast Anthony an uncertain look. "Are you bad?" he

said in what I was sure was an echo of something he'd heard his mother say.

Anthony studied him back with a tilt of his head. "I think that's subjective."

"What does *subgecktive* mean?" Max tried to shape his little mouth around the word.

I quietly laughed and pressed my lips to his chubby cheek with a loud kiss. "It means no, buddy." I set him down, and he scampered off toward the sound of approaching steps.

"Didn't expect the three-year-old to be my toughest critic," Anthony muttered, and tugged at his collar.

"Wait until you formally meet the baby," I whispered as my sister came charging around the corner.

She looked wilted and worn, and the thought I'd put the weary look on her face pulled at my heart in the worst way. But under the dark circles and the furious scowl she'd manufactured for the occasion, I saw profound relief. Her eyes softened, and she marched across her foyer to hug me.

"I'm so mad at you," she whispered in a tearful greeting.

I squeezed her back and poured every ounce of apology into it. "I know. I'm sorry. But I'm home now."

"And you're never going anywhere ever again. I don't care how hot he is."

A soggy laugh burst from my lips. I leaned back to grip her shoulders. I wiped my eyes, smiling. "Does this mean you approve?"

Libby cast a glare at Anthony. "Of him? Of course not. I meant any man in general."

I hadn't expected her to shower Anthony with gratitude for bringing me home safely, but the look on her face clearly said we were in for an uphill battle.

Anthony stepped forward and held out his hands. "Libby, I want to apologize. For everything. I'm sorry I dragged Penny into all this, but without her"—he looked over at me and swallowed like he had a hard knot in his throat—"I probably wouldn't be standing here alive, so I owe your family more than thanks."

It hadn't fully occurred to me until that moment that I'd saved his life. With a swell of emotion too big to name, I reached for his hand and laced my fingers through his. I wrapped my other hand around our grip and leaned into him. He looked down at me, dark eyes burning with the sincerest gratitude. The connection between us became something physical, and I couldn't have broken it if I'd tried.

Libby scoffed. "*Ugh.* Don't tell me you fell in love with him." She folded her arms and spun on her heel. "Mom!" she called, sounding how we had as teens and I'd stolen her hairbrush.

"Hi," I said quietly, still staring up at him and ignoring my sister's tantrum.

"Hi," he said back.

The world shrank to only the bubble where we stood. It felt much like the warm haze when I'd woken in his arms in our hotel room this morning, and I was fairly certain I could have stayed forever.

The bubble burst when my mother appeared, holding Ada on her hip. Anthony and I snapped apart like rubber bands.

"Mom!" I blurted, somehow surprised to see her there in the flesh.

She handed off her granddaughter to Libby and approached us. My mother was a tall, slender woman, with scrutinizing eyes and limited ability to smile. She studied Anthony like one of her students' papers she suspected of plagiarism. "Hello, Penelope. I'm glad to see you are all right."

"I am, yes. This is Anthony."

He stepped forward with his hand out. "Pleasure to meet you, ma'am."

"Don't call my mom *ma'am,*" I muttered under my breath.

"Oh, I mean *Doctor.* Pleasure to meet you, Dr. Collins," he corrected.

"Nope, still not it."

"What?"

"Collins is my dad's last name. She's—"

"Dr. Tanner," my mother finished for me, and cut off our hushed conversation. She took his hand and gave it a firm shake. "I hear you live next door?"

"Yes. Well. For now, at least? I don't kn-know what I'm going to do with the, um, the . . . house."

I couldn't tell if he was stammering because he was truly unsure about the house or because my mother was wildly intimidating on a good day. Thought of the former soured my stomach.

"Interesting sequence of events that brought you into my daughter's life," my mother said. From her tone, I knew Libby had given her details—biased ones, surely—and she had formed an opinion of Anthony without having met him.

To his credit, he didn't cower. Instead he slipped his hand into mine again and cast me an assured look. "Yes, it was interesting. Your daughter has been very brave."

"Well, I don't doubt that for a second. Of course she has," my mom said with a tilt of her chin. The praise fizzed through me. Anthony had been saying it for days, but from her lips, I felt like I'd been knighted.

"I'm sorry to hear about your uncle," she said. "Elizabeth tells me he was an exemplary neighbor."

Few people other than my mother called my sister and me by our full names.

Anthony looked thrown for a moment before he caught on. "Thank you. That's kind of you to say."

"I'm only repeating what my daughter said. I didn't know him."

"How long are you staying, Mom?" I interjected before she could further turn the conversation into a casualty of awkwardness.

She eyed me with a stern look. "Well, I wasn't planning on visiting at all, but when your sister called and said you'd gone missing, I came, of course." She pointed over her shoulder with her thumb. "I was just telling the detective I'd stay until—"

"The detective?" I cut her off.

My mother looked bewildered. As if she couldn't understand what I'd misunderstood. "Yes. Detective Warner. He's in the dining room."

"*What?!* He's been here this whole time?" My heart, having rather agreeably returned to normal rhythm after days of turmoil, started trampling my insides again.

"Yes. He came over before you arrived. We've been having lemonade."

Despite her boundless intelligence, my mother often missed social cues. She didn't seem to pick up on my sudden-onset fright or the way Anthony had dropped my hand and paled to a shade of bleached bedsheet beside me.

I took a breath and reminded myself Warner was on our side. I'd reported my kidnapping to him. He was probably here to talk about that, not the fact we'd buried a body in the desert less than twenty-four hours ago.

Still, I considered doing an about-face and running over to Anthony's to hide. Maybe even getting into the Camaro and riding off into the sunset.

But my sister's voice summoned us from the other room. "Penny? Daryl wants to talk to you!"

I glanced over at Anthony and could see his eyes darting back and forth. He was scrambling for a solution too.

My mother, in a rare moment of tenderness, reached out for my hand. She squeezed it and then leaned in to hug me. "I'm

glad you're safe, sweetheart. Don't keep the detective waiting."
She pulled back and gave me a nod; it infused me with a swell
of courage, silently guaranteeing everything would be all right.
She looked over at Anthony and gave him the same one before
she floated off to find her grandson.

"So your mom is terrifying," Anthony said as we walked toward the back of the house.

"I know. Not the most socially gracious person, but she likes
you. I can tell."

"You can tell? From *that*? How?"

"I just can."

We rounded into the dining room and found Libby bouncing Ada on her hip. Detective Warner sat at the table. A half-
empty glass of lemonade sat in front of him, next to a large
envelope with a lump in its middle and a closed folder.

He stood when we entered, and the fact he reached for our
hands to shake, and not slap on handcuffs, sent a dizzying
wave of relief crashing over me. "Penny. Mr. Pierce. Libby let
me know you were going to be home today."

I cringed at the memory of telling Libby this. I wouldn't
have, had I known she would invite the detective over for
happy hour. "Yep. We're back!" I said with too bright a smile.

The air filled with an electricity that felt as if it would spark
if touched.

Warner let out a sigh. "Mind having a seat? There are a few
things we need to discuss."

Anthony and I glanced at each other before pulling out
chairs opposite him. Libby's farmhouse dining table easily sat
eight. With Warner on one long side and us on the other, the
narrow gap between us felt not unlike being back in the interrogation room.

Warner looked over at Libby, who was still lingering in obvious hope of overhearing our discussion.

She pretended to busy herself with straightening glasses on the table with the hand not holding Ada.

"Lib? Do you mind?" I said when she didn't take the hint.

She scowled at me and marched off, I was certain, to hide around the corner within earshot.

"We were able to follow up on the report you made, Penny," Warner started once she was gone. "We recovered Mr. Griotti's Cadillac at the Slates' residence, along with your phones." He dumped over the envelope and out slid a pair of smartphones. I eagerly reached for mine, equally relieved to have it back and afraid of how many emails I'd racked up while it had been missing.

Anthony took his and frowned when it failed to turn on. Mine was dead too, and I found myself enjoying the idea of a little while longer off-grid.

"Thank you," I said.

"Of course. We also found something else at the Slates' house," he went on. The hairs on my neck stood. He pulled a photo from his folder, a blown-up headshot that looked like it had been cropped from a driver's license and placed it on the table.

The tweed man scowled back at us.

"Do you recognize this man?"

Fear gripped me with a cold hand. I thought back to him pointing a gun at me—twice. My mouth wouldn't offer up any words, so I simply nodded.

Warner turned the photo around so it faced him. "We found Mr. Doyle laid up in bed on the property, recovering from a stab wound."

Doyle? It sounded fitting for a henchman, but I preferred tweed man.

Despite everything he'd done to me, a tight knot in my chest unwound. Ever since that night, part of me worried I'd killed him.

"It was self-defense," I said softly as I fought off the memory of it. I felt Anthony reach out and squeeze my hand beneath the table.

"I'm sure it was," Warner said with a sincere nod. "His injuries, coupled with finding your personal belongings on the property, and your statement were enough to bring him in on kidnapping charges." He turned his gaze to Anthony. "And while we've got him, we're looking into the murder accusations as well."

"Thank you," Anthony said through a tight jaw.

"It was him," I chimed in with a sharp nod. "He told us he did it."

"All right," Warner said with a gentle raised hand. "I'll need both of you to come in and give formal statements, now that you're back."

"Of course," I said.

Anthony looked skeptical. I elbowed him. "Of course," he said reluctantly.

"Good," Warner said. He drummed his fingers on the table. "A lot of loose ends have come together because of all this, so thank you, Penny, for your tip."

"Glad to help."

He stood from the dining chair and straightened his jacket. He gathered the photo back into the folder. "Oh, one more thing. Portia Slate is still missing, and now her husband seems to have disappeared too. Do you happen to know where either of them might be?" His delivery was casual. An easy, harmless question aimed at both of us.

I felt Anthony's hand tighten on mine at the same time all the air seeped out of my lungs.

We knew where one of them was, and the other had vanished by now into a new identity thousands of miles away.

"No," Anthony said in a steady voice, betraying nothing.

I thought it best to keep my mouth shut and simply shake my head.

Warner eyed us. I sensed he didn't fully believe it, but he wasn't going to push. Not right now at least. "All right. Well, you let me know if you hear anything. About either of them."

"Sure," Anthony said.

"Thank you. Now, can I trust you'll both come into the station tomorrow to give your statements about the day of the funeral?"

"Yes," I said.

Warner nodded and expectantly looked at Anthony. "You're not leaving town, are you, Mr. Pierce?"

Anthony paused long enough to dull the glow I'd been feeling since the hotel room in L.A. After everything, it was still true he didn't live here. He'd never even planned to visit until everything with Portia went haywire. He'd told me in the desert he wasn't sure what he was going to do with the house, but his delay in answering Warner had my heart hiccupping with worry he was going to disappear as well.

He let out a breath and shook his head. "Not tonight."

Warner nodded and gathered his things. "Good. I'll see you both at the station tomorrow then."

He left us alone in the dining room. I heard his voice from around the corner, thanking Libby for her hospitality and promising he'd tell his wife to call her.

Anthony gazed out the back windows toward his house next door. The old Victorian looked regal in the fading sunlight. I traced the outline of his jaw with my eyes, feeling a nervous seed take root in my gut. I could imagine after the past several days, he wanted to go *home* home, and not back to a big, empty house.

"So," I quietly said, "when *are* you leaving town?"

He looked down at me with a softness to his eyes that made my heart hiccup in a whole different way. "No time soon."

"No?" I said with a smile.

"No. I believe a certain professor still owes me a date."

EPILOGUE

Three months later

Congratulations, Pe y, the frosting letters on my cake read. My sister had deleted the *n*s when she cut my slice. She handed the wobbling wedge of chocolate with buttercream filling to me with a smile.

"You did it," she said.

By some miracle, I had not only survived the summer without acquiring a criminal record, but also managed to make tenure. The papers were written, the grant was submitted, the book chapter done. I'd even managed to graduate a grad student and sit on three committees.

"I did." I proudly smiled back and then stuffed a bite into my mouth. The frosting squished between my teeth in the sweetest, most victorious burst of sugar.

"Who wants a slice?" Libby asked, wielding an enormous knife smeared in crumbling chocolate and frosting. The small crowd gathered in her backyard raised hands and politely waited.

I turned around from the table and found Anthony standing right behind me. He told me he'd be late, and I hadn't seen him show up. And now here he was, brooding and tall and wearing sunglasses, which showed me my own dazed reflection at the sight of him.

"Congrats on making tenure, Dr. Collins. You're a badass."

I smiled at him, remembering our night on the road when he'd first called me a badass and told me I could conquer making tenure if I could survive what we'd been through. Little did we know then we'd have much more to survive together, but his faith in me only helped. He also helped by using his fixing powers to squelch any media coverage of my involvement in the events after the fact, which blessedly left my tenure committee with nothing to side-eye. Now I leaned in and kissed him with frosting on my lips.

The summer that changed my life was winding down to an end. The new semester was a week away from starting. Libby had thrown a party to celebrate me making tenure, and as an excuse to bring everyone together for one final summer hurrah. Her backyard bustled with neighborhood friends, kids splashing in the pool, laughter, the smell of whatever her husband was barbequing. John had returned from Japan a week ago and had almost recovered from his jet lag.

I'd ended up staying with Libby all summer, but instead of giving her peace of mind over the mysterious new neighbor, I was spending almost every night at the new neighbor's house. She'd warmed to Anthony—reluctantly, but eventually. She said it was the lovestruck look in my eyes every time I came home from visiting him that did her in. Anyone who could put that look on my face was worth at least a trial period, she'd said. That was two months ago, and I wasn't sure he'd completely passed her test yet, but at least she invited him over to parties now.

Anthony hadn't taken any new jobs since Portia, other than helping me out of the pinch with the press, but he did that pro bono. Since we put Portia on a plane in Los Angeles, we hadn't heard a word from her. Public opinion regarding her disappearance was that her husband had killed her and gotten away with it, which was only compounded by his mysterious vanishing that followed. Anthony had spent the summer sorting out his uncle's estate and having items in the house appraised. To my relief, he had no plans to sell it anytime soon, and more or less made it his home over the past months. He'd gone to New York a few times, and with every trip, I feared he'd call to say he was staying, but he never did. He always came back.

With the new semester starting, I'd be back in the city teaching. When I'd informed Anthony of this, his response was to study traffic patterns so he knew when best to make the commute to see me. The old green Cadillac had been returned to the house next door, but Anthony left it docked in the driveway. He'd taken a much fonder liking to the Camaro, which I had to agree suited him better anyway.

That night in Vegas lived in a small box deep in my brain. The same box also held that night in the Slates' basement. I avoided them as best I could, but sometimes woke up trembling and feeling like I'd stabbed or shot someone again. On those nights, Anthony would wrap me in his arms, tell me everything was all right, and hold me until I fell back to sleep, listening to his heartbeat. I hated those nights, but I loved the feel of his arms.

It was safe to say I was stupidly, drunkenly smitten with him, and he with me. And with each passing day, I grew more certain what continued to bloom between us was rooted in something much deeper than simply the circumstances that had brought us together.

I reluctantly pulled away from our kiss right as Libby walked up and presented him with a slice of cake.

"Glad you could make it, Anthony," she said with a tight smile. "I hope you like chocolate."

He took the towering slice of perfectly moist layers and

smiled at her. "If you made it, Libby, I'm sure I will love it. Thank you."

"Hmm" was all she gave him before turning to me. "Warner is here," she said, and nodded her head toward the pool; she knew our complicated relationship with the detective. Then she floated off to entertain her guests.

"You're trying too hard," I told Anthony, and stabbed another forkful of cake. I kept an eye on the pool to see Detective Warner pulling one of his kids out of the water to heave him right back in with a playful grunt.

"What? No, I'm not," Anthony defended. "Your sister's desserts are in a class of their own. I was simply complimenting her."

"Yes, and she knows she's an amazing chef. You layering on the charm will only make her resist harder. You don't need to grovel."

"I think I might need to grovel a little bit," he said with a grimace.

"Okay, maybe a little bit."

"At least she hasn't threatened to kill me lately."

"Progress, surely."

"This cake *is* amazing though," he said around a bite.

"I know."

"She should open a bakery."

"Hey, there you go. You could be her investor. It would give you both something to do. Business partners."

I was only half joking. Libby had her hands plenty full at home with the kids, but I'd take any excuse to keep Anthony from fixing more problems like the one that had brought us together.

"I'll think about it," he said, smirking, which meant he wouldn't.

Max suddenly appeared out of nowhere and adhered himself to my leg in a soaking wet hug. "Aunt Penny, come swim with me!"

"Oof!" I gasped, and mussed his wet hair. He'd sprouted an inch at least this summer. "Max, I would love to swim with you, but I'm eating, and you aren't supposed to swim for a half hour after you eat."

He punched his fists into his little hips and frowned. His neon-green water wings only exaggerated his posture. "My mom says that's not true."

"Is your mom a scientist?"

"No."

"Well, who are you going to believe?"

He cast me his most dramatic glare and stomped off to the pool.

"You just *manipulated* that child," Anthony said, pretending to be scandalized.

"You don't know the half of it. Besides, it's my party and I don't want to swim right now."

He stepped closer and slipped his finger beneath the bikini string tied around my neck and sticking out from my dress. He plucked it like a guitar string. "Later?"

I met his gaze with a promise in mine. "Later."

We'd made excellent use of my sister's pool when the house was asleep. I bit my lip at the thought of doing it again.

"Huh-uh," Anthony protested, and pulled it from my teeth with his thumb. "None of this, unless you're going to ditch this party and come over right now."

A flush filled my cheeks, and I gave him a coy grin. I glanced over my shoulder, then leaned in to whisper, "I don't think anyone would notice if I disappeared for a while."

He flicked a brow and gave me a devilish smile. "Only one way to find out." He set his cake on the table and then took away my plate before taking my hand.

We stepped off the patio to head for the gate that led to his yard when Detective Warner intercepted us.

"Penny, Mr. Pierce, nice to see you."

The sound of his voice cooled my speeding blood. I felt Anthony's hand tighten on mine.

"Hi, Detective," I said. Anthony simply nodded.

"Congratulations on your accomplishment, Penny."

"Thank you. Congrats on closing your cases. I'm glad you were able to join the party."

He let out a big breath and rested his hands on his hips. I was used to seeing him in a suit and tie. The board shorts and dad polo were a refreshing break that reminded me he was a friendly neighbor.

A friendly neighbor who could lock me and my boyfriend up for life for burying Connor Slate in the middle of the desert.

"It's nice to have a day off," he said. "Things have finally slowed down after this summer."

"That's good to hear!" I said in a too-chipper voice. I was ready to end this conversation.

Warner slightly flinched at my enthusiasm. "Yes, definitely good to hear. A lot of it has to do with Mr. Doyle being behind bars. But also the search for Connor Slate has been called off. His trip to Las Vegas is a dead end. No one seems to have seen him since. After months, the consensus is finally that he skipped town and disappeared."

My breath suddenly left me, along with my ability to form a sentence. If it hadn't been for Anthony's hand in mine, I might have dissolved into a puddle of confession. But I reminded myself Connor would have killed him and Portia if we hadn't stopped him.

After the tweed man was arrested and, in some fanatic show of loyalty, pled guilty to kidnapping and murder, the search for Connor amplified. Of course he was a person of interest, not only in his wife's disappearance, but in ties to two murders. Not to mention, the FBI was still interested in his finances. The police traced his trail to Las Vegas, but it ended at the casino where a driver had reported dropping him off around

5 o'clock. They had the record of his private plane landing and report of him taking the private car to the Venetian, but after that, there was no sign of where he'd gone. Anthony called in another favor from Lou's client, who'd secured us a room at the hotel and had all security footage with signs of Connor or us wiped. We were lucky no one had heard the commotion in the room or stairwell. All anyone could prove was Connor Slate had flown to Vegas on a Thursday, was reportedly driven to the Venetian, and was never seen again.

Only four people on the planet knew he had never left the desert.

"Makes sense he would skip town," Anthony said. "All things considered."

Warner gave him an unsettling stare. "Yes, it's awfully convenient to have such resources." His cryptic statement left me wondering exactly whose resources he was talking about. "It's also convenient that the hour of public surveillance footage from before and after his driver reported dropping him off at the casino is missing. Some kind of system glitch with the CCTV. So not only is there no evidence of him *in* the casino where he was reportedly taken, but none from the surrounding public area at the time either."

Too convenient, I thought, and felt like I had GUILTY tattooed on my forehead.

It turned out Anthony had another resource to call on for help erasing footage of that night.

Me.

After things got out of hand and we realized we had left a desperate trail in one of the most heavily recorded cities on the planet, we needed someone to take care of it. The fix with the Venetian was easy enough, but the public security footage from outside in the street was another question. In a do-or-die moment once we were home and knew it was only a matter of time before an investigation into Connor's disappearance began, I'd confessed to Anthony I'd previously undersold my hacking skills and could in fact get us out of that pickle. He'd been resistant to allowing me to help until our backs were completely against the wall. As a lifelong rule-follower, it was oddly liberating to hack into the City of Las Vegas public surveillance system and remove what we didn't want seen. It made me feel way more badass than firing a gun ever could.

I didn't feel very badass now, however, what with Warner squinting at me like he knew the truth.

"That's interesting," Anthony said to Warner with a reassuring squeeze of my hand that had helped hack us to safety.

"Indeed," Warner said and mercifully left it at that. "And have you heard from . . . ?"

The implication was obvious. I felt Anthony's hand tighten on mine once more. My heart began to flutter nervously again. I fought to keep my face neutral so he couldn't see the truth written there.

"From whom, Detective?" Anthony asked, his voice steady.

Warner studied us, and I knew he knew there was more to the story. That what we'd told him after Vegas wasn't the whole truth. He knew Portia was somehow involved—why else would her bodyguard have wound up in Anthony's closet? But by some stroke of luck, Portia had not gone missing in his jurisdiction; she wasn't his investigation. His focus was on closing two murder cases, and that's what he'd done. With our help. And if the truth about our involvement somehow ever did come out, Anthony had the honest cover story of trying to help a friend get out of a dangerous marriage. It wasn't his fault his friend's vindictive husband went on a murderous revenge rampage and sucked me up in the chaos too. Warner eventually exhaled and gave us a nod. "No one. Enjoy the party."

He left us alone, and I felt like we'd escaped death.

Anthony hooked his arm around my shoulders and let out a relieved sigh. "I'm still proud of you, by the way."

I looked up at him and knew by the quirk in his mouth that he was referring to the CCTV hacking. I smiled back at him. "You're a bad influence."

"Maybe, but we wouldn't have gotten away with anything without you. You ultimately saved us all." He pressed his lips to my temple and squeezed me with his big arm.

He was right. I'd tied up the final loose end, and in comparison to going to prison, I didn't mind breaking some rules for the right reasons.

"Well if anyone asks, I'm still just a professor, not a hacker."

He gave me another squeeze and found my lips with his. He tasted like chocolate frosting and the hint of danger I'd grown addicted to. "Still want to get out of here?"

"Yes."

The mood from a moment before rekindled, and I was ready to escape to his house for a reprieve from splashing and laughing and probing eyes.

Warner had walked back over toward the gate, blocking the path we'd been taking before our chat, so we backtracked and went through the house. On the other side, we walked down the car-lined street in the late-afternoon light. The trees were still leafy and the yards lush. Although this neighborhood never really saw a season without foliage. Even in the dead of winter, someone found a way to make their yard blossom.

We walked up the path to the old Victorian, the same as I had that day that I'd met Anthony, and the now dozens of times since. He planned to invest in sprucing up the front porch and having the house painted, but was still deciding on a color. The steps creaked in greeting under our feet as we climbed to the door.

I waited while he unlocked it and pressed my cheek to his back. He was always warm and smelled good, and I just plain liked to touch him. I could hear his heart beating softly.

When the front door opened, a familiar chill curled out to

welcome us like a pair of frozen hands. He'd left the air conditioner on, but I'd come to learn the house was always cold. Maybe it was its age or lack of insulation. Maybe it was something else.

The scratchy hiss of paper being pushed across hardwood announced that the mail had been delivered. I'd urged him to mount a mailbox outside the door, or even one at the end of the driveway, because stepping on what was shoved through the slot every day got tiresome. But he'd done neither yet, so we paused when we entered, giving him time to bend down and gather the small pile of envelopes.

I closed the door behind us and locked it out of habit. I shivered at the chill in the air and thought I might need to borrow a sweater to pull on over my dress if we were going to be staying long.

Anthony shuffled the stack of mail and stopped on a small card dirtied by what must have been a long journey. "No way!" he said. His eyes lit up and he turned to face me.

"What is it?" I leaned in to read over his shoulder.

"It's a postcard. From Portia."

I snatched it out of his hand in disbelief. Indeed, it had traveled far. The front showed a generic photo of a beach, which could have been anywhere. The postage was in a language and currency I didn't recognize, but the back held loopy, cheerful writing and a message that instantly made me smile.

Enjoying my sunny days.
With love, P

Acknowledgments

I wrote this story when I was in a bit of a funk and craving something that would bring me joy. I didn't even know what genre it was or if anything would ever come of it. All I knew was hours and days would pass with me grinning like a fool at my computer screen while I brought Penny and Anthony to life. No other story has possessed me the way this one has, and to say I'm thrilled that I get to share it with readers is a massive understatement.

My agent Melissa Edwards, thank you for humoring my wildest ideas, this story being a prime example. Your knack for figuring out how to package my genre-straddling books into something publishers want to buy still blows my mind.

My editors who worked on this book: Shannon Plackis, thank you for acquiring it and getting the point from the get-go. Your enthusiasm for the screwball hijinks and love story helped it shine. Alexandra Sunshine, thank you for your thoughtful input to help polish it and for shepherding it through the publication process. I am excited for where we go next!

The rest of the team at Kensington working on this book: Jane Nutter, Lauren Jernigan, Alex Nicolajsen, Stephanie Finnegan, and Robin Cook, thank you for all your work getting this book into the world and on readers' radar!

Kristine Nobel, thank you for the absolute *banger* of a cover. Wow. I truly could not have dreamed up anything better.

My film agent Tara Timinsky, I'm glad this book was the one to bring us together. Thank you for advocating for my stories outside of the publishing world. I can't wait for where we go next!

Sierra Godfrey, thank you for enthusiastically answering my questions about dead bodies and funerals without even blinking. You make me laugh every day!

Brianna Lieberman, thank you for helping me name the fictional tech companies in this story with your brilliant suggestion to capitalize random letters after everything—literally everything—I came up with ended up being a company that already existed in real life. You're a star.

Lindsay Hameroff, thank you for reading the first draft of this book and assuring me it (mostly) made sense while still being bonkers enough to be fun. Thank you for fancasting every love interest I write as Harry Styles, but especially Anthony. You are a true gem, and I don't know what I'd do without our daily texts.

All of my agent siblings and the local authors I've met and spent time with in L.A., Orange County, and San Diego, thank you for your continued support.

The authors who read an early copy of this book and generously provided blurbs, I admire you and your art and can't thank you enough for taking the time to read mine.

The Bookstagram and BookTok communities, thank you for loving books and sharing your creativity.

The musical artists who will never see this but still deserve thanks for providing this book's soundtrack while I drafted and revised it. Your songs capture the emotion of this story in ways that words alone can't: Cruel Youth, Bob Moses, Fall Out Boy, Nicki Minaj, Goth Babe, UPSAHL, RÜFÜS DU SOL, Aidan Bissett, The Struts, Labrinth, The Dead Weather, Cold War Kids, Beyoncé, YUNGBLUD, Bon Jovi, and Turnstile. You all rock. Literally.

My friends and family who go out of your way to show up to my book events and buy copies for everyone you know, thank you for the endless support.

The Italian side of my family, starting with the historians,

Robert E. Moratto and Janet Sbragia Pisenti and your book *Italian Roots, American Branches,* thank you for creating such a rich resource of our history and journey to America. My great-great grandfather Giovanni Griotti, you'll obviously never see this, but know that one of your great-great granddaughters is living an American dream thanks to your courageous spirit and choice to come to America in 1889. The Italian Griottis and American Greeotts, thank you for letting me borrow the family name. Sorry I fictionalized us as criminals. My Italian cousins, *spero che le nostre strade si incrocino un giorno.* My grandmother Betty and grandfather Paul, thank you for a life of cherished memories. I miss you every day.

My parents, thank you for letting me read all the books and watch all the movies as a kid. My head is full of stories today because of how I grew up.

My husband, thank you for not questioning the obsessive trance I fell into while this story consumed me. Thanks for talking through plot holes with me, always listening, and acting out whatever I ask you to so I can describe it on the page. I'd bury a body with you any day.

Readers, thank you for coming along on another wild journey. I hope you had a great time!

Discussion Questions

1. When Penny and Anthony first meet, Penny has mostly negative feelings toward him. Have you ever overcome a bad first impression?
2. The title of the book refers to the central "fix" job in the story, but also to Libby's attempt to fix Penny up with a partner. Have you ever been set up on a date? How did it go?
3. Penny feels a lot of pressure to succeed in her career. Have you ever felt pressure to succeed at something and prove yourself?
4. Family loyalty is a big theme in the story. Why do you think those ties are so important to each character?
5. Have you ever had an experience where you were completely out of your element, like Penny is in this story? How did you handle it?
6. At several points in the story, Penny makes a choice that goes against her normally straightlaced personality. Why do you think she makes these choices? Would you have made the same?
7. If you've ever taken a road trip, where there any mishaps? What is your best memory from the trip?
8. When Max asks Anthony if he's bad, he says that is subjective. What do you think of Anthony's job?
9. Who would you cast as Penny and Anthony in the movie version of the book?
10. What do you think is next for Penny and Anthony?

Bonus for fun and scandal:
11. Have you ever been in a situation where you wished you could call a fixer?